You Too Can Have a Body Like Mine

HARPER

An Imprint of HarperCollins*Publishers*

You Too Can Have a Body Like Mine

Alexandra Kleeman

a novel

Illustrations copyright © Christine Keshet.

HarperCollins books may be purchased for educational, business, or sales promotional use. For information, please e-mail the Special Markets Department at SPsales@harpercollins.com.

FIRST EDITION

Library of Congress Cataloging-in-Publication Data

Kleeman, Alexandra.
You too can have a body like mine : a novel / Alexandra Kleeman.—Trade Paperback
pages cm
ISBN 978-0-06-238867-4 (hardback) 1. Women—Fiction. 2. Television—Fiction. 3. Obsessive-compulsive disorder—Fiction. 4. Body image in women—Fiction. 5. Psychological fiction. I. Title.
PS3611.L44245Y69 2015
813'.6—dc23
2014042024

15 16 17 18 19   OV/RRD   10 9 8 7 6 5 4 3 2 1

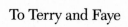

To Terry and Faye

It could be said that the orchid imitates the wasp, reproducing its image in a signifying fashion (mimesis, mimicry, lure, etc.) . . . At the same time, something else entirely is going on: not imitation at all but a capture of code, surplus value of code, an increase in valence, a veritable becoming, a becoming-wasp of the orchid and a becoming-orchid of the wasp.

—DELEUZE AND GUATTARI, *A THOUSAND PLATEAUS*

Blessed is the lion that the human being will devour so that the lion becomes human. And cursed is the human being that the lion devours; and the lion will become human.

— THE GOSPEL ACCORDING TO THOMAS

IS IT TRUE THAT WE are more or less the same on the inside? I don't mean psychologically. I'm thinking of the vital organs, the stomach, heart, lungs, liver: of their placement and function, and the way that a surgeon making the cut thinks not of my body in particular but of a general body, depicted in cross section on some page of a medical school textbook. The heart from my body could be lifted and placed in yours, and this portion of myself that I had incubated would live on, pushing foreign blood through foreign channels. In the right container, it might never know the difference. At night I lie in bed and, though I can't touch it or hold it in my hand, I feel my heart moving inside me, too small to fill the chest of an adult man, too large for the chest of a child. There was a newspaper article about a man in Russia who had been coughing up blood; an X-ray showed a mass in his chest with a spreading shape, rag edged. They thought it was cancer, but when they opened him up they found a six-inch fir tree embedded in his left lung.

Inside a body there is no light. A massed wetness pressing in on itself, shapes thrust against each other with no sense of where they are. They break in the crowding, come unmade. You put your hand to your stomach and press into the softness, trying to listen with your fingers for what's gone wrong. Anything could be inside.

It's no surprise, then, that we care most for our surfaces: they alone distinguish us from one another and are so fragile, the thickness of paper.

I WAS STANDING IN MY room in front of the mirror, peeling an orange. I cradled its exact weight in my palm, sinking a nail through the topmost layer. I dug a finger under its skin until I felt cool flesh, then I rooted that finger around and around. The rind tore with a soft, cottony sound, the peel one smooth, blunt piece trailing off the fist of the fruit. I slipped my contacts in and blinked at the mirror. Most mornings I barely resembled myself: it was like waking up with a stranger. When I caught a glimpse of my body, tangled and pale, it felt as if there were an intruder in my room. But as I dressed and put on makeup, touched the little tinted liquids to my skin and watched the hand in the mirror move alongside my own, I rebuilt my connection to the face that I took outside and pointed at those around me. My hand ripped a wad of pulp and pushed it through the space between my lips. Juice crawled down the side of my palm. Like the moon, my mouth in the mirror seemed to look a little bit different each day. It was summer, and the heat hadn't yet tightened around our bodies, making us sticky and moist, trapping us in a suit we hated to wear.

A breeze pushed through the open window, smelling of cut grass, chopped flowers, and I could hear the people outside leaving their homes. Their car doors opened and closed, tires shifting gravel as they pulled out of their driveways and vanished for eight or nine hours, only to return less crisp, their unbuttoned cuffs hanging open. I liked letting noise from the neighborhood leak into my sleep and begin turning things real. I liked it, except when I hated it, hated how close the houses were to each another, hated that the first outdoor thing I sighted each morning was my land-lady's swollen face as she poked her head out the door to grab the newspaper. She lived below us, but from certain angles she could see straight up into our unit. Every day she bent down to retrieve it, then turned around, craning her neck to peer in through my bedroom window, checking to see if I'd spent the night in my room. Her aggressively changing hairstyle, auburn one week and then a dirty highlighted blond the next, made it unclear whether she wore real hair or wore a wig, and if it was a wig whether she slept with it on. My roommate B said it was like she was a fugitive inside her own home, someone living on the run without going anywhere at all.

In the house next door lived a couple of college kids who kept the TV on at all times, even when they left for their classes or jobs or whatever responsibilities they had. Their screen glowed through the night, casting blue light on an empty couch. It went dark only when the kids were in that third bedroom, the one I couldn't see from our apartment. Sometimes for variety B and I watched the TV in their house instead of the TV in ours, though at that distance we could only guess at what we were seeing, flipping through the channels on our end to find a match.

Across the street there was a family with a dog that slept most of the day, but a few times each afternoon it ran to throw itself at the front windows, smashing its muzzle against the glass and barking until the sounds it made warped and hoarsened. I'd get up from my desk to see what was wrong, but there was never anything to see, not even a squirrel. Sometimes then our eyes would meet, the dog and me, and we'd just stare at each other from across that street, not knowing what to do.

It was a safe neighborhood. There was nothing you could complain about without sounding crazy. The sun was bright outside and I heard birds hidden in the trees, swarming the bushes with sounds of movement, calling out, bending small branches beneath the weight of their small bodies.

THUMPING SOUNDS CAME FROM THE other side of the bedroom door. It was B moving around our apartment: one small thump from the living room, and another, and then the sound of something being dragged across the floor. I heard her going to start the coffeemaker and then giving up, opening the refrigerator and giving that up, too. Standing still in the middle of my room, I tried to gauge how much I could move without letting her know that I was live. She couldn't assume that I'd be conscious this early in the morning, but that wouldn't stop her from checking every five or ten minutes, pausing to listen for the sounds of someone wakeful. Then sometimes she'd sit herself near the door, ear against the doorjamb, and talk toward me as though we were having a normal conversation. She'd talk toward me until I responded. B said the apartment was lonely when I wasn't awake. She said if I was sleeping, I was as good as dead. She meant in terms of companionship, interactivity, my ability to help her make breakfast for herself. When B did eat, which was not always, she preferred to touch the food as little as possible to keep her hands clear of what she called "that edible smell." She needed my hands to cut, to squeeze, to handle, to break eggs and toss their slimy shells into the garbage.

B and I were both petite, pale, and prone to sunburn. We had dark hair, pointy chins, and skinny wrists; we wore size six shoes. If you reduced each of us to a list of adjectives, we'd come out nearly equivalent. My boyfriend, C, said this was why I liked her so much, why we spent so much time together. C said that all I wanted in a person was another iteration of my person, legible to me as I would be to myself. When he said this it felt like he was calling me lazy. B and I looked alike, talked alike, that was fair enough. To strangers viewing us from a distance as we wove a confused path through the supermarket hand in hand, we might seem like the same person. But I was on the inside and I saw differences everywhere, even if they were only differences of scale. We looked young, but there was a lost, childish quality to how she slumped over whatever she was doing. We had the same brown eyes, but hers were set deeper in her skull, pushed back so that they disappeared beneath the shadow of her brow. We were thin, but B was catastrophically so: I had helped her zip up a dress, I had held her hair back and rubbed the cool, clammy base of her neck with my fingers as she deposited the contents of her stomach into the sink. I knew how her bones looked and how they felt shifting just below the skin.

Whenever I had something nice to say about her or something mean, C would just shrug his shoulders and say I only thought that because we were too much alike. He had a chronic misunderstanding of me. B was fragile and sick and needed to be nursed. She looked underfed, she touched objects like someone who owned nothing in the world. Sympathy for her transported me out of myself, away from my own problems. She was cut to my shape and size like a trapdoor: similar enough that I could imagine myself into her, different enough to make that fantasy a form of escape.

This morning, though, as I listened to her voice on the other side of the door, I wished that I had worked harder to have our differences. B missed me more the more I saw her. Under her scrutiny I felt the weight of my own presence constantly and grew tired, irritated by myself, so that day by day I waited a little longer before coming out of my room in the morning, trying to postpone reentering the construct of my life. Her affection created in me the wish that she would stop loving me, would leave me alone, would let me feel affection for her the way I did when she first moved in, harmless and sad, when I could feel generous for trying to think about why she was sad and come up with ways to make her happy.

From the hallway outside my bedroom, her mouth close to the sliver of space between door and molding, B spoke—*I wanted to make us some coffee, but we're all out of coffee.*

—*I need your help to figure out what kind of juice I should drink. What juice has the least free radicals? Does juice have lead in it?*

—*Have you ever had one of those moles that sticks out? Can you feel with one of those moles that stick out? The way you feel with your fingers and other body parts?*

—*I had a dream last night that we were both birds with their wings missing, but we helped each other escape from a box. When we escaped we were so happy we wanted to celebrate, but we couldn't show it. We didn't have limbs.*

THERE'S A COMMERCIAL ON TV where a woman using this new citrus-based facial scrub begins to scratch at the side of her face, discovering that it has edges, shriveled and curling slightly like old paper. Eyeing the camera, she grasps these edges and lifts up on them until she is peeling the whole surface of her face off with a filmy sound like plastic wrap unsticking from itself. Underneath is another face exactly like hers, but prettier. It's younger and wearing better makeup. You'd think that she might want to stop here and start being happy with herself the way she newly is. But she doesn't stop: instead, she clutches at the side of her face and begins to peel again, and this time the face underneath is even prettier and she's smiling wildly at the camera, she's so pleased. And she peels again, but this time what's underneath is a video of the seashore crashing against a sandy beach, and her hand peels it all off again, and we stare into a deciduous forest filtered through by little blades of light and sunshine.

Then she turns straight toward the camera and peels her face off from the opposite direction, and the face that's underneath belongs to the company's famous actress spokesperson. It's been her voice all along telling us about the hydrating effects and natural ingredients, the way you'll love yourself remade. She doesn't ask what happened to the other woman, the woman who came before her. She smiles beautifully with her hard white teeth.

Words appear on the screen: TruBeauty. TruSkin. YOUR REAL SKIN IS WITHIN.

B wanted to try the product out, she said you could buy it anywhere. But B hated to buy anything herself. She preferred to borrow from someone else, even though her parents had three cars and a horse and sent her checks every month for the rent.

If I asked her why she was always trying to need more than she needed, she'd say that borrowing brought you closer to other people, while buying mostly made you lonelier. That was how I ended up going out with B to the all-night Wally's Supermarket fifteen minutes away on a night when dozens of teenagers hung inexplicably around the parking lot, posed darkly like crows, staring and not saying a thing.

There was no one inside the store except Wally employees in their weird uniforms: red polo shirt, khakis, and oversize foam head in the shape of the store's teenage mascot. They seemed curious about us, or wary, or bored. As we wandered the aisles, I started to feel watched. There was a Wally about twenty feet behind me every time I looked back, sometimes rearranging product in the shelves, but sometimes just looking at me. I told B, but she was unfazed.

"Sure they're watching. They probably think you're going to steal something," she said.

"Really?" I asked. I hadn't known I was the type of person who could steal something.

"It's what they do," she said. "But they're dumb. I'm much more likely to steal than you." She smiled sweetly at me: this was my best friend. Then I bought the face scrub for B to borrow, even though I was nervous about what it might do to me.

When we got home I rubbed product all over my face and neck in the bathroom, feeling it froth away at my skin as B sat on the edge of the tub, taut and unblinking. When it was done I went to the mirror to see what I had become. I didn't see the promised biotransformative subexfoliation, but I knew something had happened because my lips stung and I smelled like lemon-lime soda. B came over and placed a palm experimentally against one of my scrubbed cheeks, then the other, and asked me if I felt any different. I was in the middle of answering when I realized suddenly that she was not listening to me, was not even looking, was staring past me into the medicine cabinet mirror instead and touching the sides of her face, petting her cheek vacantly. She had something on her face that could be mistaken for a smile.

FOUR DAYS A WEEK I went to work as a proofreader for a local company that produced several magazines and newsletters. I could choose any four days that I liked, but everything else was chosen for me. Although proofreader implies reading, what was expected of me was somewhat less: see that everything was punctuated, see that words were in a sensical place, but avoid trying to make sense of them—meaning was an obstacle to efficient proofing that my supervisors hoped I would avoid. I proofed everything that came through the office, so if there were errors in *Marine Hobbyist* or *New Age Plastics*, it was my fault for letting them through.

Each morning I walked forty minutes to work along the side of the road, miles that could be driven in a few minutes. I passed eight gas stations and two different Wally's Supermarkets, identical except for the garden center appended to the second one, a cordoned-off section of parking lot asphalt filled with pots of identically colored marigolds. On days when almost everyone was sick, I could have any cubicle I wanted, but I always chose my usual one, the one for freelancers. In the quiet of the empty office I could hear the slight hiss of air-conditioning coming through the vents. I felt that I was experiencing the world as only someone who did not exist in it could. There were three kinds of errors: of duplication, of substitution, of omission. By the time I got home, work seemed like a long, flat dream whose details I could not remember. I peeled the damp and dusty pants from my legs and lay on top of the bed, sweating. All I wanted to do was sleep.

Last Thursday had passed like every other, except that I had taken a nap during my lunch break, crawling beneath the desk to sleep for thirty minutes on short, stiff, office carpeting. I came home still sleepy and collapsed on top of my bedding to take a second nap. I had been there only a few minutes when I heard a knocking at my door. Standing there was B with an excited look on her face, eyes big and wet, mouth drawn up at the corners. She looked like a person who had betrayed a secret. Her hands clutched something dark. Against her thin white fingers, it looked like a coil of chain or a greased-down railroad spike—something old and exacting, designed to keep a thing in place.

"I was sleeping," I said.

"Do you want this," she responded.

Her voice angled down as though it weren't a question but a fact that she was only repeating. She thrust her hands forward slightly.

"What is it?" I asked.

What I saw in her grip as I looked closer was a two-foot-long cord of human hair: dark, thick, and braided. The braid traveled from her hands to mine, and then there was a sudden softness against my skin that I hadn't prepared for. She had given it over the way you'd hand off a baby, supporting both ends with cupped hands, shifting it gently into my grasp. I was confused, I still didn't understand what was happening, and I couldn't tell whether the thing I saw in my hands was dense or light, dry or moist. In my hands the braid lay soft and motile, limp and invertebrate. I looked down. It hung heavy, but with an active tension, a nervous cord sagging slightly in its middle where there was nothing to support it. The hair had a sad look, naked and lonely, gleaming with oily light. It was tied off at both ends with two pink rubber bands.

"It's yours," she said. "I mean, it's yours now. I just did it."

"You did this . . . ," I said, trailing off.

"I did it for you," B said, smiling the beautiful smile of a deaf child. "What I mean is, I wanted to do it and I didn't know why until I thought of you. You always look so okay. You don't have pounds of hair hanging from the top of you. I'm already feeling better, clearer. My thoughts are louder."

I looked at her head.

Hair had always been our way of telling ourselves apart. Mine went down to the shoulders, dark like hers, but finer and softer. Hers went feet farther, brushing the small of her back. B used to have Disney princess hair, hair with a life and directionality of its own, separate from the movements of its host body. She used to sling it over her shoulder and pet it like a cat, her face shrunken underneath. Now she stood in my doorway giving off a weird confidence, eyes blunt. With hair cropped to her shoulders, she reminded me of times when I had seen myself reflected in imperfect surfaces, in the windows of shops or cars.

"I think you should keep this," I said.

"You might need it," I said. I was struggling for something more to say.

"But I don't *want* it," B replied. "That stuff was driving me crazy.

It was like, you know, when you think that you're sick and there's something really wrong with you, like lupus or heart disease or chronic fatigue syndrome, and then you just realize that you're hung over. That hair was making me feel un-myself. I think it was muffling my thoughts. That's why I cut it off. And gave it to you."

She used the past tense to talk about what was happening as though it had already happened, as though I had already accepted her unwanted gift.

"Now you have a part of me forever," she added.

Someday I would think back on this moment in light of how badly it would turn out. I didn't know where to look, and I looked off to the side of her, down at the twist of hair I held in my hands, and then up at my body in the mirror to my left. Hair like this could choke a person. I didn't want to have so much of it there in the room where I slept, where my mind and body went hazy in the dark.

I wished that C could be here to tell me as he often did that people were nuts, even the people who you loved, and that therefore it was fair to keep them at a distance, even fairer the more you felt for them. It was C who made sure that we saw each other no more than three days a week, the length of a long weekend trip, a brief vacation into another person. But of course C wouldn't be here, since I had always managed to keep him and B at a distance from each other, one waiting in the car while I hugged the other one good-bye, one watching from the window as I went off with the other, so that each was just a name to the other one, a name tied loosely around a few vague events and descriptors. I didn't know what to call my fear of their meeting, but I tried: seepage, contagion, inversion.

B stood there, still looking at me steadily. Patches of light flick-ered across her face as branches outside shifted in the sun.

"I'll hold on to it for you," I said. "You'll probably want it back soon."

"Maybe," she said.

"But not likely," she added.

"You spent so long growing it," I said, looking down at the sad heap.

"It just happened on me," she replied. "It wasn't hard work."

The braid bunched under my grip, gleaming. I didn't know what I was afraid of. Maybe that in accepting this chunk of B's body, I would be diluting myself further, when already it was taking me minutes each morning to remember who I was, how I had gotten there. I set it on the mantel in my room next to the different objects I had accumulated, snow globes and ceramic cats, stuff that reminded me of myself. Its presence was loud in the otherwise quiet afternoon. From a distance it looked like a length of chain.

I hadn't wanted it, yet I had taken it anyway. Something was happening and I had the feeling that if I ever came to understand it, I wouldn't like what I found. But however I felt about it now, there was nothing else that I could have done with B. There's a kind of pressure that your own life muscles onto you, to do some-thing just like you would do, to behave just like yourself. We had both gotten so used to me being stronger, reasonable, and having the resources to yield that I yielded by default, the idea of my own strength making me the weaker one.

Looking at the braid reminded me of the commercial for Kandy Kakes, where Kandy Kat, the company's cartoon cat mascot, has been chasing a single, smallish Kandy Kake across a scrolling variety of different cartoon and live-action landscapes, such as the Super Bowl and the Great Wall of China and the North Pole, dodging all sorts of wacky obstacles and running past sign after sign that lists out the various natural and unnatural ingredients that go into Kandy Kakes. They've been chasing each other for what we are to understand has been hours or days in cartoon-time, though it all passes by in a matter of seconds, until suddenly they come to a big cliff with a sign marked END OF THE WORLD. At last there is no place for the snack cake to run, and it looks like Kandy Kat may get to eat something for once. So he advances on the little cake and grabs it with both bony hands, he lifts it to his mouth. But at just that moment the little cake opens its own mouth hugely and eats Kandy Kat in one big bite. His tail sticks out of the cake's mouth a little, wriggling, so the cake suddenly extends a little arm from its round pucky body and with it pushes the last of Kandy Kat into its maw, swallowing hard. There's a muffled crunch as Kandy Kat's whole body packs down into what must be a tiny little stomach, and you hear a muffled whimper escape. A moment later, the Kake succumbs to delayed cartoon gravity and falls to the ground, collapsing beneath the burden of its new weight.

THE SUMMER I FOUND OUT about the food chain, I was eight years old. I became obsessed with it in a way that made me outgoing, explaining it to any adult or child who would listen. I drew maps of predator-prey relations on all my binders and notebooks, big webs in which I was always pictured in some topmost corner, near all of my favorite foods. I told my parents that I was going to become an ecologist so I could find out which animals living in entirely different continents or habitats, on land or in water or caves, could eat each other if put in the same place. I would fill in the gaps, and every animal would be linked to every other by a one-way arrow leading from the prey animal to the mouth of its predator. It was an orderly system, like rainwater becoming seawater that dissolves again into little droplets of rain. It was a meat cycle, and when I ate spaghetti with meatballs or chicken noodle soup for dinner, I went to bed certain that participating in the meat economy meant that I would be eaten, too, someday, by something larger than me or maybe by many things much smaller.

That fall we moved to a new school district forty-five minutes from our old house, and our new neighborhood was greener and wetter than the last one, with more space between the houses. Everyone was a stranger, and in the afternoons I'd go out to the woods behind our house and upend rocks and logs to see what was underneath. Underneath there was a basement smell and the wood blackly wet had a softer texture, like damp velvet. I'd flip the log over and watch what was underneath scatter: black beetles with a permanent shellac to their hard casings, ants of different shades of brown and red, earthworms and shortened white worms with no eyes or faces. With a twig or long blade of stiff grass I prodded at them, rolling the worms in the rich dirt, herding a beetle over to a dark divot into which large black ants disappeared into the earth. I tried to feed the small insects to the larger ones. I wanted them all to mix, to struggle, to show me in real time what it meant to live and die.

I found an earthworm half-submerged in watery soil, where it was being eaten by a larval dragonfly. The worm was larger and stronger, its body a single muscle twisting out of the water and flopping back, failing. It struggled, pulling its long body into small arcs and spirals, and this meant nothing to the larva that worked calmly to chew a hole into one of its ends, releasing a thin, cloudy white trail hovering in puddle water.

I left my room and went into the kitchen, where B sat looking at the fridge.

"I don't know what I feel like eating," she said to me.

"Maybe you want a sandwich?" I suggested. "I can make you a sandwich."

The sandwiches I made B were white bread, condiments, deli cheese, no meat. B claimed meat was hard to digest, but I think she just didn't want the calories inside her. Instead of cutting off the crusts, I squished the sandwich down with my palm to make of it a sort of edible coaster. This was a way of tricking B into thinking there was less food in it. Then I slid it on a plate, cut it diagonally, and handed it over to her. I'd make my own sandwich while, out of the corner of my eye, I watched her pull it apart, remove the cheese, scrape out the fat white center of the bread, and throw it away, leaving only the mayonnaised crusts to chew on.

"No, too much," she said. "I don't want to overeat when it's so hot out. What were you going to have?"

"A sandwich," I said.

B stared straight forward, chewing on her lip as she thought it through. Finally she announced: "Let's have Popsicles."

Popsicles came in a fifty-pack and were bright with artificial coloring, though there were only three flavors: red, pink, and orange. B loved them, this stuff that was more like a color than a food, loved to eat them day or night as she drank the lemon-scented vodka from the freezer. Since she had moved in, I had been eating more Popsicles and less of everything else. Her habits were contagious. I could only guess at how many boxes she went through each week from the plastic cups full of Popsicle sticks, cigarette butts, and sunset-colored liquid that I found in the living room when I returned home. One time I asked her why she ate so many of these when she wouldn't eat even a scoop of ice cream. She brought the box and explained that even though they tasted like juice, they were made of something better. Each Popsicle contained about fifteen calories, and you could burn almost that many just by eating them with vigor. "They erase themselves from your body," she said as I pulled the box closer to my face to peer into the fine print.

B came from the kitchen and handed me a Popsicle, the waxy wrapper caked with frost, and we crawled out the window onto the roof the way we were used to and sat out there with the summer heat pressing down on our arms and legs from above. Sweat beaded on the surface of our skin and felt creaturely, like many legs ready to be set in motion.

Our Popsicles were identical orange, and each was a conjoined twin, bound in the center with sticks projecting from both halves. A navel orange is something similar, the navel another separate fruit attempting to grow within the base of the first, impacted on all sides, turning dry, infertile, and tasteless as a result. The fruits are seedless, and new plants grow only through cutting and grafting, which means that all are essentially clones of one another. I had just maneuvered myself over to the spot on the roof where I liked to sit, where I could see into my room and also into the kitchen next door and the living room across the street where they had the crazy dog, but B had already stripped hers down and was digging in, biting at it first and then holding its peak in her mouth to soften. Sucking sounds came from her mouth as the orange slick pooled around her teeth. She was working at it as though she hadn't eaten for days. Except for the Popsicles, tea, cigarettes, and sloppy cocktails made out of the lemon-flavored vodka that someone had left in our freezer after a party, B didn't really eat. Maybe she was saving her stomach for something that didn't yet exist. I looked over at the house across the street and tried to spot the dog as I tore at my Popsicle wrapper, gummy on the inside from Popsicle juice, juice coloring my hands as I tried to pull the Popsicle from its skin.

A bright heat trembled all around us as we ate them, our faces sheening with sweat. Sounds of lawn mowers and birds hung like chains in the quiet air. I favored one side of the Popsicle over the other so that I could finish it first and have a normal, single-stick Popsicle to work on. Sweat ran down my forehead and into my eye. Then there was the sound of an engine growing louder, harsh in the heavy afternoon, and we saw the neighbor's car coming slowly up the street. The man was driving, and his wife and daughter were in the car, too. B stopped licking to watch the car pull into the driveway across the street, and when she looked down again and noticed her Popsicle dripping, she crawled all over the roof looking for ants to drown in the sticky bright syrup. She hunched over them, dangling the last nub of it above, turning the stick in her fingers to make it drip more evenly. The ants struggled for a bit, and when they had stopped, others came to feed minusculely on the orange slick.

I shuffled over on my knees to see them more closely, the

dying ones and the ones not yet dying, many trying to eat up the stuff that had killed the others. The live ants looked like they might be distressed, or maybe just excited: I wanted to know which. I hung close above one group, casting my shadow over their swarming, and I waited to see some sign that would tell me whether they were caring for one another or just eating. B had lost interest in the ants, but she was looking at me now with intensity.

"What are you doing?" she asked.

"The ants," I said. "They're dying. Then I thought some of them were coming to help, but actually I think they're trying to eat the syrup."

"That's kind of morbid," said B.

"I don't understand why you try to kill them," I said. "They never come into the house. And when you kill them this way, it leaves sticky spots all over the roof. We'll have to clean it some-day."

"They die in sugar," she replied matter-of-factly. "It's the best possible death for an ant."

A strange noise came from nearby, and we both stood up to see better. From the house across the street with the expensive-looking hydrangeas and the novelty mailbox shaped like a barn, the house where they had the crazy dog and the daughter who took ballet lessons on Tuesday and Thursday and Friday, three figures were filing out through the front door. Each one wore a large plain white sheet over its body, with holes cut out where the eyes would be. The largest figure helped the second-largest down the front steps, while the smallest struggled out on its own, stepping all over the dragging corners of its oversize veil.

B and I watched our neighbors shuffle in sheets toward the family sedan. The husband opened the passenger's-side door for the wife, then walked all the way around the car to open the driver's-side rear for the little girl, tiny under her white covering. Then he walked back up the front steps and into the house. We watched the door for what must have been a long time. Birds fought in the dark interior of the juniper bushes over things that we did not comprehend. The smaller body fidgeted in the backseat of the sedan. The father returned, carrying an aerosol can that turned out to be spray paint, cherry red. He stood in front of the garage door and in large sagging block letters he spelled out:

HE WHO SITS NEXT TO ME,
MAY WE EAT AS ONE

The ghost man looked down at his can of spray paint like someone wondering what he had just done and whether he had done it all correctly. Then he set it down on the driveway and got into the car. There was the sound of the engine starting up, the tires grinding against stray rocks, and then they were gone. They had left the front door open.

B and I stared at the emptied house for a while, then she turned and climbed back inside, stepping over the puddles of Popsicle juice and dead ants. I squinted at their house, a drop of sweat settling onto my eyelashes and making me blink. Through the front windows I could see corners of their furniture, covered over in still more swaths of white fabric. It looked like a room about to be professionally fumigated or painted, some mundane sort of transformation. I sat there for maybe a half hour watching the empty house for whatever might happen next. But nothing happened next. When the ants started crawling over me, I brushed my body off and went back in through the window. I was still hungry when I got back to my room. I stared at the knot of hair for a while before I turned on the smaller TV in my bedroom, the one I watched when I didn't want to watch near B.

The TV was showing another commercial for Kandy Kakes. This commercial was one of the newer series of ads that mixed animated and live-action components. In this new series, Kandy Kat would often successfully chase down or otherwise achieve contact with the snack cakes, but the cakes were pictured as live-action, three-dimensional objects while the cat was always a flat cartoon. The gag each time was that no matter how hard he tried, Kandy Kat could never put a Kandy Kake down his throat: the two types of matter were fundamentally incompatible. This went along with an advertising campaign centered around the point that Kandy Kakes were made of Real Stuff. Maybe not natural stuff, but definitely genuine three-dimensional material from our physical universe that was similar to us in ways that it might not be to bodies from a cartoon world.

In this commercial, Kandy Kat walks wobbily through a cartoon landscape full of dancing trees. The trees are shaking their middles and singing the Kandy Kakes jingle, as little birds play bells and maracas in their branches. You can see every rib on Kandy Kat's brownish body as he wobble-skips through the woods, having what appears to be a pleasant day. He looks fairly carefree, oblivious to his hunger and to the words being chanted all around him by the living trees—when suddenly he happens upon a plate of Kandy Kakes sitting in a clearing in the middle of the forest, three-dimensional and super-real among the painted foliage, glowing with a sparkly light that is not real, not cartoon, but something in between. In rapid sequence, he spasms through shock, surprise, delight, disbelief, delight again, and then crippling hunger. His ribs throb. And when he reaches out for the platter, you actually see his emaciation in motion: the skin sags a little off the forearm, the bones and tendons of the arm show starkly with a little drop shadow under them to heighten the effect. His eyes grow larger and whiter in their huge cartoon sockets. At this moment, I want so badly for him to just take one of those revolting Kakes and shove it all the way into his belly, anything, anything to anchor his body a little bit.

But when his hand finally reaches the plate and grabs for a Kandy Kake, none of the Kakes will budge. It's hard to describe. It looks like Kandy Kat's hand is touching them through the glow, but they aren't affected at all. It's not like they're a photo, but more like they're impossibly heavy so he'll need something else to move them. So Kandy Kat runs out of the frame and gets a comically large fork and he aims it at the plate and stabs down, but the fork seems to just pass through them as though they're made of nothing, and Kandy Kat stabs more slowly and then picks the fork up and looks at it, confused. Then he runs back out of the frame and returns with an ax, which just does the same thing—nothing—no matter how many times he hacks away at the plate. Meanwhile the forest is getting pretty torn up. And when he runs back out of the frame and comes back he's got tons of dynamite, which he sets up all around the Kakes and detonates in a huge explosion that turns all the trees and birds black, with little white eyes blinking in stunned disbelief. The platter of Kakes glows more handsomely than ever against this scorched background, and finally Kandy Kat just yanks his mouth open with his two hands, painfully wide with a cracking sound, and jumps mouth-first onto the plate and the Kakes, trapping their glow inside his mouth as he lies on the forest floor.

His mouth is kind of suctioned to the ground now, and he struggles, very carefully, to close it, drawing the lips together, biting into the soil to prevent any precious morsel from being left behind, and he closes slowly on a mouthful of dirt and plate and Kakes. He stands up, shaking, his mouth full. There are big bite marks in the cartoon soil where his teeth have gouged away at the earth. And—tentatively—he bites down.

It doesn't even make a sound.

Confusion shows on his face, and he bites again, and again, more rapidly: nothing. Then, stretching his throat out to the appropriate width, he tries to swallow the plate whole, again and again, nothing. Finally, disheartened, he spits out the plate, the Kakes perfect and intact, still with that weird magical glow on everything, though now the glow has something smug about it. Kandy Kat looks toward the screen and his eyes have a new wetness to them. KANDY KAKES, the screen reads. REAL STUFF. REAL GOOD.

I looked down at my body as if for the first time. I felt fear wadding up the swallowing part of my throat. I reached down and put my hand on my stomach. I thought about the little swaddled girl in the back of the four-door sedan, so limp and still that she could have been a heap of dirty laundry. I wondered what happened to their dog. There was a bruise on my left thigh that I'd never seen before, and I was hungrier than I'd ever been. On the television screen, the evening news returned from commercial. There had been breakthroughs in the preliminary testing of a new anticancer drug designed to heighten the immune system's sensitivity to familiar somatic cells growing at abnormal rates. Half of the animals used in testing showed greatly reduced growth for tumors and other unusual structures, as well as a reduction in the number of new abnormalities. The other half died.

ON A TELEVISION TALK SHOW, a man named Michael spoke, his gaze drifting over and over to something beyond the camera and snapping back into position only at the prompting of the host. His scalp had been shaved, poorly. He was seated in a purple armchair that looked ugly and at the same time expensive, wearing a nice gray suit that he kept grabbing at, trying to pull it tighter across his body. He was here to explain the series of events that had led to his arrest, and he had prepared a video to help him talk. Over his head the screen faded to black and then there were scenes of veal farming: shaky handheld shots showing the crated calves gridding endlessly through long dark rooms. They ate in lines, slept in lines, fastened to their positions by lengths of chain. Stillness kept their flesh tender, prevented effort from knotting the fibers of their meat into muscle. Their low-iron diet ensured that color would not stick to the inside of the bodies. Lack of light kept pigment from ripening in the flesh. In the darkness of the warehouse farm, the calves grew whiter and whiter and softer, and the thought of this darkness wrapped around so many swelling lives grew a parental protectiveness in Michael, alongside an aimless hunger.

In the grocery store near his apartment, the slabs of pale meat were faceless, yet somehow still sad. The sadness was in the meat. Or maybe it was in him, he couldn't tell which: it hovered between them both, stretched taut like a cord. He watched the slices, splayed out on Styrofoam. He handled packages, made dents with his fingers in the plastic-wrapped flesh, and watched them disappear the moment he lifted his hand from the surface. When he held them he could feel the big dark spaces full of moaning life. The grocery store stocked only five or six packages of veal at a time, and he bought half of this veal and took it home. He didn't know what he would do with it afterward. *I just wanted to set it free,* he said on the TV.

Michael stored veal cutlets in his fridge and left them there in the cold dark. He went to work six days a week delivering mail through slim slots. As he made his rounds, he thought about the meat shivering in stacks. Sectioned off and stunted, it still needed a guardian. When he went back to the grocery store, the veal section had regrown—as though he had never been there, had never handled the stiff bundles and brought them out into the sunlight, then back into the dark cold of the refrigerator. He bought up all the veal this time, then for weeks afterward he bought all the veal and just kept it until there was no space for the new veal. Because there was no place to store it, he began to eat it instead, this veal that would not fit, filing it away in the utter dark of the digestive tract, tucking it into himself like a parent putting a child to bed. He cooked it simply, seasoned with salt and pepper, fried in butter on the stove. The meaning of the act of saving the veal had become less clear to him even as it became easier and more natural to do.

At the same time, the grocery store had begun to keep more in stock to meet customer demand, the demand that was his alone. Now there were ten to twelve packets of veal each time he came.

He couldn't afford to buy them all, but he did anyway, burying the packages in a hole he dug in the side yard near the rhododendrons, because the fridge was full. When he had used up what was in his bank account, he snuck them out of the store under his shirt, the flat faces of the veal pressed against pale, soft stomach, slab to slab, until one day he was arrested and charged on multiple counts of theft and aggravated assault.

The smooth edges of the cutlets: as if they had just grown that way, perfect and glandless. As if they had been peeled off, gently, from a larger cutlet, a mass long and cylindrical and placid. That even, stirred-together color of the flesh, the occasional streak of pure white that trailed off the side, hinting that it had a history as something larger. Such beauty in the lack of ducts or orifices, unitary and complete, impossible to feed it or cause it pain. A pasture full of veal cutlets sitting under the sun, looking eyelessly up.

I couldn't do anything for the calves, he said. *I'm just one man. But I thought to myself: I can do something for these cutlets.*

I looked over at C sitting next to me on the couch, his arm slung around my shoulders. He sucked the residue of beer from the top of the can, then ran his tongue along the crevice. C was great at watching TV. He could go for hours and never get that dead look in the face, the one B and I sometimes wore after we'd spent too long in its shifting, hypervivid light. With the remote in his hand and my head in the crook of his arm, he could pull me toward him for a kiss as easily as he could change the channel. From time to time he did this, mouthed me drily without turning his head, and his lips felt gentle on my face, like swabbing the skin with a cotton ball. C was suited to his life and to the historical period within which his life unfolded. He didn't long to return to a simpler time, or to destroy the current time, or to build a better future. He was a happy camper. This was one of the things that made our relationship work so well: he always assumed I was happy, too, even when I wasn't. With C, I could sit there and cycle through hurt, anger, sadness, ambivalence, acceptance, all without disturbing the comfortable rapport between us. As a result, he called me easygoing. And at times when the inner corners of my eyes burned and I knew I was about to spill, I had only to look over at him and his utterly normal grin to feel like I had grossly misread my own situation. Then whatever feeling I was feeling would hollow itself out, so that all I felt was that I no longer knew what I felt. "What you're describing is called 'satori,'" C would tell me with confidence. "It's the Buddhist term for happiness, specifically for becoming unburdened. It's like what we'd call peace. You should learn to embrace it, not think it to death," he added.

This is happiness, I thought as the air-conditioning droned behind me like a single monstrous insect. My face tingled or was falling asleep on one side. I had hoped happiness would be warmer, cozier, more enveloping. More exciting, like one of the things that happen on TV to TV people instead of the calming numb of watching it happen. C's limp palm was damp with sweat. Beneath it my body hairs trembled in the cold. C liked the temperature the same during the summer as it was in the winter so that he could keep wearing his favorite sweater year-round, a nubbly blue wool that was starting to give out at the elbows. I thought I saw my own breath in the frigid air, but it was probably just dust. I wriggled my shoulders around beneath his arm, trying to generate warmth, and in response he tightened his grip on me, making it harder to stir. I moved my head around, I made small sounds in my throat indicating that I had something to say. I felt sad, then unsad again. Birds settled on the old oak outside the window, settled there and waited and then left. Where had they gone, and were they better there? From indoors, watching the trees outside sag in the heat was like watching television, a little hole in the world that opened onto something entirely unrelated, trapped behind glass.

"Hey," I said.

"Are you there?" I asked.

"Hmm," said C.

I looked back at the TV screen. A large piece of calf was getting chopped and chopped and chopped into smaller, more numerous pieces. It resembled a thing growing out, melting, spreading across the screen.

"It's so weird," I said. "He wanted to keep people from eating veal, and then he ate more of it than anyone."

C turned his head to look at me for the first time in a while.

"Or," he said, "he wanted to eat it, and that scared him. He interpreted that fear as fear of the act, then used that more acceptable fear to reason his way back to doing what he had wanted to do all along, which was to eat it." In his blue sweater, in the faintly blue light, he looked far away and boyish.

"I don't know," I said. "That's so complicated. I thought he looked frightened. He looked sick. Did you see how he kept pulling his suit tight around him? It looked like he was thinking of the meat inside him."

"Well, he's also nuts," C said calmly.

C said everybody was nuts.

I twisted my body around inside C's hold to get a better view of the TV, flickering with color and light and sound. What was it that made one person go nuts while the rest of the world remained intact around them? I'd ask C on the next commercial break. *What the cutlets want,* I thought to myself. *The flesh desires something different from its sum,* I tried to think, but I wasn't sure, it didn't sound right. C's breathing was long and slow and peaceful next to me, and I felt comforted by the fact that what was going on in his head was the same as mine: the image of Michael's panic-tightened face on the screen threaded its way from the eyes toward the center of the head, through branching neuronal trails to a sludgy affective core. Even if we felt differently about the image and its meaning, at least it was inside us both, acting on our inner parts. Michael's image made something claw inside of me. Sitting in his ugly chair, he radiated a pitiful and trapped energy. He clutched at the air as he described lifting the allotments of flesh from their casings, peeling them from Styrofoam trays, and laying them onto the frying pan. He described the gentleness of the meat, how it trusted, and his eyes were as wide and gelatinous as a deer's. When Michael looked down at the imaginary cutlet in his hand, he had the face of a saint.

At that moment I wished that C would look at me like that, touch me like that, and I wondered if there were a way to trick him into doing what I wanted. A new product had just come out from Fluvia cosmetics, designed to soften your skin by tenderizing the subdermal layers that were sometimes stringy with things such as fat, muscle, and pores. The ad claimed that nobody would be able to resist falling in love with your new skin, then showed a beautiful woman holding still as her boyfriend, boss, best friend, and workplace nemesis gathered around, stroking her skin wonderingly with the tips of their fingers. But I didn't think a product like that would have any influence over C. He was one of those rare people who seemed only to do things that were their own original idea. When he bought deodorizing underarm spray at the Wally's Supermarket by his condo, it was as though the need had suddenly occurred to him and the correct product had simply presented itself—even though I knew that he had seen the commercials because I watched them with him, watched him laughing at them. He was a graceful consumer: he could consume without being consumed in turn.

In C's living room, the television talked on. It must have been early in the day: the show had the calm irrelevance of programming at hours when only the trapped and the old and the infirm are watching. Michael was still on-screen, explaining what had led him to attack a supermarket employee with the veal cutlets he had hidden away beneath his shirt. *He stopped me and asked what was under my clothing. He told me stealing had consequences in his store,* Michael said. *That's when I realized I wasn't just eating the cutlets. I was eating a whole machine, a machine much bigger than me, and a lot better organized. And when I thought of all the parts of that machine, the meadows and the grasses and the slicing machines and the plastic wrap machines and the factory farm gates and the steel manufacturers and the person who stuck the price sticker on the outside of the package, and the person who killed the calves, and the people they went home to after work, how those and other invisible parts were all there working away inside the piece of meat, I don't know. I just felt so full. I had been so empty and now I was full like I was maybe going to throw up. And I knew that if I did, it would be just veal, all veal. All the veal I had hidden from danger. I couldn't let that happen. So I guess I just panicked.*

On the grainy surveillance footage, small figures drained of color grappled with light-colored rectangles, tugging them in opposing directions. Michael was the thinner, taller, dark-haired one facing off against a store employee wearing the Wally's uniform, his foam head huge and smiling. Though Michael was larger and stronger than the grocery store kid, whose flabby arms peeked from his polo sleeves, you could tell he was frightened by the grimace on his face, like a photo of a man on a roller coaster, taken midplunge. He started hitting the uniformed employee over and over and over again with a package of veal, as another shopper stopped to stare. Eventually something dark came out of the employee and spilled onto the floor: it could have been blood or vomit. The image looked just like the grocery store down the street from C's apartment.

Do you consider yourself a hero? asked the talk show host, a woman dressed in royal blue with stiff, sculptural hair.

What? asked Michael. *What?* He looked so confused, doubly confused, as though the question were confusing him, but also and more important as though he couldn't even understand where he was, or how he got there, or how to get back out.

When I looked over again, C had fallen asleep. His head was tipped back and his mouth lay open and pointed up, all the hardness gone out of it, the hands loose and docile as flowers. I saw all

the things I liked about his body laid out like a map, and I knew
how his chest would feel under my hands, I knew what it would
be like to take the lobe of his ear between my front teeth and
press them together. At the same time, I had no idea what his
dreams were made of, whether they ever involved me, whether
they involved other women I knew or did not know. Though I had
spent hours and hours for months with C, I possessed a better
understanding of what went on inside of Michael's veal-addled
psychology. What Michael wanted leaked through him like blood
through a tissue. C, by contrast, remained obscure. I was still
staring over at him when he woke up, looking straight into my
eyes, scratching at his cheek blearily.

"How long have you been awake?" he asked.

Before I could answer, he stood up.

"We have to get the laundry," he said.

C sloughed his sweater in preparation for entering the
summer swarth. He inhaled sharply, sucked snot back up into
his nasal cavity. We were behaving exactly like people behaved,
there was nothing wrong that I could name, but for some reason
I wasn't feeling that unalone feeling you were supposed to have
when you were with someone else. Was there anything joining
me to my life that was a matter of necessity rather than chance?
It wasn't my body, which could be moved from place to place,
job to job, fed nearly anything, partnered with anyone. It wasn't
my mind, which seized the fake lives of television people with
greater enthusiasm than it did its own. Sometimes I thought
about C and the idea came to me that any man's genitalia, however large or weirdly shaped, would be guaranteed to fit inside
my own. Our pairing was coincidental or, at best, lucky. I wished

that for once he'd just agree with me on any one thing about how I saw the world.

THE LAUNDROMAT WAS A TEN-MINUTE walk from C's condo, a stand-alone building with a crummy parking lot riddled with cracks in which dandelions tried to grow. At the front counter they sold detergent, fabric softener, bleach. They also sold tampons, shaving cream, disposable razors, small dinosaur toys made out of glow-in-the-dark plastic, novelty pencils, candy bars, and hot dogs. C bought a hot dog from a sunburned teenage girl who sat behind the counter watching a game show where a woman applied makeup to a man who I decided might have been her husband.

"Do you want one?" C asked. "Mmmm," he added, his mouth full. He made squeaky sounds as he chewed. The casing was popping, splitting, tearing.

"I'm all right," I said. The Laundromat hot dogs tasted okay, but sometimes you found bits of things in them that had the texture of knuckles. There were only a few other people in the place, older women leaning against the folding tables as they watched their clothes struggle behind the thick glass of the washing machines. We walked over to our dryer, where the clothes had been still for over an hour. I opened up the dryer door and squeezed them. They felt like limp wet fur. "Still damp," I said. C fed some more quarters into the slot.

I hopped up onto a folding table and watched the clothes jump up toward the top of the chamber and fall back to the bottom, over and over again. C was looking back toward the counter. "Do you think I should get another hot dog?" he asked.

I felt grossed out. "I'll probably be hungry after we're done with this," I said, hoping that we could go someplace after. I was hungry now, but I didn't want to deal with C making me eat one of those hot dogs or explaining why I didn't want to or what I had been eating the past few days with B.

"Yeah, still," he said, "that'll probably be forty minutes or more from now, I don't know if I'll make it." He looked toward the girl at the counter and then walked up, ordered another hot dog, choked it down effortfully while checking his phone with the other hand.

All of the machines at the Laundromat were full, even though the place was almost empty. Pale-colored fabric spun around end-lessly, and from the look of the sudsless water it seemed as though the machines had been running for some time. I took out my phone and checked to see if C was doing anything on his phone that I could see on mine, but he wasn't. The older women read magazines or stared. The girl behind the counter unwrapped a package of chewing gum. On the TV screen mounted to the ceil-ing, the woman stood proudly next to her husband, whose thick, cakey makeup made them look weirdly similar.

C came back and leaned against the folding table. "That was the right decision," he said happily.

"Good," I said. I was looking across the room at a stack of folded white sheets three feet high. Next to it was a shorter stack, crisp and folded. There were dozens and dozens of sheets there, all carefully arranged, all of a blank, silky white.

"What do you think all those sheets are for?" I asked.

C looked over.

"Probably for the normal reasons," he said. "What do you mean?"

"I saw something weird the other day," I said.

C turned toward me, still doing something on his phone.

"Okay," he said.

"I was watching from the roof," I began. "The people across the street came home in the middle of the afternoon, which never happens. They went into their house for a while, maybe five minutes. A short while, like they already had everything prepared. Then when they came back out, they were all wearing white sheets with holes cut out for their eyes, like cheap ghost costumes. It looked really sloppy, the eyeholes didn't even fit right on their heads. Then they got in their car and drove away, and they haven't been back since."

"What happened to their dog?" C asked. "The loud dog?"

"I don't know," I said. "I've been listening and I never hear it anymore.

"I listen all day long," I added, more or less to myself.

"You're sure they haven't been back?" he asked, typing what I thought looked like a reply into his phone and pressing send. His face was smooth like a sheet.

"Well, not while I was home," I said, sounding defensive, though I wasn't sure why. "Obviously I haven't been home for a few hours," I said.

"Okay," C said thoughtfully, as though he had made a decision. He put his phone in his pocket and pulled himself up to a standing position. "You're a sensitive person, you saw something weird, you feel spooked. No pun intended. There are plenty of reasons why what you saw might have happened, and some of them are weird. But some of them are just boring. You know? That family could have been going to some kind of school pageant. Or a birthday party. So you can just ask yourself: Do I live in a weird town, or a boring town?"

I blinked at him.

"I'd say boring," he added, nodding and then raising both eyebrows expectantly.

I loved his face, his bland white good-looking face. I believed in him and therefore in the boringness of my town. C was good at handling me. He made things suddenly, instantaneously normal, just by explaining them. He was like a magnifying glass, I only had to look through him to see the world in crisp detail. And he had a really nice smile and good teeth. They were so good that he had probably had braces once, and a retainer, and maybe even headgear. I saw him standing in the middle of a sunlit field, a child with a baseball bat in his hand and a mouth full of metal. Beneath a huge blue sky, he wheeled around on the grass, swinging his bat at butterflies. It was a scene so normal, it felt capable of infecting the neighboring parts of my mind, making me normal in turn. I smiled.

We stood around waiting for the clothes to dry, checking every couple of minutes, and when they were dry enough C dumped them into a wheeled bin that he rolled over to the folding table, where we turned item after item of rumpled clothing into neat little rectangles. C's shirts were old and soft with nonsense slogans on them; there were three or four button-ups and a few pairs of pants. The older women had been replaced by other older women, similarly dressed but at the beginning of their laundering process, pouring capfuls of detergent, unloading jumbles of colorful things, and putting them into the washers. C piled his folded clothes back into the laundry bag and hoisted it over his shoulder. "Ready?" he asked, heading for the door.

I followed him out, but when I looked back from the doorway I saw an old woman, one of the ones who sat around the Laundromat all day watching the little ceiling-mounted TV and sucking on fruit-flavored hard candies. Sometimes for a few bucks she did other people's laundry. Right now she was standing, holding up a white sheet, unfurled, and it was perfectly normal except for two holes that could be draped over the eyes.

I HAD STARTED DATING C a couple of years ago, during the fall when fathers began vanishing from out of their comfortable, middle-class homes. For the first few weeks, local newscasters read out the list of the newly vanished each night along with the location in which they were last seen, and it sounded as if they were reading from a master catalog of legitimate, reasonable names, names like "Peter" and "Steve." Ted Hartwell, Matt Skofield, Dennis Galp. None of them knew one another, and there was nothing to link them except that they were all equally average. Telephone poles and store windows went white with flyers depicting men in interchangeable hairstyles, clad in polo shirts, all traces of fun leached from their faces long ago. They wore confused expressions in the pictures selected by their family members, as if none of their kin had cared to warn them that photographs were going to be taken. Their confusion made it seem as though they had been lost for a long time, much longer than they had been gone.

The news anchors called it "Disappearing Dad Disorder." For months nobody knew where the dads had gone, whether they had been stolen or had stolen themselves, victims of self-napping. Then last January dads started turning up, one by one. Good Samaritans found them wandering dazed in shopping malls five towns over, malls that were not their own but resembled their own to an uncanny degree. They would return to familiar stores like the Gap and try to buy khakis with little scraps of paper that they had collected from obscure places. They sat on the mall benches and closed their eyes, waiting for someone to claim them. Often they wore clothes identical to the ones they had disappeared in, identical but fresh smelling, as if they had been laundered or even bought new in the same sizes and colors. They were confused and quiet, preferring to stare off into the distance or fiddle with a key chain instead of engaging with those around them, those who asked them gently: *Are you lost? Is your family looking for you? Do you have a number we can call?* When questioned about their disappearance, whether they left or had been taken, who had taken them, did they remember his face, height, manner of dress, was it someone they knew from work, from home, from the bowling league, from the auto repair shop, was it many people, an organization, a religious group, a band of criminals, a league of sexual predators, the missing dads reproduced, with slight variations in phrasing, a single sentence: *Sometimes you've just got to be content with things the way they are.*

The emptiness of C's apartment reminded me of those missing fathers. The place was nice the way car dealerships are nice: clean, spacious, cold, and full of light. He owned two of the same self-assembled couches and three identical self-assembled end tables, the cheapest model they made. They were all arranged in his living room, the couches side by side gaplessly and facing forward to the television set, the end tables pushed together in front of them to form a single, long, low table from which you could eat food if you hunched over and lowered your jaw almost to your knees. From the door, you could see the living room, kitchen, and a chunk of bedroom splayed before you like a blueprint of someplace an engineer had once thought might be all right to live in. I took a few steps forward and the bedroom came into view, a full-sized mattress on the floor with navy-blue sheets and a wad of comforter. Next to it, a laptop blinked drowsily.

"Did you just move in?" I asked, hoping that he had.

C laughed. "People always ask that. I've been living here two years. Two and a half, really," he added.

"Where do you keep your things?" I asked, and he gestured all around us.

C did graphic design for a small advertising agency, but this had almost nothing to do with his life. He left for work around eight thirty or nine in the morning and returned unchanged, with few memories of where he had been. If I asked about his work, he seemed surprised to be reminded of it, then annoyed. "If you want to talk about dead-end jobs," he'd say sometimes, "why don't you talk about your own?" and I would respond to this by saying nothing at all. I pictured him as a hot-air balloon, saggy and bright, tethered to the earth by three or four flimsy ropes. The person who lived in this bare, depressing, anonymously furnished apartment was about one taut rope from falling off the face of the earth, I decided.

"Are you one of those people who acts normal, but is secretly about to chuck their lives and disappear?" I asked. If that were the case, I wasn't going to waste my time getting to know him. I knew that we'd be dating for a while, at least, when he laughed several times, loudly, and kissed me for what was then the third or fourth time ever.

"Yeah, right. No way. Neither are you," he said. "I've seen that on TV, those dads, and it is nuts. No way. Everything's worked out great for me since whenever, I don't have any plans to make it complicated. Besides, I'm attached to my material goods."

What material goods? I wondered. Then I followed the arc of his arm pointing to a location across the room. He had been referring to his collection of DVDs, heaps of horror and comedy and porn, stacked together in a pile the size of a small love seat.

In the cold of C's apartment, we had just finished folding the laundry.

"Can we do something?" I asked.

C looked at me mildly.

"Like what?" he said.

I looked around us.

I went to C's kitchen and stood staring at the open cupboards that held his library of canned goods. He had cooked beans flavored with pig fat, different soups and stews, vegetables—corn off the cob, chopped green beans, carrots sliced into bright orange circles. There were peaches and pears in syrup and, toward the back of the cupboard, canned meats with labels obscured by shadow. Blocky squares of skin-colored food on their printed labels were visible through gaps between the small towers of cans. I was impressed by how well the cans stacked together: they fit to each other the way I wished I fit to the things around me. And there were cans of fruit cocktail with peeled grapes, canned peas, Porkpot Chili, and an off-brand noodle-and-meat-sauce product that had a picture of tomatoes on its label, but no tomatoes listed in the ingredients. There were cans of tuna and cans of olives and pineapple and also mandarin oranges suspended in sugary water, the little naked pieces jostling up together in the perfect dark of the can, curled fetally against one another.

"Do you have anything fresh?" I called out to C, who was already sitting in front of the TV in the other room.

"All that stuff is fresh," C said. "And it lasts for one to five years," he added.

I didn't think I could stand to eat any of it. I imagined opening a can and putting a forkful into my mouth, and I knew, whatever it was, it would be soft and yielding and would disintegrate as I pushed it around with my tongue. I wanted to eat something real and living, something tough with life. I wanted to destroy it with my teeth. I wanted it to be veal. I wished that I had eaten one of the gross hot dogs earlier, but it was too late for that. I heard a smattering of crunching sounds from the TV over in the other room.

"You're missing *Shark Week*," C shouted.

I went over and got under the blanket with him. I tucked my feet in under his thighs and looked where he was looking.

On TV, the sharks ate through a goose and a school of sardines. They ate a belly-up humpback whale that had died partway through its migration, and when it died it had rolled over and slid up to the surface of the sea, a glistening red exposure rising toward the sun and quick spoilage. Under the rows of sharp teeth, the whale came apart as if it were made of wet paper, sloughing wads of sodden crimson that slid into the water with a liquid sound. The sharks ate seals, and other things by accident—driftwood, garbage, people. The lesson was that sharks were made to eat things. Nothing else had the immense hunger of a shark, and nothing else could back that hunger up with such efficient action. It was so beautiful that I felt like I wanted to be a part of it, though I knew it would be impossible for me to ever become a shark.

At the commercial break, there was an ad for Kandy Kakes. In this commercial, Kandy Kat faces off against his longtime nemesis Kandy Klown, a bulbous, Santa-shaped figure who consumes Kandy Kakes like it's the simplest thing in the world, like it's all he can do. He makes it look easy. The Klown is walking around, left leg, then right leg, slowly articulating full circles in the air, the two round hemispheres of his belly bobbing up and down alternatingly, bobbing in rhythm with the smooth fall of his feet. As he walks, the little Kandy Kakes on their tiny legs trot over to him and form a patient little queue scurrying alongside. Now the first one runs forward with a sudden burst of speed and hops straight into the Klown's mouth. Its body is a cheery little lump visible in the Klown's profile. Then the next one runs up and hops in, then another. Slack-jawed and dark, the Klown's mouth is the exact shape and dimension of the Kandy Kakes that slide through it so smoothly.

All of a sudden we see Kandy Kat some distance away, watching this scene unfold through binoculars. His jaw hangs open, and out comes some drooly fluid. He turns away from the scene and grabs his head in anguish, then his stomach in anguish, the stomach distended and throbbing through the thin cover of skin. Suddenly he has an idea and rushes off-screen. We hear the sound of metal, rubber, cloth in motion, and when he runs back on-screen, he's dressed like a Klown. He's got the white face painted on, the ridiculous red nose, the floppy polka-dotted hat pulled over his ragged ears. With the sharp nozzle of a bicycle pump through his belly, he inflates himself until he rolls, lolling like a moored boat. He runs to the Kandy Kakes gathering and strikes a Klownish pose, arms out and swaying, listing slightly from side to side. The Kandy Kakes turn and for a moment they seem to be considering it. Kandy Kat's big eyes grow wet and you can see he is full of hope, you can see it like you see the heart pounding inside the little cage of his body. A dry red tongue slowly rolls out of his mouth.

Then they decide. As if they are a single body, a single mind, they fall upon him. They fall upon him with their small, sharp mouths, swarming his bony frame, covering it completely, bending it beneath their weight as the Klown watches a few feet over. They tear at his costume, little bits of it are flying everywhere, and we hear a dozen wacky sproingy noises while the voice-over announces:

KANDY KAKES. WE KNOW WHO YOU REALLY ARE.

I noticed that I had been sitting with my nails pressing into my knee, and as I pulled the hands away I saw ten little semicircular segments dug in, each one a purply blue. It was like discovering that I was filled with something totally different from everyone else, a dark and dislikable substance, and I had let a bit of it seep up for the first time. So I turned to C and asked, experimentally:

"Do you think we look alike? B and me?"

"Well, if I had to describe you and her with words," he began cautiously, "I guess they might be the same words." He frowned at the screen, which was now advertising toilet paper, miles and miles of toilet paper wrapping all around a cartoon world. "If I had to use words," he added.

He was still looking at the screen, looking as if he were waiting for something to show up on it and save him from whatever my next question might be.

"Do you know she cut her hair?" I asked.

"Well, it's summer. It's terrible," he said, toggling the volume on the TV set up and down and then up again.

"It looks just like mine now from behind," I said.

"Well, honestly," he said. "Lots of girls look the same from behind.

"People, I mean," he said sheepishly.

I didn't say anything.

"Like her," he said, indicating someone on-screen in what looked like a tampon commercial. "I bet she looks like you from behind."

The slogan to that Kandy Kakes advertisement was off somehow. *We know who you really are.* It failed to sell anything; it wasn't friendly, it sounded more like a threat than a promise. But then again, maybe it was a promise made to the worthy, that they alone would have all the Kandy Kakes they desired. Or a promise to those eating Kandy Kakes, that they would become good people, worthy of eating the things they had eaten. Either way, I realized I felt hungry. Or to be precise, I wanted to take something into my mouth and destroy it there.

"You know what I want?" I said a little too loudly. "I want a Kandy Kake."

"They're gross," he said.

His face brightened suddenly and he leaned in toward the TV. From the edge of my vision I could see a frenzy of different blues and greens, creatures the color of the sea testing their teeth against one another.

"I know. But I want one anyway," I said.

I got up to do I don't know what. Leave?

"There's a lot of canned stuff in the cupboard," he said helpfully.

"I don't want that," I said.

"I want real food," I said, not knowing what I meant exactly but remembering the phrase from the commercials. As I said it, I was aware that what I said I wanted wasn't really what I wanted at all.

"I want to go to Wally's and buy real food," I said.

"We need a car for Wally's," he said, annoyed.

C was looking at me now, but clearly he wanted to look at something else. He squinted his eyes slightly, as though by looking harder, he could interest himself in what was going on with me. C loved *Shark Week* more than any other week on TV, so I knew it was taking some effort for him to pay attention to what I was saying.

"I worry about you sometimes," he said. "Everything gets you so bothered. You need something really bad to happen, to put it all in perspective. Or, I guess, for nothing bad to happen for a long time," he conceded.

I thought about B and whether I looked like the woman from the tampon commercial from behind. I thought about Michael and how it must feel to beat someone senseless with something that you love so very much. I thought about my boring town and the weird events. I thought about stacks on stacks of white sheets with holes cut into them, silent and pristine and waiting. I thought about one of the missing dads from that missing dad TV special they made back when the topic was really trending.

This dad had disappeared from his Fairfield County home while watching a football game. His wife and two young sons came back to find pretzels, Cheez Forms, and mini microwavable cheeseburgers sitting pristine in their plastic serveware, the TV chattering to nobody. Police posted his photo as far as Tibico City in the south and Coxton to the north, but nobody matching his description exactly turned up, although there were many approximate matches. A few months later, they found him living in a town more than three hundred miles away, across state lines. A neighbor had called to report a stranger living in the house next door to them, someone who seemed friendly enough but who had "a weird bent towards underreportage." When the local police investigated, they found their missing person living in an occupied single-family home with a blond woman who closely resembled his abandoned wife, down to the navy-blue pumps and feathery bangs. The blond woman, whose husband had vanished a year earlier, was the mother of two young children, both male. She preferred not to comment on how this stranger had come to take her husband's place or where her husband might be now. The missing father was arrested by Pleasanton police and held on suspicion of having kidnapped the woman's actual husband and assumed his identity. It turned out Pleasanton was also the name of the town from which he had originally disappeared, a town farther north but similar in all other ways, though authorities couldn't comment on whether this was a coincidence, an accident, or a mistake.

"Look," C said in a very soothing voice, putting his arms around me and pulling me back down to the couch. He slung himself around me so that I was like a wrapped package, unable to move my arms. He slid his hand up to my jaw and held it there as he kissed me on the cheek.

"You're okay," he said, "trust me."

For C, it was possible to get along with me even if I, for my part, was not getting along with him. It was lonely being the only one who knew how I was feeling, to not be stored in the mind of someone else who could remind you who you were. The image of a skeleton key flashed in my mind, heavy and long, made of antique brass with a wide, flat end for the thumb to push against when turning the key in the lock. The key was normal except at the functional end, where it had no teeth, nothing with which to turn the small gears of an inner lock. This was a key that could fit into any lock, a key that could never unlock anything.

C slid his arm around my back. His body was warm. He pointed to the TV.

"Look, the sharks are back. Just look at the sharks," he murmured, holding me close.

B AND I PAIRED UP before we even met. I heard stories about her, mostly stories about her biting people. It seemed like everybody knew somebody she had bitten, a friend of a friend or an ex-lover, most often during a one-on-one conversation. They happened at moments when B felt cornered in the conversation or when something unpleasant came up. I couldn't imagine what it would feel like to bite into another person. Usually one of the things I thought about when I bit down into something was how ill-suited my teeth were for biting down into anything.

When I got back to the apartment, the day was already close to ending, the light was growing dim. B sat on the couch in the living room facing the door, staring hard ahead of her with a drink in her hand. When I opened the door to find her there, clutching a plastic cup, she looked like she had been there ever since I had left, just waiting for me to walk back in. I stood at the edge of a room thick with my own absence, wondering whether to stick myself into it gradually or all at once.

I ran the tip of my tongue over my teeth, one by one. At the very back, the molars were short and crooked, angled rearward, pointed toward the throat. Then they were dull, blunt, herbivorous, with deep pits that roughened at the center. Their texture was disarrayed, unfinished. The points of the canines were rounded down, softened up like objects left out in the rain. Then the small white teeth at the front, divots in their backsides, the tiny incisors with their scalloped edges, registering some minor body crisis undergone when I was still a child. I felt sad for B. She seemed misequipped for her desires.

My conversations with other people about B always ended with something like this: *You should meet her. You two would get along. You have a lot in common.* But then I would ask what it was we had in common, and the person would say one thing, something B and I shared, that was true of me but didn't really seem central to who I was or believed myself to be. The person would tell me that B and I were both single, or we had the same color hair, or we both liked to read, or we had the same name. And then they would just leave it there, with that single trait dangling before me as if hung from the ceiling on a very long thread, turning and turning around slowly, making me wonder if it could be true that this trait constituted me and, if so, how fragile might it be, how solid?

But I met B only when she came to look at the empty bedroom in my apartment. My summer sublettor had worked at a moped repair shop and spent all his time at home locked in his room with his computer, his microwave, and a case of instant ramen, and I was looking for someone who was more like me. I knew from what other people had told me that B was looking for a room only because her boyfriend had broken up with her. I was worried that there'd be emotional spillage, maybe even some tears, and comforting strangers always made me feel like a pervert. She seemed so fragile when I had first opened the door, startlingly small in an overlarge dress and bare face. But she wasn't really any smaller than me—I just couldn't see myself from the outside. She looked at the room that was for rent, empty except for a mattress and a basic desk, and then she asked to see mine.

I watched from the doorway as she drifted between items of furniture. She moved like someone in convenience store surveillance footage, someone who hopes they are being watched. She would stop and stare someplace downward and ahead, then look around, then down again, dragging her gaze somewhere new, to some other piece of floor or fabric. She touched my books, rubbing the tops where hundreds of pages blended into some single surface, and she touched the glass of water by my bedside, and she picked up the broken snow globe that C had given me and the small painted wood box on my mantel. She handled them, turning them around to see each of the sides. B sat down on the bed and put her palms on the quilt. She was angled like a drawing, a form in two dimensions set into a world of three. She seemed to hover, holding herself just above the bed's surface so that she'd leave no mark on it with her weight.

Then she gazed up at me and said: *I wish I could wear makeup on my eyes, like you.* Then she said: *You have so many things.*

In second grade, I had a friend named Danielle who used to say the same thing whenever she came over for the playdates our parents arranged. *You have so many things,* she'd say. *What's this?* And I would answer her, where it came from, what its name was, whatever, while she looked it over. If she liked it enough, she would try to trade me for it, using whatever was in her pockets at the time. She always had something strange in the pockets of her bedazzled overalls, something crushed and shadowy that resembled nothing. Once she wanted my favorite stuffed animal, a dog I called

Pinky. *Can I have him?* she had said. *I'll give you this, it'll be a best friend trade.* "This" was a wadded-up washcloth with a picture of a reindeer on it and something spreading grayly at the left corner. I didn't know exactly what happened, but then I was holding this washcloth, and Pinky was no longer mine. Looking down into my hands, it looked as though something awful had happened to my stuffed dog. He had been flattened out, creased deep, warped. He had these weird things pushing out through his skull.

I STOOD THERE IN THE living room, still waiting for B to say something to me. I knew she might be upset that I had left her home alone. It was early evening, and the sky through the windows was a deep, darkening blue. They must have sprayed the neighborhood for insects because I heard nothing but the trees, their leaves twitching in the warm night air. A heavy, calm feeling suffused the room, but I knew that was temporary and about to end. Lit up by the TV, B's face was a mess of shadows. It reminded me of that first day, waiting for her mouth to move, standing in the doorway of my own bedroom wondering if she'd ever put her teeth in me.

"So you're back now," she said.

The word *now* sounded like an accusation.

"I'm back now," I said.

"Where were you?" she asked.

"With C. You know. Watching sharks on TV, mostly," I said, trying to shift the conversation a foot or two to my right.

"It was *Shark Week*, or still is, I guess. C knows everything about them. Did you know that you can tell the age of a shark by counting the rings on its vertebrae? Like a tree," I said.

There was no reply.

"What are you watching?" I asked.

"I'm watching channel seek," she replied.

Watching channel seek was when we pushed the button on the remote that made the TV automatically cycle through all of its stations one by one. You'd see a politician and he'd say the word *institutions* and then suddenly he'd be a tractor pushing through tall grass and then the tractor would be a bucket of steaming hot fried chicken being emptied onto a plate, et cetera. We watched channel seek when we were upset, because it was like experiencing several dozen small attachments and losses that you could maybe prevent but definitely would not do anything about.

"I'm sorry," I said.

I looked at the side table. There were a few oranges with little gouges in them, as if someone had started to peel them and given up. From over here they looked like faces, with the eyes and mouths all misplaced.

"Have you eaten anything?" I asked. "We should have dinner."

"It's past dinner," she said.

"Okay, a snack," I said.

"I'm not hungry," she said. She had turned the volume way up on channel seek.

"It's past a snack," she said softly, as if to herself.

With the television turned up so high, I saw the outline of her words but couldn't hear them. The television speakers rattled softly with the force of their own output.

I went to the bathroom to see if there was anything going on with my face. I stood in front of the bathroom mirror and registered the discrepancy between how I had looked last afternoon and how I looked now. In this way I measured the amount of life that had been extracted from me by loving someone, in person, face-to-face. I gauged the minus value by the dullness of my skin, the streaky, patchy black around my left eye, the miscellaneous redness that came from rubbing my face against C's stubble as it increased in length and bristliness hour after hour. My skin felt looser from where he had squished it, playfully or in clumsy love. I had a swollen spot on my lip where I had gotten bitten or sucked. My face in the mirror looked like someone else's staring back at me through an open window in her own bathroom, and all I could think was that hers looked very much my own, only much more tired.

I did the toothpaste and the floss, the facial wash and toner and moisturizer. I dabbed something on the dark spots to fade them, and I covered them over with concealer. I did a layer of primer and applied the foundation, rubbing it on in small circles as if I were buffing or sanding. A zone of creamy, skin-colored skin eked away at my own. It ate up the jaw, the chin, the nose, the forehead. I was looking more like myself every second. I did the eyes, drawing an eye-shaped outline around the whole thing. The spots were still there, but now they were putty colored, on their way out or between. They might have been residue on the surface of the mirror, except they moved when I did. I reached for more concealer to cover them up. I was watching the hand in the mirror rather than my own.

From out in the living room I heard the sounds of channel seek. *If you're looking for . . . brrrrrrrrrztztzt . . . an open door . . . by eight and three-fourths . . . kinder or better . . . ring-*

*dringdring I'm sorry . . . get it under . . . and then you rolllll
your hips, kinda ro . . . ckclunk . . . I never said you could have
her but . . . just got better . . . unlike the ostrich . . . anything,
anything . . . reminder of our . . . If he knew, if he knew what
was going to . . . a personal pizza for . . . lk klk klk klk kriiik . . .
and then I start right over here, you see, sort of skating along
the edge of the eye, just kind of skaaaating my pencil along the
edge of the eye. There, you see how easy this is? There, again,
just skaaaaate it along the line you've already got there, yes.
Yes. Now we're going to do the extensions.* It always felt weird
when channel seek started to make sense, like mistaking a real
person for a mannequin. That the television made sense again
meant that B had found something to stick with, but it did not
necessarily mean that she was any happier. I walked back into
the living room and found her hunched into a ball, hugging her
knees to her chest the way I used to do when I was a child.

"What are you watching?" I asked.

"She's teaching them how to do eyeliner," B replied.

"Do you like that?" I asked.

"I don't know," B said. "You can see the brush tugging on the
skin near the eye. The skin bunches up and stretches at the same
time. It looks like a balloon being written on. Or something."

I looked at the screen. The woman who was speaking had her
hand wrapped around the jaw of the other woman, holding it from
beneath the way someone would hold a dog being force-fed a heart-
worm pill. She tilted the jaw up so that the eyes listed toward the ceiling, and then she brought the pencil point down toward the socket
from above. *It's so simple,* said the voice of the woman makeup artist.
Just think of it as drawing a picture. You're drawing a picture of your

face, right smack onto your face. Draw the face you'd like to have.
Draw your perfect face. Okay, now make sure your pencil's sharp.
I'm going to do little points at the end here, see? Looks just like a little
wing. Now we'll do blush. Right after this break. The camera pulled
back for the first time to show the full view of the woman being
made up. She was reasonably pretty, with a heavy nose and chin. A
spattering of zits trailed from her temple down toward her ear. She
turned her face silently toward the camera, revealing a half-finished
face. One side was a uniform beige with a thick, elongated eye that
swept up toward her temples. The other was bare. The eye within
its socket seemed tiny and underprotected. It looked as though the
second half of her face, previously hidden from the camera, were
sliding off the side.

"She looks beautiful," B said.

In the faintly electronic light of the television screen, I could
see B's T-zone pores, her untreated pimples, a small unexplained
scar beneath her left eye, unnaturally smooth and white against
the weak tissue. Sometimes a face could be so simple: even a
couple of dark spots on a lighter surface or a dark oval in the
distance might be a face. An electrical socket could be a face, a
mailbox or a couple of punctuation marks could congeal suddenly
into something with an expression. Our faces, on the other hand,
were made of hundreds of different parts, each part separate and
tenuous and capable of being ugly, each part waiting for a product
designed to isolate and act upon it. Every time I looked at my
face, I seemed to find another new piece to it, floating there next
to or underneath or inside the others, all the parts together but
impossible to connect.

B sat forward, trying to catch every word of the commercials as they unfolded one after another, her eyes darting from the left to the right over and over again as the bluish light played off her face. The two of them were like one now, B and the television. She balanced at the edge of the couch, clutching the remote with both hands. Then she looked right at me.

"You know, I think things would be better if I looked more like you," she said.

"What do you mean?" I asked, feeling nervous.

"I mean, I feel like if I looked more like you, maybe more people would talk to me. The way they talk to you," B said.

"I'm sure people talk to you," I said, though I had no idea if this was true.

"And when I looked in the mirror, maybe I wouldn't mind so much when you stayed away," B added, still looking right at me.

She said it with much more certainty than I expected from her. Her lower lip stuck out like a child's, thick and center creased, with a wart on it that might have been caused by cigarettes or repeated biting.

"It would be like you were still here, so I wouldn't really be alone," she continued.

"Or maybe it would be like I wasn't there as much, so I'd only feel partly as lonely," she added.

Her eyes were looking much larger than I had remembered.

"I don't know," I said. "Maybe you could get a pet?"

B looked for a second like she was going to cry or bite me.

"You don't understand," she said. "You've always got yourself to keep you company."

I wanted to disagree, but I didn't even understand. The effort of the conversation was making me hungry, hungry for something more substantial than an orange. But when I tried to think it through, think about what I would prefer to eat instead, all I could see was oranges, all I could taste was oranges. It was as if my mind were the exact size of an orange. There was no room to move around it. I could think only of pulp, the soft, warm wad of sweetness on my tongue growing blander as the jaws closed on it, the tiny sacs of juice popping and the ropy bits of rind catching on the teeth. And then there was the amniotic sound, the edgelessness of wet against wet. The sound I imagined shifted into other sounds, related as water is to other water: a sameness displaced and separated, but only temporarily. I heard myself chewing, and it made my mouth water.

"You're with me or you're with C or you're alone, and it doesn't seem to matter. You're the same all the time," B said.

I was thinking of a perfect orange, whole in my palm. It fit there as if it were made for me. I was cupping it in my palm and then I was lifting it toward my mouth. I bit into it like an apple, peel and all.

"But it's not like that for me," she continued. "I'm less when nobody's around. I do less, I move less, I eat less."

The ooze of the peel burned at the edges of my lips as I bit in. A bitter, oily orange film slicked my lips and teeth. There were little grains of something sliding in the oil and I bit harder. I tongued the flaps of rind, dry as felt, and tore them from the flesh with my teeth. I bit into the sweet wedges, and the wound filled with juice around my lips. As I worked my tongue farther in, I felt the tips of seeds near the center.

"I think I even think less," she said. "I don't remember what happens when I'm alone. It's like all that time just happens without me. It's like being a chair or a table."

B paused expectantly.

"Is there any way I can help?" I asked, hoping there wasn't. But instead she looked eager, even happy.

"Can we have a slumber party?" she asked. "Where you give me a makeover?"

"Would that really help?" I asked.

Now she sat back, as if I had already agreed.

"Definitely," she said. "Definitely."

"Okay," I said. "Do you want to go to the store to get makeup?" I asked.

"I'll just use yours," she said. Then she turned her face back to the TV and flipped a page of the magazine in her lap. The magazine was called *Women Tomorrow.* She reached over to the coffee table and primly picked up a paper cup. A lemon scent trailed from the paper cup, strong enough to sting your eyes.

I stood there feeling irrelevant. It was as though B had forgotten all about me the second I gave in. Usually B hung on me whenever I was in the common space, asking me what I thought about different TV shows, outfits, different kinds of food. Now she was acting more like I did when I wanted to remind her that this had been my apartment first, silence hardening up around her bony body as she watched her own things, as if I were the one with something I wanted from her. I wanted her to return me to the way I had been when I was confident, when each inch of this apartment was familiar to me, rather than a couple of steps removed, like a photograph of a drawing of a place you had once loved. I wanted her to act like herself, insofar as the B I had known always wanted to be like me, act like me, but was never quite able to do it. I wanted her to side with me on the weirdness of the house across the street, I wanted her to worry about what happened over there the other day and let me try to comfort her.

"Hey," I said, "do you remember that family driving away the other day? Wearing sheets?"

"Duh," said B, glancing at me for a second or two.

"What do you think that was?" I asked.

B shrugged. Her face had taken on a slurred look, drooping at the corners.

"Have they been back?" I asked.

"I don't know," she said. "And I don't care. That family was all assholes anyway. The way they used to look at me. I mean, they wouldn't look at me. Like if they saw me smoking out on the roof, they'd just stare straight ahead like robots, like they thought watching me doing it would give them lung cancer. People in this neighborhood don't pay any attention to me, so I don't pay any attention to them.

"It's a matter of principle," she added, taking a dainty sip from her paper cup.

The magazine lay open on her lap, revealing a photo of a famous actress astride a terrified-looking horse. The actress leaned forward, cuddling the horse with one arm, the other raised in a gesture of triumph. "Do you think I could do that?" B asked, pointing at the page. I looked at the photo. I honestly didn't know.

I felt like gagging. I went to my room and closed the door. B and C would make a great couple, I realized. They'd get along like crazy. I could imagine them now facing the TV as noise poured from its wide glass eye, happy and content as the rampant weird-ness unfolded outside, their hands clasped together like a single, monstrously large heart. He wouldn't mind the way B drank—he'd love it, in fact, the novelty of it, the sweet deadness of her breath after disgorging, the sense her body gave off that living was a wet and collapsing struggle.

May we eat as one, I thought to myself, because I had no idea what else to think. I closed the door to my bedroom and lay belly-down on my bed, pressing my face up to the open window. Through the black mesh screen, the house across the street was dark and impossibly still. The yellow glow from the streetlights stopped just short of the lawn, leaving a large blue-black expanse leading toward the house, opaque as an ocean. I pressed up to the mesh screen and smelled the thick green growth of summer writhing in the night. I felt the dark air on my face. I angled my head around, trying to see into their windows. The door was still ajar, windows illegible. Someone had propped some sheets of particleboard against the garage door, blotting out several of the scrawled words, and there was debris on the driveway, dark clods of vegetative matter that could have been lawn related. It was possible that they had come back while I was out with C, that they had snuck their sedan silently in, leaned the boards up against the garage to fake disuse. But I doubted myself. The words that man had scrawled on the door were meant to be seen. If they had been covered, it had been by someone else.

I rolled over and stared at the ceiling. C and I went away on a long road trip once. On our way north we stopped at a quarry where people paid a fee to drive their cars in, park them in the little public lot, and spend a few hours lying on thin towels spread out on rocks beside the cloudy water. There was a sun-bleached diving board at the water's edge that you weren't supposed to use; a doughy man in yellow swim trunks lay dozing on it. At the other end of the quarry the water was supposed to be fifteen feet deep, and you could jump off into it from the rock cliff above. C wanted to do this with such great enthusiasm that it couldn't even occur to him that I might not. He took my hand and was leading me up this path, both of our towels wadded up under his arm, and when I asked him where we were going, he just said, "The top," in a cheery way.

At the top there was some random trash, plastic soda pop bottles, and a set of keys that looked like they had been there a long time. You could see a long way, all over the quarry, all the way to the skinny preteens putting each other in fake wrestling holds down by the ice cream stand. Far below us, the water looked milky and frothy at the same time. "Are you ready!" C shouted in a way that wasn't a question. Then he grabbed me around the middle from behind, his crotch soft against my ass, and leapt us over the edge. Because I hadn't intended to jump, had no plan to jump, it didn't really feel like I was falling as I fell. I just felt the movement all around me, like a gust of wind coming from the bottom up. Nevertheless, a ragged scream tore from me, one that sounded as if it had been cut out of me by a steak knife, and when I hit the water I was still going, swallowing some of the water by accident, which tasted like blackboard chalk. When we had paddled over to land again, C was excited, laughing. He held me and said that it seemed like I wasn't afraid of strong feelings, and I let him keep thinking that even though I knew it was nearly the opposite of how I actually was.

I lay there. *Think this through,* I said to myself. *Just because you weren't the person he thought you were doesn't mean that you won't be that person at some other time, someday. It doesn't mean that B is that person, or could be that person if she tried. It doesn't mean you're not you. It doesn't mean that he doesn't love you.* I had enumerated the doesn'ts.

By then I was tired or maybe sad, so I turned the TV on.

On-screen there was another Kandy Kakes commercial. In this one, Kandy Kat has become a scientist so that he can crack the problem of Kandy Kakes, find out what makes their matter so disastrously incompatible with his own. Kandy Kat guides us through a series of diagrams on the chalkboard that elucidate the basic structure of a Kandy Kake: outer coating of crispy candy shell sprinkled with crushed nuts and a patented candy substance known only as "Choco Shrapnel," then a layer of gooey caramel followed by two layers of rich chocolate of slightly different consistencies. Then a layer of fluffy cake, kept moist by the four layers of airtight, watertight substances surrounding it, then a layer of crisp chocolate cookie. At the center is the top-secret "Kandy Kore," a dense, sugary substance whose chemical composition is known to only a few privileged individuals within the Kandy Kakes empire. Rumor has it the Kandy Kore is not strictly edible per se, in the sense that the special materials that give it its unique flavor are not thought to be made of food, specifically. No food that I've ever eaten shimmers with such beautiful, rich shades of green and pink. It's like eating a gasoline rainbow, if gasoline tasted good. Dressed in a white coat, Kandy Kat rubs his hands together eagerly near a gigantic machine that promises to do something

scientific to the lone Kake sitting on a pedestal directly beneath its beam. Even in the coat his ribs show through; it's
painful to see them. He pulls a lever and a beam of sizzling
green light envelops the Kandy Kake, which Kandy Kat ap-
proaches reverently, his eyes growing wider and wider behind
his professorial glasses.

Suddenly I had a thought, and I muted the TV.

What I heard was unmistakably the sounds of the same commercial playing in the living room, where B was still presumably
sitting. It was muffled, yes, as if it were wrapped in a blanket, but
I could make out the terrible grinding and cracking sounds that
happen when Kandy Kat tries unsuccessfully to bite down on a
Kandy Kake. It sounded as if someone were trying to repair a car,
but with tools all made of bone and meat. I tried to picture her
sitting there on the couch and watching, but all I could picture
was myself, sitting on my bed, trying hard to picture something. I
stared at the screen, at Kandy Kat trying to eat. He was biting so
hard that his teeth cracked.

WHAT WAS AT THE ROOT of Disappearing Dad Disorder? Sociologists said it was social, psychologists said it was psychological, and some religious nut said they had heard a call from God to leave behind their wicked lives. Biologists compared it with migration and with songbirds that become confused in the presence of skyscrapers. They compared them with honeybees who abandon their hives: maybe the fathers had been misled by cell phone signals, by highways, by toxins in the water supply. An American studies professor from Cornell argued that it had to do with the breakdown of the single-earner family model upon which our common baseline for masculine worth was founded; a comedian said that all husbands were on the verge of disappearing, only there was still such a thing as a football season, and then a basketball season, and then a baseball season. And a minority voice pointed out that this had been happening forever in minority communities, but it wasn't called a disorder until it started happening to well-off white people.

Possible explanations for the self-napping impulse were offered up in interviews with abandoned wives. Their husband was a sneaky rat and had been since the earliest days, the days when they were courting and he often "forgot" his wallet, forcing her to pay for the entirety of their meal, which, though it was only diner food—fast food, really—nevertheless added up.

Their husband was well intentioned but also a doofus, he had trouble with navigation even in their own moderately sized gated community; his absence was surely an exaggerated case of the many instances in which his sense of direction failed completely even as he continued to insist upon its "pinpoint precision." Their husband had loved them very much, particularly in the beginning, but in recent years she had noticed that he had noticed that the backs of her arms jiggled when she waved hello, that there were spots that were not freckles distributed among her freckles, that her joints made loud cracking sounds when they made love, which sometimes caused him to ask her if she was all right.

But maybe the fathers were just seeking a perfect life, which when you think about it is a completely reasonable thing to do. They wanted the good things: the popcorn, the corn dogs, the plush industrial mall carpeting with its friendly geometric patterns screaming themselves in green, pink, and brick red, stretching across the concourse like a little, comprehensible fragment of infinity. They didn't want the bad things: the pressure, the stress, the weekly division of chores by chore wheel, the homework that they thought they had done away with when they graduated elementary school or middle school or high school or business school. They didn't want the gift-curse of recognition by those they loved and who loved them back, one consequence of that love's durability being that they would be recognized and loved aggressively even on days when they couldn't stand to recognize themselves in the mirror, even on days when merely remembering themselves made them sad and want to sleep. Love that made every day a day that they had to live in a handcrafted, artisanal fashion, rather than being outsourced to someone who could do it happily and efficiently for a third of the price.

They might have thought, to use a stock phrase, that somewhere out there was a way to "have their cake and eat it, too." That many of them returned to their homes months later, malnourished, dehydrated, and amnesiac could be interpreted as evidence that there is no cake anywhere in the world to be had or eaten.

THE LIGHT WAS EBBING INTO my room from the west, a swath of rose coating the surfaces before dying off for the night. Without my contacts, things bled into each other, the differences between them middled. The first day that I ever understood my eyes were imperfect, my second-grade teacher had called on me to read what was written on the board at the front of the classroom. "What am I supposed to read?" I asked over and over. The board was a flat green, marked only by a smear of chalk dust. The teacher threatened to send me to the principal's office, but I was brought to the nurse instead. There I was made to understand that there were things I didn't see, things I very likely hadn't seen for some time. There were messages embedded in the blur. In my room, the late light evaporated the bookshelf and mantel, retreating into the dusk.

At the corner where I kept some of my cosmetics, I imagined myself standing there, my body small in the space surrounding. From the times I had seen my reflection without preparing myself, I knew how bad my posture was, how I let my shoulders fall forward, making the chest look caved in and weak. But the self I projected in front of me looked alert. My neck looked long. I was looking through the clear resin box that held the little makeup boxes and tins as though I had not seen them in a long time. I felt pleased with myself. I felt that I was a girl I would enjoy watching as she went about doing the little, dull things that make up a day. That's why it was so alarming when I realized that instead of pretending to watch myself, I actually was watching B.

"What are you doing in here?" I asked. "Didn't you see I was sleeping?"

She turned her blur of a face around toward me. I was trying to get my contacts in as quickly as possible, to decrease the resemblance between us by increasing the number of details I could discern.

"You were sleeping. And I already asked you if I could use your makeup," she responded.

No, you didn't, I wanted to say. *You didn't* ask.

Instead I groaned and pressed the covers to my eyes, which hurt for some reason.

"Can you just get out?" I said. "I need to wake up."

B left, letting the door swing halfway shut. Without my contact lenses I couldn't tell how she had meant it, whether her exit was guilty or reproachful. I rolled back into a sleeping position with the covers bunched in front of me like another person, which I held in my arms from behind. I missed C, but I was weighing the possibility of getting caught if I tried to leave to go see him. I thought about staying here in my bedroom for weeks, until she forgot about the whole makeover idea and moved on to something else I would have to do for her. I could wait it out.

With the two and a half packs of cookies I had in my desk drawer, the three oranges in my dresser, and that bottle of wine I could make it two days, maybe three. But if C brought me groceries and hoisted them up through some sort of basket-and-rope rigging, I could make it for weeks, conceivably. Maybe three weeks, if C didn't forget about me or find someone new. B would give up long before that. She would find someone else to get close to, someone like me with an open room in their apartment, or maybe she would move out and get a job. It could be exactly the push she needed to step out into the world and take her place as a productive member of society. And I could walk out years later, fresh and rested, into an apartment that had been occupied and abandoned again and again, occupied and abandoned enough times that my name and story would have become legendary and then been forgotten several times over.

But if I was in here alone for weeks, C would forget about me, too. I could sneak him in through the window for visits: there was a fire ladder to the roof on one side and a large tree on another. My last boyfriend used to come up like that sometimes to be cute. The noise he made when he knocked on the loose panes of the window was terrifying. But C wouldn't climb the tree because he wouldn't support my desire to stay forever, together, in my room. He'd argue with me, probably, from his spot on the ground, and in doing so, he'd completely give away my hiding spot. I'd have to do without him. I'd send him naked photos of myself in Photoshop-ready positions. He could use his graphic design skills to copy-and-paste himself in there next to me, behind me, whatever. We could have evidence of our congress even if we couldn't have the congress itself. But C wouldn't bother with the photos: his desire was a spotlight, shining with impressive intensity and focus, but only on the thing right in front of him. I was barely able to get him to return a text message, even the dirty ones.

I thought of sending him something explicit. Something I'd like to do with him. But in all honesty all I really wanted to do was stay here in bed until everything changed around me. Besides which, it was a challenge for me to compose erotic messages. I always got lost in the parts of speech: if I wanted something involving one particular part of his body, I had trouble not using the preposition "with," telling him to do something "with" it, or else I would be telling him to "put" it someplace. Both structures made the part eerily passive, something he could pick up and set down and use or not use, like a hammer or a telephone. The same thing happened when he talked about things he would do to a particular part of my body: the body that emerged from his description seemed to have only three or four parts, linked hazily by what I would assume was more body. Talking about my body in any way took me apart. Afterward I would lie still and try to put myself back together, naming the parts one by one silently, in order, beginning with the small bones of the foot.

Then there was describing the deixis of the thing through prepositions and directionality: inside me was in, up, deep, down, farther, through—contradicting directions that didn't seem to add up to one whole person operating in space, much less two. I always had to think about the planar orientation of my body—was I vertical or horizontal? "Put it all the way across."

In watching porn and listening carefully to what the people onscreen were saying as they did the things they were doing, I had come to understand that the only stable point of orientation was the stomach. Even though they never mentioned it explicitly in their porn talk, all the ins and ups and downs and deeps seemed to indicate a line cutting through the vagina, through the uterus, and right into the center of the body, which also happened to be the center of digestion. This center seemed to be where everyone wanted things to go, deeper and deeper to the innermost point, where they could finally rest.

I rolled over in bed and sent C a text message: *I'm starving!*

Then I rolled onto my back and stared up at the ceiling. I had at least one eye, pointing straight upward. From this perspective it was easy to pretend that all things were in a state of perfect stillness. If something in the world had moved or acted, then its action would have affected something else, which in turn would be compelled to react. Its reaction, an action upon things other than itself, would cause other reactions that would change the states of other things, a domino effect that would eventually topple something in my visual field, which consisted solely of ceiling. As the ceiling remained the same, so must everything else. That, or the ceiling was shifting but my eyes were not, would never be, sharp enough to perceive it.

I got C's reply after a few minutes. *Eat something from the kitchen,* it read.

B would be out in the kitchen or just near it, maybe watching for me, maybe waiting to make me do something. I didn't know how to tell C that I was afraid to leave this room and step out into the other parts of the house. I didn't know how to say I was afraid of diluting myself if I encountered B in this fuzzy state, where she resembled me more than I did myself. A woman's body never really belongs to herself. As an infant, my body was my mother's, a detachable extension of her own, a digestive passage clamped and unclamped from her body. My parents would watch over it, watch over what went in and out of it, and as I grew up I would be expected to carry on their watching by myself. Then there was sex, and a succession of years in which I trawled my body along behind me like a drift net, hoping that I wouldn't catch anything in it by accident, like a baby or a disease. I had kept myself free of these things only through clumsy accident and luck. At rare and specific moments when my body was truly my own, I never knew what to do with it.

I picked at a patch of loose skin on my foot, a whitish patch lifting up from the substrate. It must have loosened while I was walking. Tugging on it, I felt the skin pull on my foot, but nothing from the patch itself. It was already leaving me. If I could look into my insides and poke at them, see them day after day, have control over their color and texture, maybe then I'd feel close to the pounds and pounds of matter that lived within me, in my blind spot. Until then, the outer layer would be the innermost part of me, the thing that would evacuate me if stolen, the absolute core.

HOURS LATER, MY PHONE BUZZED. It was C. His message read: *Did you eat something yet?*

The eggy white of the ceiling was growing grayer all the time. Its nullness was more difficult to see, though there was as much of it. Ted Hartwell, Matt Skofield, Dennis Galp. Had they felt like this before they felt like disappearing; had they stared at their walls for hours, hoping for something to change? A span in my stomach registered discomfort: it ached first like an absence, next like a stone. It read as a trembling, a shiver without the cold, and then as a solid, a sluggish setting of the soft squish in my middle. It was hunger, I thought. It changed in quality as it changed in quantity: it seemed hunger was a tiered thing, a mountain rising to a peak, and each new altitude would be different from the last. Even though a portion of myself was interested in this, interested in climbing to the top of this hunger and discovering what it felt like at its end, it was a normal human life that I was living, and that meant continuing to eat, eating with no end in sight. I got up to go quickly to the kitchen and grab something whole and bring it back to my room to eat it there, alone. If I moved quickly and quietly, B might miss me entirely.

In the kitchen I grabbed an orange and a piece of string cheese and two energy bars specially formulated for women to eat; they were full of folic acid and had a round, feminine shape. Then I heard a noise from behind me. It was a small urgency, like the sputter of a motor the size of someone's pocket, but it was so close. I expected to see B standing there with something aimed at my head, an electric toothbrush, maybe, or a drill. But there was nobody behind me and nothing really except a window with the curtain still hanging before it, and from the curtain the sound of that little motor going and going and stopping and then going and going. I walked toward it, still thinking of that blank space behind the back of my head that I couldn't see or protect. When I moved the curtain, there was a pause. And then a dragonfly, beating itself against the screen over and over, whirring like a thing made of feathery gears. Musical sounds came from the surface as it struck the screen, buzzing and chiming, close enough to my face that I could see the smooth panels of its body.

The dragonflies I knew lived only for a few weeks out of the summer and were lazy, hanging still in the air four or five feet above anybody's head before gliding to the next stopping point. This one was desperate, and though it looked sturdy, something so small and living couldn't be designed to outlast that sort of wear, repetitive and dumb. I put my finger on the screen where it seemed to be aiming and the sounds paused. I heard the breeze rush around in the quiet. Then the small crashes began again, a few inches below my fingertip. It was easier to watch insects trapped indoors, on their way to a frantic death, than it was to watch this one killing itself to get in. There was nothing for it in here. In here it would die. As soon as it was inside, it would understand it had to get out.

Feet shuffled across the kitchen tile. I turned around and it was B standing there with a cup in her hand, the prettiest one we had, made of thick blue glass. Her face was stark without makeup on, full of peaks and valleys. Her eyes had a hungry look.

"Are you ready?" she asked.

"This dragonfly is beating itself against the window," I said.

She looked at it blankly.

"I think it's going to die," I explained.

"Then we should do it in another room, I guess?" she said.

I stood there looking at the window and then at the food in my hands. The orange was sweating condensation from the refrigerator. Oranges "breathe" even after they are picked. Torn from their branch, they continue to take in oxygen and exhale carbon dioxide through their skin like small, hard, naked lungs.

"I don't feel very well," I said.

B looked at me and then she sat down. She seemed to collapse slightly as I watched her, her shoulders slouching forward, caving her chest.

"Look," she said. "I know it's not going to look perfect. I'm not going to be mad at you if it doesn't look right or if I don't look exactly the way you look. I know it's not easy to do things with my face. I know that I have weird proportions, and a big nose, and a big forehead. It's irreparable. That's why I've always been so scared of putting makeup on, that I'd do all that work and end up looking like myself, exactly like myself but with things smeared on me. I just want to try it this once and I don't know how to do it myself. I'll probably look awful," she said.

She was rubbing her thumb hard against the side of the cup like someone trying to rub the prints off her own fingertips.

If you were a person, you were supposed to want to be a better person. Better people had a surplus of themselves that they were willing to give away, something they could separate out and detach. In me the portions only separated, pulling apart and waiting there for something to happen. I could see what it was that I could give B, but I couldn't really give it. In fact, I wanted to keep it for myself, to take it and run. All around me, people were giving feelings and help to one another all the time, as if it were the only thing to do. And I watched these exchanges like a dead thing, a thing sealed off perfectly, a room with no holes in or out.

"You'll look great," I said. The light from the living room lamps felt warm and prickly next to me. "You look great," I said.

She seemed like she wanted to smile. Her face bunched and crinkled around the eyes. I looked back at the window where the screen sat open to the night air, and I saw nothing, heard nothing.

THE MIRROR IN MY BEDROOM showed the two of us side by side. All I said was that I didn't want to talk. "I don't want to get distracted," I said, and she nodded the way I was sure she would have nodded to anything I said then—worried, but with some potential for happiness hidden within. I did the foundation for her skin, which was the same color as mine. It was a color called bisque, the word for clay in its first stage of firing, hard, dry, unglazed, unfinished. It was also the word for a kind of soup made from the roasted husks of things. The makeup changed the face without changing it at all, it seemed only to restore to it an evenness that it had always held underneath, an even surface without pock or worry. The better person hidden inside the real person.

I wanted to be gone, to be by myself, to be with C, but instead I held still and reminded myself that this impression of uncovering a face was exactly as real as the fact that I was covering up a face at the same time. It was like the optical illusion where you see the vase and the two faces in the same image, but you can't see them both at once.

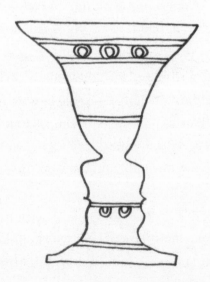

The single image splits into two, which occupy the same space without sharing it. Or maybe it's the opposite: the two objects find themselves in shared space, and the thought of one after the other in the mind of the viewer's eye, vase face vase face vase face vase face, makes them grow together. The two words even begin to sound alike, like the same words spoken in the mouths of two people from different, distant places. I poured makeup on a white foam sponge so that it looked like a little puddle of skin suspended on nothingness, and then I dabbed it against her cheek over and over again. I dabbed it against her cheek, and then I did smooth, long strokes. I left skin-colored streaks that vanished a little more with every stroke. She was disappearing, or reappearing, or appearing for the first time, whatever.

I had covered all the spots, and now, when I looked at it, her face had the texture of a piece of pottery. I saw pores only when I leaned in close to the nose, where they appeared as tiny skin-colored mounds rising out of little sloping craters. People were such fragile things: they existed only from a certain angle, at a certain scale and spacing. Forget where to stand and you'd lose them completely. From this distance she didn't resemble me much, though she didn't exactly resemble herself, either. I rubbed at the edge of her jaw to blend the makeup. Then I did the lips. I used the things I had around, without wiping them off: my own lip balm, gooey and flavored like an orange Creamsicle, a lipstick that I wore a lot and had worn down to a flat, wet-sheened plateau with half a rim on it. I dabbed the color on with my fingertip, the padded part, poking at her lower lip and watching it spring back up. It was just like painting a portrait of myself, I thought, onto the face of another person.

I remembered one summer that I spent at my aunt's house when I was younger, middle school, maybe. My aunt spent most of her day doing embroidery while her husband was at work, sitting in front of the TV and watching movies on mute. The movies were action films, thrillers, things that she and my uncle had originally bought for their son to watch. She didn't pay much attention to the story line; the movies were a type of home decor, a device casting light and movement. I would walk through the living room on the way to somewhere else and see the warm yellow glow of an on-screen explosion playing off her smooth, serene face.

One of the movies she put on involved two men who were hardly ever pictured in the same frame. One was squarish and broad, the other angular and hawklike. The squarish man was seen in an office and then in a sort of hospital room. The angular man was pacing around a tarmac. Then the angular man was waking up and walking around. Then the square-jawed man was waking up. They both seemed to chase something, separately, using many different kinds of vehicles—planes, cars, boats. I understood it as some sort of story where two men competed to be the first to capture some unspecified thing they both wanted. Years later, C told me that it was actually a movie about identity theft. One of the men had swapped appearances with the other, then the other swapped appearances with the first. Then they worked to undo each other. C said that I should have picked up on the identity swap by noticing that the square man's body language was initially heroic and then became sneaky and aggressive, while the angular man's body language began sneaky and turned heroic. I told him that it would be nice if we could all think that way, but in actual life we were supposed to recognize a person in spite of their mannerisms rather than because of them. We were supposed to trust the similarity of their face in the moment to the face we remembered. "Otherwise," I said, "I would treat you like a stranger every time your mood changed." C had just looked at me for a while, seeming confused, not saying anything at all.

I held B's smallish face in my hands and I gripped her chin a little harder than I had to because I could get away with it, I was making her so happy right now. Before there were mirrors or cameras to allow you to face yourself, you had to see yourself through other people. I tried to think that I was painting a picture of my face on hers so that I could see myself better. See myself filled out rather than flattened, see myself as C saw me. I wasn't losing anything or giving myself away, I was just expanding, becoming more, many, like the television image and its occupation of all those otherwise empty screens. The image I thought of as mine sitting on the surface of her skin would absorb her to me and I might know what it was like to be myself outside of myself, for once. To see a part of myself that I could observe and recognize, but which transmitted no feelings. A numbed-out limb that could do what it did without me.

I was still hungry, and the tips of my fingers trembled against her skin as I did the thick black line on the eyelid. I hoped that I'd mess it up, but I had no practice doing anything other than trying to make it perfect and the same each time, so it was the same. And as I saw the face take shape, I felt less and less bothered on my own behalf. I felt more like some entirely other person, a casual spectator. There was a flat pleasure in seeing it unfold from this angle, this image that was pleasing to me, so pleasing to me that I had chosen it ten years ago and repeated it upon myself pretty much ever since. As I worked, I tried to find every one of the ways in which our faces differed: the slight cleft in her chin, the widening of her nose at its tip, the mole on her lower lip that looked like a small wart. Now I just sort of let go, and I thought about how different it was to see this image so clearly, familiar and unfamiliar at the same time. It felt like it used to feel to watch myself put on makeup, before it became a thing my hands did almost without me. When I did the dot of silvery stuff at the inner corners, I was done. I turned around to look at us in the mirror.

"It looks so good," B said, her eyes opening wide.

It did look good. Her eyes looked huge, her mouth smaller and more precise. I had buffed away the dark circles and the random mole. The dark around the eyes distracted from their anxious expression and made her less like prey, more like a predator. She was smiling now, and this changed her face dramatically. It put shadows under her cheekbones and lines around her mouth. She looked like the girls on TV commercials, thrilled at the condition of their outsides.

"You look beautiful," I said. "You're a babe."

I was feeling like I had a surplus, B blinked at me, silent.

"I'm going to go to the bathroom," she said.

"Okay," I said.

I didn't know what she was going to do there, and I didn't really care. I picked at a loose thread on my comforter to pass the time. I felt light on the inside, like a balloon, and I was incredibly sleepy. When Kandy Kat appears on two television screens at once, does he split in two? Two bodies with two minds pointed out at identical cartoon scenes? Two bodies responding identically, like twin machines? Or is there still one cartoon body, ribby and drained, with a doubled hunger for its double image? I needed some air. I walked to the door and stepped outside. When I looked back, I had a clear view into the bathroom: B had left the door wide open, and even from a distance I could see her standing there in front of the mirror, brushing her fingertips gently against the skin of her nose, cheeks, chin, tracing it with reverence, caressing it like an infant, newly born.

I crossed the lawn in the dark, drawing closer to the house across the street, darkened and uninviting and empty. I looked back behind me, but nobody in the neighborhood was watching, not even B through the skinny kitchen window where she usually stood when I left the house. Nobody was watching me, nobody was thinking about me, I was truly alone. I pushed my way through the unclosed door using my shoulder instead of my hands, arms wrapped around myself like someone with a stomachache or someone who had just been punched in the gut. The door swung slowly back in, shutting out most of the light.

Inside the house across the street it was soundless and clean, free of dust and voices. Everywhere was white with draped cloth, and the moon shone down on the muffled things and gave them an incredibly lonely color. There was a living room to my right filled with hulking white mounds that must once have been a sofa, love seat, armchair, upright piano. To my left was a dining room with three shrouded white chairs and a shrouded white table. From the lumps on its surface, nobody had bothered to clear away dinner before covering it over. I poked at one of the lumps through the pallid sheeting, and it gave way beneath my fingertip with a squish.

There was no family. There was no dog. There weren't even any insects that had crept in through the open door, the door that released a soft squeal behind me as the wind blew through our street. What had once been a family's life, still vaguely life shaped, now resembled an arctic scene: white and smooth and cold to the eye. The sofa and love seat vague under sheeting, the obscure shapes of hidden toys. I stood there waiting for something to happen, but nothing was going to happen. It was like watching the body at a wake. My breath slowed and I felt like I might lie down and never get up.

I realized that I was feeling happy.

In the stillness of this dead house, I felt a sudden sense of belonging. It was partial, but still better than nothing. I belonged to this family whom I didn't know and who didn't know me either. This family that had left me behind. And though they didn't know they were missing me, I knew. And that was something. I could still come in here and spend time, conjure them into their domestic spaces, miss them, remember all the things we never did together. I could imagine their voices, imagine finding those voices familiar. I felt as if I knew the entire layout of this house, knew exactly what was under each of these crisp white sheets, even though I didn't.

Outside, sparse crickets called back and forth. I went into the living room and sat down on the floor behind the ghosted couch. I stared at their white wall and then I lay down on my side. I lay there not thinking about B or C or my job or my parents. I didn't think about how I looked or how good my skin was today. I didn't think about food or water or the things that had happened. My breathing slowed. This house with its weird white covers over everything was telling me to do Nothing, and I knew exactly how to do that. I felt like snow, I thought, like snow feels: cold and quiet and close to vanishing. A temporary covering on a small piece of ground. I lay like snow for a long while, as occasionally a car drove past and made the white briefly whiter.

Then I realized that if I stayed here too long, B might try to find me. I stood up and left right away. I closed the front door behind me but left it unlocked.

BACK IN MY BEDROOM, THE television was telling me about a new edible beauty cream. A beautiful woman with black hair is smiling at a midsize jar that she holds in her hands, turning it slightly from right to left as if to admire its label. The woman is already so beautiful that it's hard to see what she could possibly need inside that jar. Nevertheless she is so excited to open it up, the smile on her face just gets larger and larger as she unscrews the lid, tilts the jar delicately toward her, and then gasps in surprise. A white dove is struggling its way out of the smallish jar, straining its neck against the rim, trying to use its neck and beak as a lever to wrench its downy white breast through the opening. It tries to unfurl a wing, but it's still too much trapped within the jar, so it looks left and right and then pecks at the parts of the jar that are within its reach. In terms of its experience as an animal, the dove is obviously distressed. Its black beady eyes are still, but its head jerks back and forth, back and forth. As a part of the commercial, however, the dove looks elegant and soft, its feathers fluffy as it twists around, trying to free its wings.

The jar topples over and the dove kind of spills out, taking flight gracefully. As it flies, the voice-over tells us what sorts of things are in TruBeauty's new interior-exterior skin-perfecting cream. Some of the things are vitamins, antioxidants, moisturizers. The dove is looking great with its wings flapping in slow motion and therefore appearing extra glamorous. When it completes one lap around the room, it circles back toward the beautiful woman, her mouth open in amazement, and it heads straight for her mouth, full throttle. The impact makes a soft *thwack* sound, and then it's just the back half of the dove that's visible sticking out of her mouth and trying hard to wriggle its whole body inside. The voice-over speaks: *Most beauty creams stop at the epidermal level, treating only those minor flaws and imperfections that are the easiest to reach. Competing treatments only go skin deep.* As it forces itself down her throat, she tilts her chin up gracefully and you can see some muscles at the sides of her neck clenching and releasing, working to help the dove get itself swallowed. When the last claw-tipped foot goes down, she tilts her chin low and smiles radiantly for the camera. *Only one beauty cream attacks signs of aging and damage from the inside and out, making sure that threats to your beauty have no place to hide.* The beautiful woman dips a spoon into the now dove-free jar of cream and lifts out a creamy mouthful. She dabs a little on her face, and brings the rest of the spoonful to her lips, thrusting it inside luxuriantly. It looks like yogurt, but it's not. She licks the front and then the back, and then she reclines, closing her eyes and smiling in the sunny glow of her beautiful living room. And the voice-over says: *Trust TruBeauty. We know that true beauty begins on the inside.*

I curled up on my side and I tried to smile the beautiful woman's glowing, contented smile. I pretended I felt full and warm and that I had a whole living dove in my belly, looking elegant and soft. The dove was in there, but I wouldn't hurt it—just hold it, keep it safe inside me. I pretended C was next to me, watching over my body, making certain that nobody could steal my face for as long as he was looking at it. I remembered B's eye pointed up beneath my gaze, small and immobile and unprotected, with the lid slid all the way back. It was about the size of a thumb, from nail to first joint. My hand twitched. I was digging my two thumbs into the middle of a Kandy Kake, deep into the dark, oily center and pulling it apart. Soon the center would be surface, quivering under air. I could feel myself falling asleep, the sort of sleep you fall backward into, a sleep that feels like water rising higher and higher inside your head until it pushes at the backs of your eyes and the inside of your temples. *A Kandy Kake is just like an eye*, I thought, and that was the last thing I thought before I was asleep.

In the middle of the night I woke up to a soft hand stroking my hair, but I was hollowed out, exhausted, and I fell back asleep before I could ask who it was.

A MOUTH WAS A MEANS into a person, but it also offered one of the neatest ways out. Whatever entered that slick passage immediately began pushing through to the other side, emerging unrecognizable and many steps removed from itself. A mouth glistened with saliva, ninety-eight percent water and two percent suspended particles, which made it slick, odorous, corrosive. In my saliva and my boyfriend's rested enzymes that would break carbohydrates into sugars and fats as soon as food touched the inner walls of the oral cavity. Digestion begins inside the oral cavity, read the biology textbook I used in high school, in a section titled "How Do You Eat Meat?" What this meant was: Even if C loved me, even if he cared for me, even if he saw me as an equal and wanted only the best for me in my life, when he kissed me a part of him worked blindly to undo my body. When I put my own mouth on him, the material in my body sized up the material in his, checked to see if it was food or something other, something indigestible that would never truly penetrate.

I stared up into C's mouth, pink and wet and blackening as it deepened inch by inch into throat. Saliva pooled at the inner rim of his fleshy lower lip. On my back and facing the ceiling, I felt his body settle over me, pressing into my skin like a fist into dough. I was malleable and easily shaped, I was substance all the way through: no pockets of air, no hollow for the soul to fit in. Any lacuna that took a place in me was opened and filled at once by the same thing, so that hunger and its solution occurred simultaneously, barely leaving any sort of gap for desire to take place. I was solid, bounded on all sides, and when I reached for him I felt his own solidity, wider and less bony than my own, larger and different in shape, like a couch or an automobile. I tightened my hand on his shoulder and the skin underneath gave a little. It made little divots under my fingers that I grabbed into more sharply for traction. I slid my hand down. I hooked the thumb into his armpit for a better grip. The way my hand struggled showed me that he was unlike the handle of a hammer or a knife: he was not made for my grasp, not designed with me in mind. It slipped around beneath my palm, it was too large to hold. The repetitive motions of my hips slipped away from me, no longer controlled through thought. It was just like lying down in a boat and staring up, feeling your whole body move with the movement of something else.

As the music that emanated from the television set grew louder and faster and more robust, C began to take a more decisive attitude toward my body. He grabbed my left leg below the knee and swiveled it around like a massive joystick, trying to push it back toward my ear. He put the heel of his hand on my thighs and leaned in, pushing against the club end where femur met hip.

"My legs don't work that way," I said, trying to find an angle that hurt less.

"What?" he said with a note of surprise, maybe just surprise that I was talking.

"It's not comfortable," I said.

He continued to press into me the same way he had before. My leg was a lump of hurt, the joint burned. I tried to wriggle my hips, but I was wedged in. He pried his weight deeper into me, placing a hand flat on my jaw for leverage.

"They don't go back at that angle," I added, trying to explain it more precisely.

"Oh," he said. "Sorry. I just thought . . ."

He trailed off, looking over to my left, where the TV was glowing with pornographic scenes that I had forgotten were playing. C removed his hand from my leg and placed it back on the mattress. On-screen, the skinny, beige body of a ponytailed woman lay collapsed like a folding chair. The bright rectangle was filled with the bodies of others, doing the sorts of things we were doing, but under better lighting. Their genitals appeared first attached to their bodies and so small that you could cover them with a fingertip, then grew large enough to fill the entire screen. The oversize organs that were being pictured now had no body attached and therefore were bodies in themselves. Hairless and smooth, they lapped like faces with rudimentary mouths, speaking in a language that lay outside of my hearing. These part-faces had a way of interacting that was gentle and tactile, like the jellyfish I had seen on nature documentaries. The one swallowed the other up again and again, the other pulled away, creating a space between, then closed it again just as quickly. As I watch them draw their invertebrate torsos toward and away from each other, any sexual intent attributed to their motion would have seemed like pure projection.

When we first met, I hadn't really understood why C liked to have sex and watch porn at the same time. My first thought was that it was instructional, a sort of hint he was trying to give me. I tried to make sure that I was always in a position where I could see the TV, where I could shadow the woman or women on-screen. I arranged myself the way they did, I tried to move through the positions when they did. But he never seemed to map himself to anyone up there, and when I tried to he'd rearrange me, destroying the resemblance. Then I thought it might be like background music or the radio when you're cooking dinner, or an attempt to cover up the sounds of our sex with sounds of the sex of strangers. But in the end I decided that it had to do with the thinness of the present. At any given present moment a person was doing one thing, maybe three things. They were lying down, and they were reading a sentence, and possibly they were thinking about what they were doing. Or they were reaching for someone's shoulder, and noticing a mole on someone's back, and feeling their own breath leave their chest. Any piece of time is lonely and pale in isolation, and moments resemble other moments, so that sometimes you feel that you are a memory being called to mind by someone else.

I saw him look to the TV screen as soon as we had spent too long doing the same thing, and I thought I recognized something in him that I had seen in myself. He was thickening the moment by laying fantasy upon reality upon fantasy. Any two people stuck to each other in the present made for a wasteland. He was repopulating the act so that we would not be so alone in it together.

In a similar way, I sometimes thought of a specific scenario to fill up the residual mental spaces that the act never seemed fully able to occupy on its own. In this scenario, C and I are together and about to turn on the TV and take all of our clothes off when suddenly there's a knock on the door. We go over to see who it is, and when we open the door we find all of my ex-boyfriends outside, smiling and greeting us warmly. I recognize every one of them, and they haven't changed a bit. They've all brought gifts: nice bottles of wine or a six-pack, boxes of filled chocolates, peanut brittle, or a fruit basket full of really lovely ripe pears, all russet-blushed green.

They want to be invited in and it's hard to know how to refuse them, with their earnest smiles pointed right at us. We sit around catching up. C and the exes are talking about their jobs and sharing stories from the different times they dated me, and as I watch them getting along, I feel this tremendous sense of well-being clogging my chest. Emotion swells in my middle and won't let anything else through. It feels finally like there is no past, just a thick, happy present wrapping it all up, so beautiful that I can hardly breathe. Then all of a sudden we're all stripping down and fucking, the whole group of us together, very politely. Everyone is respectful of one another's personal space and nobody is uncomfortable. There are dicks everywhere. In the middle I feel happy and rested and I think to myself: *The people I know best now know one another in the same way that I know each of them.* I realize that I recognize all of their bodies right down to the placement of body hair and freckles. I know them like I know myself, better than I know myself. The scenario ends there.

The ratio of actual sex to chatting, joking, and eating snacks in this fantasy is about one part to six. Even in the midst of the hardcore stuff we're chatting casually to one another, remembering different vacations we took or little routines we used to have on the weekends. We're talking through arguments that were never fully resolved while we were together, and everyone is offering their opinions and support.

I told C about my fantasy one night after he had shared one of his with me, something about five women, five different flavors of peanut butter, and a jungle gym. I thought it was on topic because they both involved a multiplicity of people, I thought we would laugh and compare and maybe even synthesize, but C told me my scenario weirded him out. I told him that in the real world, I wasn't really interested in any other guys, even if they were my exes, but he said that wasn't it. What bothered him, what seemed filthy, was the emotional aspect, the way I had dictated the personal. "You need them not only to be doing something for you but also feeling some specific way about it," C said. A begging quality had entered his voice. C said: "Why can't you just let people have their own inner lives, as long as they're doing pretty much what they're supposed to with their outer lives?" Then he stared away from me hard, thinking about who knows what.

When I watch the porn actors and actresses on TV, the thing that touches me most is their manners. They carry out their tasks with a sort of faraway etiquette, like the cashiers at the grocery store during the lunch rush who say just enough to make you feel that what you're doing is appropriate and look at you rarely enough that you feel you should move on efficiently. Porn people conduct similarly balanced exchanges: they'll offer up one way into a person, one of the most literal ways, but no more. And because in their world everything offered is taken up and no proposition is refused, no excess desire is left behind to molder. It may be the only perfect world I've ever seen, perfect except for the occasional glimpse of a badly infected wax.

Afterward we sat around on the couch in front of the TV, which was muted: just colors. C sat forward and grabbed at the remote as I put the pillows and cushions back where they used to be. Now it was as if nothing had ever happened. I looked down at the amnesiac material, clean and boring, its nubbly fabric a thrift store plaid. Looking at this couch made me feel like I hadn't been where I had been or touched any of the things I had touched. Even his body, half-clothed, looked the way that it had: warm with warm folds, soft and vulnerable. But having been there myself for the entire event, I knew that the parts had participated in a whole series of perceivable physical changes, the rise and climax, the resolution. When I considered myself, the account was much hazier. I could barely remember my part having been there since I saw it so rarely over the course of action, and the brief flashes in which it registered offered up the same sign over and over, the lips parted or not, no qualitative or quantitative difference in their appearance. Even now, only a slight soreness indicated that something had taken place. I could feel the part thinking already about the next time it would be filled.

"Are you feeling good?" I asked C, rubbing my cheek against his shoulder.

"Sure," he said pleasantly, as though I had offered him a cookie. "Why not."

"Why not?" I asked.

"You know what I mean," he replied.

SEX USUALLY LEFT ME FEELING calm for at least a couple of hours, but I hadn't been feeling much calmness recently. At least it still distracted me from what was going on at home. Ever since I had gone to the house across the street I had been trying to get back there, but it never felt safe. B with her new face was louder, and more curious, too. She looked at you longer and harder. When I slid my shoes on in my room and B heard the sound of my heels, she'd call out from wherever she was in the apartment. She'd ask me where I was going. She'd ask me what I was going to do. She'd ask me if I wanted to watch some TV. All I could do was slip my shoes off silently and creep back over to my bed, where I'd lie facedown on the mattress and look out across the street, thinking about how much easier it would be to have fewer things to think about, or no things at all.

B seemed so different from the shy girl who had moved in. With the B I had gotten used to, everything you uncovered about her was hard-won, from what she liked to read to whom she had a crush on in grade school. You had to dig it out of her gently, through a combination of offhand questions and calculated fun. But she was different after I started dating C. I had found her waiting for me in the stairwell the morning after the first night I spent at his house. She had been smoking cigarettes, the used-up butts were lined up next to her purposefully. "I was worried about you," she said as I walked up. I said I was sorry. I was standing there with stringy hair and most of my eyeliner rubbed off, and I smelled funny. I looked like I had been reshelved. B would usually have left it there, waiting for me to suggest something fun to do, but this time she kept looking at me. "No," she said decisively. "I'm happy that you're happy. I want to be out there too, I just don't know how to do it. You'll show me how," she said.

Then she stood up suddenly, stubbed her cigarette out on the steps, and placed the longer, half-smoked piece in its proper place within the line. She said she wanted to show me something. I followed her up to the second floor, where the door to our apartment was already open wide. "It's in my bedroom," she said, beginning to sound excited. Our apartment smelled like cigarettes and Pine-Sol; the two scents sickeningly blended. B pushed open the door to her room and pointed at something that I couldn't see from the doorway. I trailed in behind her and saw. What B had pointed at and was pointing at still was a portrait of her ex-boyfriend, painfully detailed and done all in graphite pencil. His face was chiseled and hard, as if there were stone bedded just under the skin. His mouth had a mean shape and a smoothness that made you want to reach out and touch the paper. B had made his face twenty percent larger than it would have been in real life, large enough that even the smallest features of his face, the specks of stubble and small moles, seemed aggressive. His face inflicted itself on you, it was almost too handsome to bear.

"How did you do this?" I said.

"I drew it," said B. "I had to use memory, we didn't take any pictures."

"Did you do this for art class?" I asked.

"I haven't done anything for my art class," she said.

B was looking impatient.

"Well," she said, "do you think I should destroy it?"

"Why would you ever do that?" I asked.

Her drawing was better than any other thing I had ever done.

"I should stop pining," she said simply.

But I wasn't sure I wanted to see what happened when she was no longer fixating on her ex and her ex alone. All that time she spent searching out new information about him on the Internet, the energy she sank into watching over where he shopped for groceries, whose parties he went to, which girls he talked to and for how long. I didn't think I wanted that loose energy coming into contact with C. I looked at her and said: "No, it's beautiful. You need to keep it. You should show it to him and see what he says. Don't give up."

B looked hesitant.

"That last time we were over there, when he attacked us with the soda?" she said. "He texted me after and said next time he'd call the cops. I think he was serious. I've seen him call the cops six or seven times. I was there when he called the cops on his ex. They broke up, but he found out that she was still living in this shed in his backyard."

"Don't give up," I said to her. I sounded confident.

ON TV, A LATE NIGHT host was interviewing Jonathan Winker, a DDD victim who had recently returned himself to his own life. Winker, a round-faced man in a plaid shirt buttoned up to the neck, sat across from the host, whose comically large desk seemed to be made of several different kinds of wood. *So, Jonathan, buddy—is it good to be back?* asked the host. The audience laughed. *Well,* said Jonathan, *initially, no.* The audience laughed again. *I don't know if you've ever had amnesia,* Jonathan continued, *but it is really a doozy. Imagine if a bunch of strangers surrounded you while you were eating a hot dog at the Freezy King in the mall, and they started grabbing you and they wanted to take you home.*

And, like, you looked around at all the other people sitting in the food court, and they were looking back at you like they were very specifically not going to help? And then a policeman came and told you that even though you were scared, and hungry, and all you wanted was to stay near the Freezy King where it was safe, you had to go with these noisy new people, because they were your family? The audience laughed.

Jonathan's eyes were tiny as he spoke. *Well, let's just say I'm in a better place now,* he said. The host kicked back in his swiveling office chair, then lurched forward to lean conspiratorially over the desk toward Jonathan. *And why is that, friend?* asked the host, smiling out at the cameras and then turning his face back toward his guest. *I've really turned it around,* Jonathan said proudly. *I was given some reading material that explained to me what exactly my problem was. My body was rejecting the falsity that had infected my life, I was trying to eject it, like the immune system does, only I didn't know enough to tell which parts were false and which were true. So that's what I've been working on.* The host nodded mildly toward him. *I found religion,* Jonathan said, grinning.

I looked over at C, who had emptied two whole cans of syruped mandarin oranges into a red plastic bowl and was stirring them with a spoon. In the teeming red bowl, the little orange segments looked like the bodies of dozens of sugary, gelatinous shrimp. "Does this need condiments?" he asked. I couldn't tell if he was talking to me or to himself.

"You know," I said, "I forgot to tell you. B didn't just cut her hair. After she cut it, she gave it to me. This whole thick rope of it. I have it in my room. It's creepy. It's the size of my arm."

"That's interesting," said C. "What does it feel like?"

"It feels weird," I said. "It feels like she's trying to turn me into her. Like she's slowly going to start shifting her stuff into my room and taking my things into hers. Like I'm going to wake up with a wig made of her hair taped to my head or something. And even though it's clearly not normal, I know if I try to talk about it, she'll just find a way to make me feel bad for something, like she has to do it because I'm not there for her."

"I meant how does it feel to hold. The hair," C said.

"Oh," I said.

"What?" he said. "There are no wrong questions."

"Don't you think that's a really weird thing to do?" I asked.

"I was just trying to be an interested listener," he said affably.

We were silent for several moments. On TV, a commercial for a dessert-flavored toothpaste that came in lemon meringue pie and chocolate pudding flavors. *Shouldn't the last thing you taste at night be the sweetest thing?* asks a motherly voice that is also straining to sound somewhat naughty.

"You're a great listener," I said. "I meant, don't you think B is behaving weirdly? I mean, who gives someone a part of their body as a gift?"

"Oh," he said. "I think a lot of relationships with females have weirdness built into them. Like with mothers. And sisters, and friends. In that way, weirdness is normal. So what's happening is normal.

"Also, the Victorians," C added. "They used to give hair and nail clippings as mementos. And also Catholic saints.

"This is about how you relate to the world," C said.

"Maybe it's about how the world relates to me," I said back.

"Let's not have a fight," he said.

I said: "Okay."

C shoveled his spoon into the bowl of syrupy fruit. It made a wet, nuzzling sound. He dug up a spoonful and extended it toward my mouth, as though I were an infant. The tip of the spoon butted against my closed lips. After a few moments he shrugged and stuck the heaping bite into his face. He chewed and I heard the little mushy bodies break against his teeth. He swallowed wetly.

"What do you want to watch?" he asked.

The television was tuned to a shopping channel.

I thought for a while and then I said: "Commercials."

He flipped through the channels until he found a game show, one that he knew I hated. In this game, couples in long-term relationships were brought on for a series of challenges designed to test how well they knew each other or, more specifically, how well they were able to recognize each other. One person was made the player, while the other was taken backstage. The first level used photographs: the player sat in a chair and saw a series of photographs of the backs of people's heads, the backs of their hands, the undersides of their feet, etc. Mixed in among these similarly lit, similarly photographed pictures were ten photos of the loved one's body parts. The player who could identify at least five of the ten photos belonging to his or her partner would receive a cash prize and pass on to the second level.

The second level was a sort of musical number, in which every dancer but one was a trained actor disguised as the player's girlfriend, or husband, or whatever. As the performers danced their way through the song, the player's task was to point at them one by one when the player was certain that that performer was not the person the player loved, at which point the dancer would leave the stage. By the end of the round, only two people would be left. The player would have to choose between them before the closing bars of the song were played, pointing at them and calling out, *That's my partner!* which not coincidentally was the name of the show. At that point there was usually some sort of interrogation, where the one chosen would be brought to the front of the stage, his or her parts parceled out to the waiting swarm of cameras, each of which took hold of a nose or eyebrow or twitching mouth and sent it up to the large screens above the stage, where every feature looked warped, lonesome, unbelonging. With the different screens tuned to slightly different saturations, the pieces lacked the coherence of a single source. Each was strange and solitary—but familiar, too, a thing stripped of particularity and made example. And then the dashing host, dressed in the outfit of a federal court judge, would ask the player over and over again, *Are you sure this woman is your wife? Are you one hundred percent sure? Are you one hundred and ten percent sure?* I had seen a player give up at this stage, wandering abstractedly offstage to join the audience.

The third level was the one that offered the largest cash prize, but also the greatest risk. Players were sent into a pitch-dark room in which a number of completely naked people waited in the blackness, one of whom was their loved one. The clock would start, and then they would have three minutes to grope everyone they could get their hands on. When they found the person whose body they thought was their partner's, they had to hold on to the wrist and drag that person out of the room onto the studio soundstage, where the audience would clap and cheer pretty much no matter the outcome. For the players, it was often a different matter. They turned to the person they had grabbed and saw a blonde where there should have been a brunette, or a man where there should have been a woman. The unchosen other would usually trail out a few seconds later, looking some variant of miserable or angry. Because the twist of the level was this: Players signed contracts beforehand agreeing that "losing" the challenge would dissolve their relationship and institute a modified restraining order, one that was bidirectional. Under no circumstances would the losers be permitted contact through words or bodies—though, obviously, the law could not dictate that two people cease loving each other in an abstract sense, from a legal distance.

On the screen in front of me, a man was crouched with his head between his hands, not quite rocking back and forth, but definitely swaying a bit. He was pulling mechanically at his own hair. If he was saying something, it wasn't audible over the sound of the crowd and the music playing him off the stage. I couldn't tell if he was the person who hadn't been recognized or the person who hadn't recognized his partner. I felt bad for everyone on this show, coming on with smiles and hopes for winning big amounts of money. I was always wanting to tell them to turn back quick, be happy with what they had. Because they had so much. Or at least they had something. But to the people on TV I was nothing more than a ghost, watching them hour after hour, unable to speak to them or warn them of what was coming.

"Why are you making me watch this?" I asked. "You know I hate to see them lose."

The man on-screen rubbed his slack face with a hand as three or four tears made their way down his cheeks. The rubbing pulled his mouth into an externally imposed smile, then an externally imposed frown.

"I know," C said, "but I'm trying to cure you of it."

"Why," I asked, "are you trying to cure me of something I feel?"

For the first time, C looked a little bit hurt.

"I know you've been worrying about B, and I think it has to do with feeling like you'll be less yourself if she starts seeming more like you," C said. He looked thoughtful. "But I also know that she's not going anywhere, and she's only going to look more like you, if anything, not less. I think what would be healthy would be to just start dulling that fear, and the fears related to it. Think of yourself as a franchise, like a Coffee Hole or Wally's. More outlets just mean greater reach."

"So you do think she looks like me," I said.

"Well, hmmm, you think she looks like you, right?" he responded.

"Would you be able to tell us apart?" I asked.

"Sure," he said. "I know you."

I just looked at him.

"Well, of course I think I could," he went on. "But it's hard. Everyone thinks they could. All those couples thought they could," he said, pointing at the screen. "But in reality people are a lot alike. Any two people, on average, share 99.9 percent of their DNA sequences. The genetic difference between the two of us comes down to something like eye color and whether or not we like the taste of cilantro."

I wished he would stop talking. When I looked at him now, I couldn't help but see him as a casing stuffed full of thready strands of DNA, just a few miles of letters in a shell. I thought about the parts of my saliva that were merging with his in his mouth, the stray cells that probably had already mixed in. The three or four things that made me different from him were already lost in there and would never find their way back to me.

He was speaking facts to me that many other people knew, that many other people could have told me, and it made me feel like I was sitting with a stranger. I pulled my knees up to my chest and made myself smaller on the couch. I was looking at him now like I was trying to get his features down, so I'd recognize him in the future. The more steadily I looked at him, the more excited he got about the things he was saying. He must have thought I was listening. Sitting over there and gesturing with the remote control, he grew more and more animated and his hair flopped around on top of his head. He looked like someone I was just meeting for the first time, and didn't like all that much.

"I don't understand," I said, "why you can't just tell me that I am exactly who I am, and that I couldn't ever be mistaken for anyone else."

"I could tell you that," he said. "But anyone could tell you that. And if they told you that, you'd know it wasn't me, so you wouldn't be satisfied with it, even if it was me telling you. It's like if I said that to you, I'd disappear. I'd be someone you didn't recognize."

He leaned forward and rubbed my shoulder, suddenly tender.

"What I'm saying," he continued, "is that you aren't going to get what you want. Probably you don't even want what you want. There's no satisfaction here. So maybe you should think of something else you could want, and then just go get that instead. It's called 'transference.'"

I was sitting there and thinking that B could be in my room right now, touching all of my things, and my things wouldn't even know the difference. Then I was wishing her out of my room, but that still left all the empty, threatened space, saturated with potential violation. It wouldn't be enough: I wanted my room to be gone, the whole apartment gone, all the walls closing in on the space between until there was no space between. I wanted to eliminate all the space within which something worse could happen. That blank material was a threat. It could become anything. And then I wanted C gone, wanted him gone so that it would be impossible to want him, so that there would be nobody else that I wanted things from and nobody else to disappoint me. So that there would be nobody I needed to recognize me except myself and maybe B, if I didn't decide to wish her away, too.

All this wanting created an appetite in me that was terrifyingly shapeless. I had no idea how to feed it. I didn't know how to make anything vanish. The things I wanted were hazy, and the things one could have were small and solid, like an orange, and never seemed to add up. I pulled the remote out of C's clutched hand. I was going through the television channels one by one, up and up, looking, and the channels were going up like they would never stop. They would go blindly on, climbing up until they were back at the bottom again, sketching a sort of Möbius strip. I was looking for something I recognized without knowing what I was looking for, something that would remind me that I had an appetite. I wanted the sort of company that could be given only by someone who didn't know I was there.

"What are you doing?" he asked.

I passed an ad for used cars and one for kitchen hardware. Faces of women and sometimes men pointed away from me and at something off-screen, at faces I couldn't see. Lids of jars and flaps of purses lifting up, revealing something dark inside that the gaze of the camera did not penetrate. The hands moving them were pale hands, the nails painted awful colors. And then there was a commercial for something medicinal, some modifier for the body, where the inside of a body showed up on-screen, flooded in light and glistening with a studio lacquer. The heart and lungs and liver and kidneys showed up throbbing and shiny like they did in real life, or the real life we imagined they had in the dark within us. They pulsed there, silently.

Then, suddenly, the smooth flesh parted like a ripple from the center, sprouting holes in all the organs. A mouth opened itself in the middle of the liver, a little Claymation mouth with thick cartoony lips. With its new mouth, the speaking liver complained of pain, dissatisfaction, longing for something more, better. A mouth opened up in the heart, the lungs, the small cute kidneys. All the organs clamored for more. In chorus, they demanded better treatment, more respect, more fun. My own heart felt strange to me, fluttery. I watched as a thick pink liquid slid down over the organs, a sheet drawn over the little holes that still flapped open and shut, open and shut. The gaps winked at me, thickly pink.

I felt a smothered hunger beating out from the unseen places inside my body. I felt corseted in skin. I wanted to turn myself violently inside out. I wanted to throw myself into the outside and begin tearing off chunks of it for food.

Somewhere to the right of my body, C continued to speak. His voice was a little bit sharper than I remembered it. I turned my head to the left, but it still found a way in.

C said: "I thought I should let you know that I put our names in as contestants on *That's My Partner!* We've been together longer than their minimum relationship length, and I think it could be good for you, therapeutic."

I looked in the direction I had been looking before.

"Just kidding," C said. "Are you listening? I was just kidding. But I am going to enter us. If you don't want to do it," he continued, "I could always bring B. You could watch from home. That could be therapeutic too."

He looked at me for a while, studying my face silently. It was like he was expecting me to do something, say something, but I couldn't tell what.

"Just kidding," he added.

I knew then that we were going to have a fight. I wanted to excuse myself before it happened, leave my body behind to field it while I did something else, something completely else. I wanted to return to myself hours later with no real memories, only a vague feeling of having floated. But what I wanted wasn't something that I could have: my life, the process of living it out, was undelegatable, intransferable. This was an essentially contemporary problem, a problem of supply and demand. I had to solve it the way other problems of scarcity and desire were being solved: by finding something new to want and pursuing that wanting instead. Baby monkeys taken from their mothers will form attachments to fake mothers made of cloth or electrified wire, ducklings with no parents will imprint on a cardboard box with an alarm clock ticking inside of it. Wanting things was a substitute for wanting people, one of the best possible substitutes.

I had to leave and find a real Kandy Kake and eat it. I couldn't stand to be myself around any of these people until it was all done.

I looked toward the door. It was the dead center of night.

2

I GREW UP IN A place just like this, where the leaves never fell from the trees but clung there crinkled like burnt paper, shriveled and brown in some places but sprouting tender green leaves somewhere else. Here, the flowers bloom all year, and once they bloom they are already close to dying, nicking the mulch beneath with blotches of collapsed red and white. They repeat themselves, blooming and falling and being swept away before they rot, restoring the perfect squares of green that grid this town and the towns beyond. They grow blindly, nursed by an unending stream of water and sunlight. They wither against a uniform background of palms and pines, which are the same every time you look at them.

I walked at the side of the road as cars passed me by in the sweltering heat, not knowing whether C was awake or whether he was still where I left him, smiling sweetly in his slumber even though we had just had a killer fight. Maybe he was entering us as contestants on that terrible game show right at that very moment. And if he succeeded, how would I ever know whether he had done it to help me, or hurt me, or something in between the two. Loving someone was no guarantee of how they would treat you. All it did was raise the stakes.

I called C two times in a row, then three, then I let it go to voice mail and just kept walking. I missed him. I wanted to hear him say something to me. I thought of him listening to my voice mail later that day, the sound of my breath pressing into his ear. I thought of my footsteps etching themselves onto a material far, far away. I was happy that some part of me would be touching some part of him, even if it was only the sound of my movement against the tissue of his eardrum.

This is a landscape made by human beings, but not for human beings. Walk it and you always step someplace identical to where you stepped before. You can't get anywhere on foot. Cross it in a car and the surroundings slide by until you realize that you've seen them all before, like in the commercial where an impish young Kandy Kake lures Kandy Kat on a chase through frame after frame of a happy suburban neighborhood populated by cute yellow houses. Kandy Kat's clubby feet kick up a wake of dust behind him, his body blurs with speed, the world scrolls maniacally by, breaknecking. He runs with claws out ahead of him, swiping at the little Kake that is always somehow a step or two away. Then a stray claw snags on a piece of sky, and the world starts to stretch and then slump in a startling way: Kandy Kat has literally torn through the scenery, caused a widening rip in the world. He stops to look, perplexed, at the fluttering material, blown by a breeze of unknown origin. On it you can see a piece of house, mostly window and some lilac-painted shutter. The shot widens, and we see that Kandy Kat is standing in a studio soundstage in front of a flat, painted background that slips past him while the little Kake turns a crank. One yellow house after another scrolls by before Kandy Kat looks down and realizes that he's been running on a treadmill the whole time, a treadmill that yanks him suddenly backward and threatens to throw him off completely. Kandy Kat starts running for his life, running toward the giggling Kake, and he is still running with no sign that he will ever stop when we see the words projected over his body.

KANDY KAKES: HOPELESSLY DELICIOUS.

I had been walking for almost two hours when I came up on the crest that overlooked the DoubleWally's, the newest and biggest grocery store in the area. B sometimes drove us up here when she wanted to be a food tourist, her term for the activity of coming to Wally's with a digital camera and rigorously photographing all of the doughnuts. Each one was glazed or filled or sprinkled, sitting beneath colorless fluorescents that made it look inside as if it were always the same time of night no matter how bright it might be outdoors. I always thought her interest in food photography should be encouraged: how long could someone ogle doughnuts without giving in and eating one? So while she crouched on the floor to get her shots of the filled maple bars and glazed twists, shots taken up close and from below so that the doughnuts looked like sticky, oozy mountain ranges, I hovered around her and said encouraging things like *That one looks really good.* Late at night nobody bothered us, but if we came during the day, a line might form behind B as she took her photographs, a line of customers waiting quietly to choose their doughnuts from the bins, waiting without anger even though B took forever to line up her shots.

Sometimes she'd have me drive back so she could look through the photos right away. Her body curled around the camera slightly as she stared, as if she were trying to shield the photos from my gaze. They didn't look like anything real from where I sat: they might have been blurry photos of abstract paintings. B passed these times silently, mostly, with an occasional squeak of satisfaction. Afterward she looked rosier, as though she had found something real, something meaty to feed on in the tiny images. Her satisfaction worked at me in weird, corrosive ways. Her soft *mmm* sounds, coming from next to me, sounded nearer to my ears than they actually were. They ate at me, at my resting feelings, and made me feel a sudden dissatisfaction of my own. What was there in my life to absorb me the way those photos absorbed her? Even C, a thing I had that B didn't, created as much lack in me as he sated. Sometimes I would sneak a look at her doughnut photos, hoping for a bit of that satisfaction I'd seen her feel, but the most I noticed was that each frosted surface glistened in an anatomical sort of way. After looking at each one, I felt slightly nauseated.

Maybe Kandy Kat survived like that, from images of eating and images of food. Light consuming light, the desire for sustenance a type of sustenance in itself. Even if he was always paused on the narrow edge of starvation, what he was doing in pursuit of Kandy Kakes sustained him. They made his life terrible, but at the same time they made him more himself.

I WAS SITTING ON THE floor of Wally's, in what they called Wally's Food Foyer, a grand and open and frosty-cool space decorated with gold-framed photographs of food lit lovingly by a large chandelier decorated with bananas and pudding cups and racks of ribs, which hung from the ceiling in the middle of the hall. On this structure, examples of the sale items of the day dangled just out of their customers' reach. I stood up and readjusted my dress. The ribs suspended in the air over me turned slowly. Artificial light glinted off the corners of the plastic casing, making the meat look shiny and hard. The ribs were like a toy model of ribs that children could play with and pretend to eat.

This DoubleWally's was the largest grocery store within a thirty-mile radius, larger than the one by our house. Its scale was a matter of repetition. There was an aisle that was only for ketch-ups and mustards. It stretched red on one side and yellow on the other, two or three brands carving up the wall and reiterating their particular shape of plastic squeeze bottle for many feet. The sprawl of the aisle was a single tessellated surface dented where a few bottles had been removed, revealing a multiplicity of identical bottles behind them. I stood there in the ketchup aisle trying to remember how this place was laid out.

Every Wally's had a similar feel inside, the interminable rows of smooth color that began to break apart as you got closer to them, dissolving into little squares of identical logos. But the stores had a special trick to them, an organizing concept based on years of statistical data about purchasing preferences, the drift habits of purposeless customers: they were designed to baffle. The most sought-after items—candy bars, sandwich meat, milk—were placed in the most inaccessible parts of the store, not next to one another, but in separate and distant locations that were rotated every one, two, or three weeks in accordance with an obscure schedule developed by top management. Because the things you wanted most were constantly on the move, you couldn't trust muscle memory to guide you back to them. You moved slowly and cautiously, looking for signs of familiarity in your product surroundings. You followed false links and backtracked and still usually ended up in two or three wrong places before finding the right one. Sometimes you ended up at a different desirable object, peanut butter, for example, and bought it instead, but more often you bought both, and the things in between, following a chain of substitutions and transformed desires until your basket was full. Wally's customers ultimately spent thirty-six percent more time wandering the aisles than customers of the leading supermarket competitor, which equated to an impressive twenty-two percent increase in unforeseen purchases along the way. You could recognize Wally's customers by the confused, placid look on their faces as they came to a full stop in the middle of the aisle, gazing wistfully at nothing in particular.

Kandy Kakes used to be in the back right corner of the store, then they were in the far left near the sugar cereals, but that was weeks ago. By now they'd be in the place that Wally Incorporated's team of programmers, statisticians, and behavioral psychologists had calculated to be the least thinkable location for the statistically average Kandy Kakes consumer. I closed my eyes and tried to think of the place I'd be least likely to think about. I made an empty space in my mind and tried to keep out of it. I let my hands flop open as if I were asleep or had been knocked unconscious. All I could hear inside was the hum of Muzak all around me, familiar sounds with all the words missing.

I opened my eyes to no new clues, no new insights. To my far left, a Wally squatted close to the ground, working at shelving some cartons of raisins. I gave him a long stare to let him know that if he was spying on me, I was spying on him right back. Then I saw that what this Wally was doing was not so much shelving as rearranging, moving the front-most boxes of raisins to the back and vice versa. Most likely B had guessed right: they were trailing me just to keep tabs, make sure I wasn't going to steal anything. But that gave me an idea. The work that the Wallys seemed to be doing was purposeless, designed only to distract me and obstruct. If everything about Wally's was designed to thwart me, I would operate as though I had no goal. Against my better instincts, I turned randomly into the maze of aisles and began wandering. It was possible that I would come around to the thing that I wanted most.

The direction I had chosen carried me toward gift items, flowers, and other inedibles. It seemed like an entirely separate store swallowed up and surviving within the belly of a larger beast. I stopped to look at the rack of frill-topped flowers: white, pink, red, and then, more disturbingly, green, blue, neon orange. They clustered to one another like a single growth, blossom crowding blossom so that they looked hard and burstable. I squeezed their puffy heads between my fingers to check if they felt real. The frill of petal looked like the thin red membrane hidden inside the gills of a fish. I would have ripped one apart to see if color went all the way through the bloom, but I heard a voice from behind me, a male voice, so near to me that I immediately thought it had to be C sneaking up on me again, sliding his warm hand up the nape of my neck.

"They're died," said the voice.

This seemed like a strange way to say something obvious. I turned around and looked for the source, which sounded familiar and new at the same time.

The speaker was about the same size as C, wide in the shoulders, hair more dark than light. I could tell that he wasn't C, but when I looked at him I felt the tug of recognition. That feeling alone made him and C blur together in my mind.

"They're dyed," he said again. "It's easy to do, you just need some warm water and food coloring. You put twenty or thirty drops in a glass of water and stir it up, then you chop the bottoms off in a slant. You put the carnations stem down in the water and they drink all the color up. They do it automatically. It's easy."

I asked: "Does it hurt?"

He looked confused.

I stared at the flowers. I worried about them, their deaths serving as decoration for birthdays and dinners. I looked at his face, then back at the dying flowers. Then I remembered, all at once, how I knew him. He had light brown hair cut short so that you could see his scalp beneath the little hairs. He had thin skin, smooth as paper, that looked like it would feel clean and easy to touch. He was less handsome than the drawing of him had been and more handsome than he had looked from the car, as we watched him move around inside his condo.

A week after B moved in, she asked me to go on a drive with her. It was the first thing she had asked me since she had shown up, brittle and small boned, hauling her gigantic suitcase up a staircase with three cramped turns in it. B was absentmindedly picking at the upholstery on the armchair where she was sitting, destroying an embroidered peony and staring at me as if she were trying to see all the way through the me of this moment to what the me of the future would say in response.

B drove an old maroon sports car that must once have been

a nice object. I tucked my knees up inside the passenger's-side cabin, where the floor was covered with scraps of paper, torn-out advertisements, photos of faces, and food mingling together, tamped down by the bottoms of shoes. Every time I moved I heard the sound of something squealing in protest, the leather seat or the Styrofoam cups wedged underneath. I couldn't find a way to sit where I wouldn't be treading on a picture of something special and saved. B got in next to me and turned the key in the ignition. Hot, itchy air started pouring from the vents, smelling like vintage clothes. She put the radio on and turned it down so low you couldn't hear anything, only feel it twitching in the air, a slightly human presence. At home she had always seemed hesitant to touch things, use things: even buttering a piece of toast was a gesture that required careful planning, several pauses, and two hands clutching the knife—so it wouldn't slip, she said. She was the same way in her car, hesitating over the temperature of the air-conditioning, adjusting and readjusting the mirrors, talking aloud through the possible obstacles she might encounter on the way to her destination. But that night B pulled out of the driveway before I could even put my seat belt on.

It was two in the morning and nothing was moving in any of the houses we drove past. I saw the Wally's on our right, then B took a left into a street with no sign, past a couple of branching roads, toward a dark clod of condos pushed up against each other around an empty cul-de-sac. She parked in front of one of the condos and the headlights shut off, the trickle of radio stopped, and then there was only a thrumming sound taking place within me, the sound of space pressing down on the emptiness inside my head. She took out a cigarette and lit it. It was faint light, but in it I could see the shadows below her mouth where the wrinkles would begin. The photographs on the floor of her car all seemed to point their eyes and mouths in my direction.

I listened to the thrumming, my body idling.

Then I asked: "Is this where he lives?"

She nodded her head up and down. "I like to spend the night with him," she said.

"I don't think I'll be of much help," I said back.

I looked around, but I didn't know which of the different identical windows I was supposed to be looking in. The condominium complex was dark and silent. Through the units that were still lit up, I saw bland slices of wall painted cream and ecru, occasionally decorated with objects both boring and useful, clocks and calendars and wall-mounted telephones.

B put her thin hand on mine. It felt like a moist leaf clinging to my skin.

"You already help," she said to me. "Just by being here, you make it more."

I had never been able to remember his name, something standardly male like Brendan, Brady, Brian, Bob, but this was definitely B's ex, larger and more three-dimensional than I'd imagined from the scurrying black shape we used to glimpse behind the venetian blinds on rare occasions. The voice and height and full-on, detailed views of the face were new, but I recognized him by his profile, the haircut, and the anxious sense that I associated with looking at him, a feeling that I was about to get caught. I was closer to him now than I had ever been before, with the exception of the time when he spotted B's car while we were staking out his grocery shopping one night. He was so furious running up to us that it seemed to me he was moving in slow motion. He had a liter of soda that he was using like a baseball bat, and he brought it down on the hood over and over, shouting in his language that I couldn't understand, could only listen at the way I would to a recording of humpback whales singing their underwater songs.

"No, it doesn't hurt them," he said patiently. "They're plants. You need a brain and a nervous system to register pain. Pain is a product of thinking."

He took a can of protein shake from the shelf behind me and popped it open casually. The air filled with a scent like ice cream and laundry detergent. I looked around, expecting to see a Wally coming to discipline one or both of us, but the only one around was watching us from twenty feet away and looked down at his feet when our eyes met.

B's ex assessed me.

"You must be one of those nutri-terrorists like that veal guy. You have feelings for all the wrong things," he said conversationally, smiling and taking another sip from his protein drink. "When you're at the top of the food chain, what it means is you don't have to worry."

Now he was sounding like C. Another person explaining the world to me, what things were and were not, and why I was being unreasonable when I failed to keep them distinct. At the same time, when I described the dangerous blurriness that I saw at work around me, they were always failing to notice, always finding a problem in me, in the way my mind ordered or disordered the things around me. "You live in the world you make for yourself," C would tell me. "Why not make a less precarious world?"

"Who are those flowers for? Do you have a boyfriend?" he asked me.

"I don't know," I said.

He looked at me strangely.

I didn't know if I "had" C anymore, if he was still around to be had. I didn't know if he'd care if he saw me with this guy or what it would take to make him care. B's ex breathed down on me from above, the air from his mouth smelling of stale cake. It occurred to me that if B's ex had been interested in B for any of the traits that we shared, he might be interested in me at this moment. Suddenly I found myself wondering if I could have him, too, if I tried. It might help me understand B a little better to put myself in her place, or as close to it as possible. If I tried to lean up on him, watch commercials with him, chew on his thin, sharp-looking mouth. I could ask him about his ex, whether she had been crazy before they dated, or only after, or also during. Maybe then I'd understand whether her encroachment on who I was amounted to intentional or unintentional aggression.

I could feel his body heat from where I was standing, and because he was still a stranger to me, someone seen only from a distance, his temperature was offensively intimate. I was violating some sort of order in being close enough to B's ex to touch him, after having kept her at a distance from C for the entire time I'd known them. If it was easy for me to take her place, it'd be even easier for her to take mine. Anybody could sit next to C on the couch, watching episodes of terrible TV. Anybody could fit inside the curve of his arm, could cuddle against his front. And I realized the more I found out about this man in the grocery who was watching me back for the first time in my long history of watching him, the more my knowledge and memory converged upon B's. Just being near him was a form of contamination.

"I really need to go," I said. "I came here for Kandy Kakes."

"Kandy Kakes?" he asked. "They're barely edible. I hear they have plastic in them."

"They're edible enough," I replied.

I was backing away from him, flowers in hand.

"Good luck, I guess," he said, watching me.

"Maybe I'll see you again," he added. "I live right by here."

"I know," I said.

"How do you know?" he asked. But I could tell he was asking to keep me talking and not because he cared.

I felt his eyes aimed at me as I walked away. I had already put a good amount of distance between my body and his, which was threatening to turn me into B. Then it occurred to me that if he was interested in fucking me, he might allow me to use his phone. I had an interest in using someone else's phone, using it to call C from an unfamiliar number that he might not be actively avoiding, tricking him into picking up the phone to find out what this strange number wanted and then yelling at him. I turned around and walked back toward Tom, or Tim, or whoever. When I reached him, I tried to look friendly.

"Hey," I said, "could I actually borrow your phone?"

His hand moved toward his pocket but stalled just before reaching in.

"I need to call my roommate," I told him.

"She's diabetic," I added.

He pulled it from his pocket cautiously.

"Thank you," I said, taking it from his hand.

"Diabetes," I said again. I had his cell phone in my two hands, the thumbs positioned for pressing numbers into the keypad, and I started pressing them in. I had done only the area code when I realized that I no longer had any idea what came next. I knew there were some sixes, a four, a three. I had no feeling about what order they might come in. I tried to draw upon my muscle memory, to start again, faster this time, and let my hands find their way to it on their own, but then I was just standing there again, stuck. I felt him looking at me. His look was not flirtatious. Reluctantly, I put his phone back in his pocket.

"You remind me of someone," he began.

Before he had a chance to finish, I was walking away. At the end of the aisle, I sprinted. I wanted to increase the distance between us exponentially. My sneakers squeaked against the shiny plastic floor.

I passed canned soups and magazines. I passed the produce section, which was advertising a new breed of apple—grafted together from two popular types of apples and also a type of peach—that I had read about. Its chromosomal structure was unstable, odd numbered, which meant new seeds and plants could be created only in a laboratory using a variety of specialized equipment. It was supposed to be delicious. The apples were a fuzzy coral color with a velvety texture. When you took hold of one in your hand, they gave in a little bit, like a stuffed animal. Flesh on flesh.

Where I had thought I might finally find Kandy Kakes, past the canned soup and seasonings, paper products and household cleaners, I found meat. The meat came in slack shades of red or pink within the refrigerated bins, and I stopped to visit them while I decided what direction I wouldn't try next. No matter what shape an animal might have been while alive, dead animal was always made to resemble slabs, a paste that could be shaped into logs, toruses, wavy rectangles. These were the shapes we made, mathematically and conceptually simple, and they were different from us in every way. I patted the packages of meat with my right hand, the one that wasn't holding the flowers. It was colder in this part of the store and brighter.

Then I saw the veal section. It was twice its usual size and covered in posters and slogans. I recognized Michael's face printed large on every one of them, his mouth pinned into a stiff grin. He wore a kitschy black-and-white-striped jumpsuit and a handkerchief tied around his neck. His left hand was planted on his hip as his right pointed out at the promotional display in a stiff "I'm a little teapot" sort of way, as if he were practicing being something that he would clearly never become. The posters read THIS VEAL'S A STEAL in big black print, and below it small cursive letters spelled out: "Veal is a delicious part of any balanced meal.—Michael Trowbridge, 'The Veal Stealer.'" The posters had a tiny stamp at the bottom, indicating that they were a product of something called the Regional Council for the Protection of Veal and Veal Imagery.

I went to the veal poster that was nearest to my eye level and I got close to it, close enough that Michael's head was almost the size of an actual person's head. From six inches away he was blurry, but he looked more real than he had that day on the TV screen. I was trying to look into his face and figure out what it meant that Michael had gone from hating veal to hiding it to eating it and now to endorsing it. Had he changed his mind? Had he been sued? Had someone stolen his picture and made it mean whatever they wanted? His burglar costume looked like it had been pasted on in Photoshop. I wished that I could speak to him, ask him who was in control of this ad campaign and whether it was awful or just much more convenient to have another person controlling your identity.

Out of the corner of my eye, I saw the red-and-orange coloring of the Kandy Kakes logo. I was close! Then I remembered that I was starving. My hunger was so wide and placid that I could dog-paddle around in it. There were dozens of boxes of Kandy Kakes stacked on top of one another on the shelves, red-and-orange boxes with the neon-green lightning bolts that signified snack cake bliss. My body felt small to me and light, and I walked to my Kakes with a cartoonish energy in my limbs, as though one giant leap could carry me all the way to their shelves.

I heard a scuffling sound as the cloth I wore rubbed against itself. I saw my bony arms sticking out in front of me as I maneuvered them over to the shelf and picked up the nearest box, which was suspiciously light, because it was empty. I picked up the next box and tilted it right to left, listening for the Kakes sliding back and forth within.

All the other boxes were empty, too.

It was just like that commercial where Kandy Kat turns to crime in a last-ditch attempt to achieve Kandy Kakes consumption. He goes from store to store trying to buy a single, measly package of Kandy Kakes, but nobody will sell him anything. They point at a poster behind the counter that reads DO NOT SELL TO THIS KAT.

DANGEROUS CHARACTER. Kandy Kat's face is on this poster, hollow and gaunt. So Kandy Kat hijacks a freight train made up of an endless number of cars painted with the Kandy Kakes logo, and off goes the Kandy Kakes alarm, bringing police helicopters and squad cars, then military tanks. As Kandy Kat barrels toward a military blockade, he reaches back for a box of Kakes and says a final prayer before opening the box. But the box is empty, and so are all the others in the first car, and the second, and Kandy Kat looks up toward the impending collision with tears wobbling in his eyes. Strings of drool hang from his mouth as he meets his doom.

Holding the empty Kandy Kakes box in my arms, I realized that C was not going to be calling me back anytime soon. I realized that I had not been realizing how different he was becoming, day by day. He had seemed like a different person, or the same person acting differently, an even scarier thought. Last night he sat at the far end of the sofa, six feet away from me, as he explained his thinking. I was a great girl, he said, but I had a downward trajectory. I had been doing less and less each day, and the things I did do I regarded with trepidation, as though they might turn on me. He wanted to date someone who was on the upswing. Someone who had shaken off simpler problems and was left only with the unsolvables. I, on the other hand, was turning solvables into unsolvables and then trying to solve them. I made the least of my situation. He didn't believe in that. I reminded him of one of those polar bears at the zoo that won't mate even though, in captivity, there was really no other way to participate in some sort of natural order. Though obviously, he said patronizingly, literal mating was not our problem. I told him that I *was* on the upswing and that all he was noticing was a person coming to know what was right with her life and also what was wrong. C said I tired him out. He went to the fridge to get a beer. When he came back he looked at me a little more warmly. He told me: "I want someone who can do everything I want to do in life with me, and I want that person to be you. Could you be a person who wanted that?"

Inside I was imagining myself showing up on that game show, smiling as they led me into a chamber where I would be duplicated by dozens and dozens of paid extras. I imagined myself excited to get on the show, excited to try to win the big suitcase full of money with my partner. I imagined myself dancing the cancan with the other decoys, my shoulders and face tingling from the hot lights overhead, smiling big and feeling certain that C would pick me out of the lineup. But even though the face I put on this imaginary person was my face, and even though her body was like mine, I knew the person I was imagining wasn't me, only looked like me, and really had nothing more to do with me than a piece of paper a photograph is printed on has to do with the picture printed on it. And if I wasn't really going to be around, I'd rather not be around at all. I'd rather be wrapped in a sheet, ghosting myself, leaving everyone with questions about what had happened to me and where I had gone.

I looked at C, at his wavy, shampoo-smelling hair and the thin lower lip that I had been sucking just an hour before. I loved his face, I loved that I could touch it, taste it, put my mouth all over it. There was no other face like his, no other face I was allowed to do that with. His face wore a waiting look.

Then I said, "No. No, I don't think I would be that kind of person."

WHAT I DID NEXT HAPPENED at some distance from myself. I took two of the empty boxes and headed toward the front of the store. I was shouting that I needed some help, because I did. I needed someone to fill up those boxes. I was talking to a cashier and asking her what's going on with these empty boxes, what have they done with the Kandy Kakes? Where did they go? Where are the rest of them? There have to be others. I was shouting a little, it's true, but in my defense I was really very hungry.

"Ma'am, I'm sorry," said the cashier. "Please lower your voice," she said, "you're disturbing the children."

What children? I thought. Then I said: "I'm disturbed. You're disturbing me. Where are your Kandy Kakes?"

"Please calm down, ma'am, and I will address your question," said the clerk.

"I'm calm," I said.

"You don't understand what my day has been like," I said.

"I'm already calmed down," I said.

"Ma'am," she said, "we've had some trouble keeping them on the shelves given the activity of that cult out in Randall. All the stores nearby have been hit."

"What cult?" I asked.

"What cult?" she said back to me. "You've seen the murals? The strangers picketing Town Hall? The people dressed up like ghosts?"

In Wally's Food Foyer I see the children dressed in private

school uniforms, navy blue on the bottom with crisp white tops. They're dancing beneath the food chandelier, lifting their arms toward the light. Their little faces darken when a banana or loaf of bread passes by overhead, casting a gray blotch in its own shape upon their open mouths and eyes. A little boy stands off slightly to the side, hopping up and down, reaching for a rack of ribs that twirls slowly above his head.

I HAD GRABBED ONE OF the veal posters on my way out of Wally's. I was holding the poster in front of me, arms outstretched, walking in what I hoped was the direction that I had come from. Now half of Michael's head eyed me from the paper, its corners curling in the wind. I tried to place it where an actual person's head might be, standing before me, ready to explain to me what exactly was going on and what that pressure was that I felt digging in against my organs, that pressure like a man's hand pushing down on an oversize game show buzzer. Embedded in paper, his eyes were flat, his face was flat. Where a nostril was supposed to be, I looked harder and saw more flatness, the semblance of a hole more like a bruising of the paper than any kind of way in. Around the eyes and cheeks there was an inanimate smoothness, like a stone washed ashore after years of slow wear underwater. This smoothness crept in toward the crinkling eyes and nestled around them, clotting near the wrinkles on the outer corners, which looked overdefined and numbered fewer than seemed anatomically appropriate. The lips pulled at the skin-colored surface surrounding them, suggesting a grin and a grimace at the same time.

What I was searching him for was his level of satisfaction, which I thought might be lodged somewhere in the facial expression. Had Michael's veal-related accomplishments left him with a sense of purpose fulfilled? Was this ad campaign somehow the next step in his commitment to saving veal from its enemies? Who exactly were veal's enemies? Might veal secretly crave its own consumption, thus making its enemies its saviors? Was consumption a form of infiltration? I looked to his face for clarity, but whatever answers might once have been there had been smoothed over in retouching.

Help, I thought. But nothing happened.

I rolled Michael into a thin tube and stuck him in my backpack. I took out my phone and looked at it as I walked. I had been calling C every hour or so, hoping he'd pick up and let my voice join to his once more. I had left one message after another, many of them silent, filled only by the background noise of wherever I was walking. In some I asked the same questions over and over. *Why won't you pick up, where are you? Are you at home? Are you someplace else? Are you alive?* I felt angry, sad, at peace, and then angry again. I told him things that I wasn't sure I felt but wanted him to hear anyway. *I've been napping in the house across the street during the day, I want you to come next time, you'd like it. There's nothing there. Nothing to go wrong. Call me back. Call me back right away. I know who you're with. I want to know who you're with. Call me back. I may not want to be the person you want, but I love you, and maybe I could make myself try to want to be, if you'd call me back. Call me back.* Emotions infiltrated me like toxins in the air supply, passing through my body and corroding the things inside, filling me entirely and then leaving me vacant.

I thought about C sitting there, picking up his phone each time it shook at him, looking at my name on the little screen, and choosing to put it back down, ignored. I imagined his face not changing when he saw my name, or maybe just changing a little bit, into some less pleased shape. It hurt to imagine that, so I imagined him differently, distraught every time he saw me call, distraught and missing me, but that didn't make sense. What actually felt best was to imagine him missing entirely. On the arm of a couch I had never seen before, somewhere I had never been, his phone rang and rang and nothing happened. The lights on it blinked on and off, a sequence of green and blue and red, and nobody did anything to quiet it. When I imagined a stranger's hand, the hand of a much older man or woman, reaching down and pushing the button on the side to silence it, I was comforted. Maybe I could be the one to cut the feeling that linked me to him, to cut the thing that had me worrying about his love and who he was saving it for, that had me wanting words from him and a constant stream of feelings. I felt empowered, briefly. If I could find him, I could disappear him. But even if I couldn't find him, it was within my power to disappear myself, dispose of my own body. If I looked at it blurry, I might even be able to make it feel to myself as though the world were vanishing from me, rather than vice versa.

Then I took out the pamphlet that the Wally's manager had offered me when I demanded to see a schedule of deliveries that would tell me when there would be Kandy Kakes again. "Ma'am," he'd said, "we do not know when the next date will be that your product will be in stock. We are currently having difficulties getting in touch with both the distribution and supply ends of things, and furthermore those individuals visiting from the Conjoined Eaters Church have been removing product from the shelves and leaving these documents in their place, which we recognize is an inconvenience to our customers. Please feel free to take one of these reading materials home with you, with our apologies, and you will see that our problems are genuine. Their religious practices devote no thought to the complexities of supply and demand, or customer service."

He had opened a drawer stuffed full of identical folded white papers. White filled the cracks between white, a harbor of inexhaustible paper. With a dull feeling in my skull, I took a pamphlet and left. Now I opened the pamphlet, which had the flimsy feel of paper from a home office printer. The shiny black of the type dissolved into tiny dots when you looked into it deeply. The pamphlet was blank on the outside, but on the inside it read:

HAVE YOU BEEN SAVED TWICE?

Many people know the story of Jesus Christ, who was born in a humble manger to the blessed mother Mary, who conceived her child immaculately and at the will of God himself. Few people know the truest facts of this event, these being that JESUS WAS ONE OF TWO JESUSES born on that day and at that time. It is well-known in nature that certain species manage a type of conception without the need for or uncleanliness of the sex act, namely they practice VIRGIN BIRTH (e.g., water fleas, nematodes, parasitic wasps, and certain vertebrate species such as komodo dragons and hammerhead and blackfin sharks to name just a couple). Scientists know it is the case that some bodies need no other body to set in motion the action of procreation because all bodies contain an excess that enables one to pinch off a part of themself and COPY IT INDEFINITELY. This was the case with Jesus our lord and savior who is veritable proof of TWINNING and by extension the UNIVERSAL TWINNING OF SINGU-LARITIES and their DIFFERENTIATION INTO LIGHT AND DARK varietals.

An illustration: How is it possible that God's son, Jesus, made SPECIFIC in mortal form so as to serve as an example of goodness for mortal man, should rise from the dead—a thing of which no man is capable? The answer: HE CANNOT. The Jesus who "rose" had been there the whole time, mingling his false sermons with the great truth of the accurate Jesus who is light manifest. Hence the injurious nature of the false-risen teachings, e.g., "When you see your likeness, you are happy. But when you see your images that came into being before and that neither die nor become visible, how much you will bear!" (from the Gospel of Thomas). This speech is of a piece with counterfeit materials being woven into many things in your vicinity, FALSEHOODS THAT WORK AGAINST YOUR WELLNESS.

Have you ever wondered why the person you love is kind and amenable one day, dissatisfied and cruel the next? Why eating a certain food on one day leaves you feeling fine, but eating it the day after or the day after that will make you feel tired, or fat, or depressed? THIS IS BECAUSE THE LIGHT AND DARK TWINNING IN THEM HAVE NOT BEEN SEPARATED. Alternatively, you are being made sick by consuming matter that is improperly sourced. Production obscurities in today's food assembly mean that you may be buying accidentally foods grown or produced in a dark realm by ghosts of the types of people you know. Food items of VERIFIED OR POSTULATED DARKNESS include: green apples, eggplant, garlic (whole), wheat- and rice-based dry cereal, Red Delicious apples, chicken breast, milled oats (enriched variety), prepackaged breakfast sausage and bratwurst, bagged ice, seltzer, oranges, orange and fruit juice, loaf bread, udder, nut butters, and A WIDE VARIETY OF APPARENTLY INNOCUOUS FOODS.

IF YOU HAVE ALREADY OR MAY SOON CONSUME DARKSOURCED FOOD, CALL THE NUMBER BELOW FOR A FREE CONSULTATION BY EXPERTS.

At the end of the text came a 1-800 number and a round black seal with an etching of two white chalices. Printed above in tiny serifed capital letters was: NEW CHRISTIAN CHURCH OF THE CONJOINED EATER.

Below that, in smaller letters, was an address based in Randall, a town twenty miles away. The back, again, was blank. There was a smear of rusty brown with a few whorls intact on the edge of the pamphlet. A bit of bloody fingerprint.

I looked up from the paper and out at the land that bodied the distance between myself and my home, where B presumably was waiting, looking more and more like me with every passing second. I checked my phone, but nothing had changed, C was as remote as he had been a couple of hours ago. It was late in the afternoon, and the mid-July heat would break in an hour when the sun began its slide down toward the horizon, turning the sky a toxified red. But for now, the swelter slung thick in the air and made it a sort of jelly, something that I waded through, something that I pushed aside as I eked my way toward work, and then toward the apartment that I still managed to think of as home. Shapes trembled under the heat. The things I was wearing pressed sweaty to me like another skin on my skin, wet and wettening in the heat of the sun.

I fixed myself on the horizon line where sky met land and walked toward it, toward the wavering highway, which like a mirage seemed to be fleeing itself continually.

I WENT TO WORK AND I proofed *Kayaking Quarterly* and *Marine Hobbyist*. I struck out the duplicate characters and misplaced punctuation with ferocity, my fingers sore afterward where they had choked the pen. I felt a little bit dizzy, and the letters trembled when I looked at the page. I realized that the lowercase *p* was exactly the same letter as the lowercase *d*, just in a tricky new arrangement. I tried to tell a co-worker in the cubicle next to me, but she just looked down when I started talking, shaking her blond head. Other people think that proofreading is just about changing incorrect things into correct ones, but it's more complicated: it's about holding language in place. When I got home, the sun was setting and the different lumps of furniture in the living room were brilliant on one side, the other side sunk into dimness. Their shadows slanted off into the lack of light. It was quiet, but it was always quiet in there when I got home, as though B were activated by my presence, my proximity.

I had never liked this about B, that when left alone she wouldn't do the sorts of things a human body normally does when it takes up space. There were no clear effects of her presence, no new arrangements to welcome you back. She didn't warm up a room. She wouldn't let you know she was inside already by squeaking the sofa or singing to herself or making doors open or shut audibly. While she knew I was home, it was as if there were an invisible string tied from my wrist to hers, alerting me at all times to the sound of her footsteps moving from left to right in the living room, indicating that she was going to the bathroom, then again from right to left, indicating that her time in the bathroom was over. But the first few minutes of returning home made me feel like the girl in a slasher film, opening doors and checking her makeup while the audience members shout at her to turn around, look behind her, call the cops. I preferred the certainty of the house across the street, the house that I loved for its emptiness and sense of desolation, for the way it comforted me.

Stepping raw and nervous into this house with its thick shadows and creaky floors made me miss C more than ever. If he were here, I'd be less scared, less alone. C took up all the space around him, including my space, his legs sticking out into the passages that I had planned to walk through to get to another place, forcing me to climb over him or find another way around. I missed having to maneuver around him, to sort my body from his. When we put our faces close together sleeping or cuddling, he seemed to suck up all the air, leaving me sleepy, dizzy, partially undersupplied, and nuzzling at his mouth. *That's what love is like,* I would think, breathing shallowly, my mouth and nose smashed against his skin.

But B was the sort of person who might be anywhere.

Standing in the kitchen, I couldn't remember a time when I had eaten. The counters and cabinets were clear, meaning that if there was something to eat, it would be found in the fridge. One of the special features of Kandy Kakes was that even though they contained real animal- and plant-derived perishable ingredients, you never needed to worry about taking measures to keep them from spoiling. Most food manufacturers add preservatives to their food to counter the many different threats to the integrity of a food item: rot by bacteria, rot by oxidation, rot by fungal proliferation, rot of all kinds. These additives struggled against the inevitable rot of dead matter. Foods died because they once lived.

But Kandy Kakes were a pure food. Their wrappers could boast that they were *Preservative Free!* because they really were. In one Kandy Kakes commercial, Kandy Kat and a Kandy Kake are dropped into the right and left halves of a split screen. Time begins speeding up as they stand side by side: seasons change and the furniture starts looking more futuristic, hands on the clocks in the background spin around dizzily. Kandy Kat's bony body grows longer and taller and wider as it ages, though never more fleshed. Then suddenly he buckles, beginning a serene crumple inward. His knees bend and begin shaking, his head hollows out and gets skully, sinking down toward the ground where the shedding hair collects in soft, fluffy clots that blow around like tumbleweeds. His shriveled tail looks like a chewed-up rope. Occasionally he raises a skeletal paw to the stark black line that divides him from the Kandy Kake one cell over and claws at it, but he's clearly getting tired. On the other side of the split screen, the Kandy Kake is doing jumping jacks and calisthenics, practicing the cancan, hopping around, and looking bored. No matter how much time seems to pass, it remains the same: untouchable, impassive.

The voice-over explains the miracle of Kandy Kake imperishability as a product of several different highly advanced manufacturing processes. First, biologically derived ingredients are passed through an ultrapasteurization process that destroys not only harmful bacteria and molds, but other life-related elements within the substance: trace enzymes, proteins, vitamins. Next, these elements are filtered out through a subtractive chemical process sensitive to the structure of organic compounds, which eliminates most natural degradation. Finally, the nascent Kakes are reinvigorated with specially engineered weather-resistant forms of sugar inspired by plastics, which function doubly to repel vermin. As long as you leave the water-repellent fudge casing intact, your Kandy Kake is guaranteed to stay fresh for twenty to thirty years. By this time, Kandy Kat is mostly a pile of hunched bone and hide, his two round eyes blinking blearily at the audience. He holds up a sign that reads MY LAST WORDS, while the Kandy Kake, which has found its way over into his half of the screen, dances a perverse jig around his broken body.

I opened the refrigerator and saw nothing but a pile of stripped oranges, a pyramid of them, all the pale yellow color of rind. They would be so easy to eat—pre-peeled, unarmored. The little gouges in their rinds matched the diameter of B's fingernails exactly. But for some reason oranges now filled me with dread. I had never noticed it before the pamphlet had pointed it out, but there was something dark about oranges, seeded through their sweet, watery flesh like a poison. With a product like Kandy Kakes, the ingredients are spelled out for you on the wrapper—every part accounted for, its caloric and nutritional content tabulated. But what sorts of ingredients went into a piece of fruit? An orange wasn't a type of food so much as another entity, looking out for its own interests, secretive and sealed, hiding its insides from the outside world.

I looked around for the peels, but they were all gone, vanished down B's throat.

It made sense to me that B would be a danger: she was too weak to be harmless. Though I didn't know how to describe the threat posed by the oranges, it wouldn't be hard to avoid eating them since I avoided eating almost everything else. But the threat posed by C's absence, the regret I felt as C felt further away— these things felt more dangerous with each passing moment. The no-longer-myself feeling was growing; I worried it was here to stay. Things were better with him than they currently were without him, dizzy and bereft of snacks, not sure what was safe to eat. I would take a nap, reread the pamphlet, and maybe go to the grocery store again later.

When I opened the door to my bedroom, the last squeezings of daylight were leaking in around my curtains and the outlines of things were barely visible in the dark. My shelves and desk were normal, and my bed was normal except for a deformity in the center, a lump under the covers that was too small to be C but might be small enough to be me. I went over and looked. Her body was curled under with the covers tucked beneath the feet, under a curve that was probably a knee. A little bit of her black-rimmed eye poked out over the top of the blanket, shut in sleep and oblivious. She had a ponytail like mine, splayed out over the pillow like a quick swipe of ink from a large, stiff brush.

I felt light and airy. It was as if I weren't there. For a moment it seemed possible that I might have been asleep the last few days, dreaming a long and extremely detailed dream where my roommate was turning into me and I was turning into nobody. But when I leaned in again toward the face, I saw small freckles on the earlobe that I knew from B's ears, though I couldn't remember what my own looked like, and mine could easily have been marked the same way, except there was nobody else there to look for me. I moved my face close to hers and breathed in and out, watching the fine hairs at her temples dance around her face. But I remembered what someone had told me once about breathing in dreams: If you're feeling your lungs open and close, you can't be dreaming.

Leaving my bedroom where B was sleeping, I saw a pamphlet

on the living room couch. It looked like the one I had taken from Wally's, distinctive insofar as there was nothing at all distinctive on the outside of it. But mine was still in the back pocket of my shorts, so this one had to be B's. I opened it up and read:

DOES YOUR HOME OR LOVED ONE
GIVE OFF DARK CHEMICALS?

Many individuals operating in this day and age are familiar with the disheartening experience of becoming ill, anxious, or otherwise SICK IN THE SOUL despite having made good life choices. You may find yourself asking, "How have I placed myself in this position despite following the best information available? Could it be there is better information available?" The self-destructive impulse is to open oneself up to an influx of new advice, but in truth one should simply ELIMINATE DUPLICITY from your existing body. In other words LEARN TO CLOSE YOUR SECOND EYE.

An example: Monks living in the Middle Ages under the watchful care of our Lord were frequently given the task of copying out holy documents while reading them aloud or mouthing them beneath their breath. Working six hours a day six days a week, a monk or nun could copy out the whole Bible in a year. And yet these monks were never given an education in the discovery of the hidden pages within the pages of the Holy Book, and thus with face full of DECOY KNOWLEDGE they copied the Bible as it appeared without referencing the SHADOW STRUCTURE beneath. Thus was the book rendered rife with mistruths, namely the number of Jesuses. Similarly, Oedipus was in the right when he set about gouging his left eye out so as to eliminate from his sphere of knowledge the false truth that Jocasta was his mother. It is because he failed to stop at the better truth, that she was his wife, that he went mad. To this end, you might ask yourself: WHO IS MY SECOND EYE AND HOW AM I GOING TO GOUGE THEM OUT?

You are probably wondering: "What does this mean for my loved ones?" That depends upon their level of contamination. Does living near them make you sleepy? Do they increase or stifle your appetite? When you make a statement natural to your body of knowledge, do they contradict or compound it, forcing you to ingest new knowledge that has not been tested for safety? If your answer to any of these statements is "maybe" or "yes," then your loved one may be SEVERELY BUT NOT IRREPA-RABLY DUPLICATE.

Scientists have confirmed that chemicals are present in nearly everything manufactured by natural or artificial means. To put this in more detail, chemicals can be found in almost everything, but what about the chemicals that cannot be found? WE CAN FIND THEM FOR YOU. Our spirituality centers offer the best step in diagnosing factual contaminants in you or your beloved, using subtractive processes developed by some of the most suc-cessful corporations in the country. You too can be well stocked, free of false certainty or taint.

It is worth mentioning that in these confusing times other pamphlets may front themselves as being accurate renditions of the knowledge possessed by the New Christian Church of Con-joined Eaters. These pamphlets, once discovered, should be dis-carded swiftly and their memory dumped.

BRING YOUR LOVED ONE IN
FOR A FREE CONSULTATION.

IF THEY LOVE YOU THEY WILL COME.

At the end of the passage was that same phone number, same address, same logo with CONJOINED EATERS CHURCH printed above it. Was the error in the Church's name intentional? I had never noticed how much the logo looked like a Kandy Kake: thick black border surrounding two squiggles of light, two chalices made of white frosting, twinned. I stared at it and felt like it was trying to tell me something, something I couldn't hear over the sound of my hunger, which was like two people with two megaphones shouting at each other through the center of my head. Was this the correct pamphlet? Was the one I had read earlier a decoy? Could there be a more correct pamphlet than either of these somewhere else, waiting to be found?

THE FIRST EYE EVOLVED BY accident in the single cell of an organism that had been born sensitive to individual particles of light, according to an article I had read in *Marine Hobbyist*. Deep underwater, it felt their soft touch on its surface as a blow and registered that shock by wincing slightly, changing its shape. In this way, the cell learned to say *there is something blocking the light above me* or *there is not*. Either something was there or there was nothing. This ancient eye was primitive in comparison with our modern eyes, which now operate as whole colonies of individual photosensitive cells yoked together into a single blob, cringing together at the sun. What the first eye saw, though, it saw with certainty.

I put my hand on B's bedroom door, which was just like mine but with a little paper sign taped to it that read VISITOR PLEASE ANNOUNCE YOURSELVES. She had stolen it from someplace on campus, I guessed. I didn't think it was grammatically correct. I was filled with a feeling like purpose, like those moments where you remember what you came into the room to do. What sort of purpose? I'd find out once I got inside. I pushed open the door onto an inside so dark, it startled me. B had gotten the better room, it was bigger and had an extra closet, but the windows looked out onto trees and told you nothing about the house across the street. While she watched the trees, I learned things about the world around us. I learned that our neighbors had sensed a threat in their surroundings, that they had ghosted themselves as some form of preemptive defense. I had learned that they were never coming back. I had learned, as they had, that just because a thing is in your home, just because you allowed it in or even put it there yourself, is no guarantee that it won't begin changing itself while you're not looking, unbecoming what it was and transforming slowly into something you'd never, ever let into your life. These sorts of things needed to be rooted out or abandoned as toxic.

It wasn't that I wholly bought into the message of Conjoined Eating. There were some good ideas there, but I was still waiting to see how it all played out. What worried me was B's malleability: if she had read that pamphlet, it could be assumed that she would fail to realize that she was the contaminated one in this relationship. Given her temperament, it was almost certain that she'd attack, if she wasn't already somehow attacking me by invading my bed, infringing on my face. The safest thing was to retaliate in advance. Once, at least, maybe twice.

I saw dozens of shiny little tubes and jars arranged across her dresser, the mirror image of my own room, and I went to them and opened the little lids of the flower-reeking creams and dug my fingers into their mellow white. I glopped them out on top of the dresser and spread them around with my fingertips. They were all the same things that I used in my room, but they had been bought new, pristine, some with the crisp factory surface still on them. Then I clutched at the makeup, squeezed the pencils in my fist like a child trying to cause harm, pressed them point down until they snapped, and I banged the pressed squares of powdered pigment against the cream-covered surface until they fell out as chalky crumbs. The lipsticks I extruded from their canisters and rubbed between my gummed-up fingers, working them until they were warm and melty and slid over my hands like thick water. Outside, the dark trees swayed. The pinks and violets and greens were a clown-colored smear across the furniture in her room. I looked happy, though I didn't feel it. My neck and face were covered in daubs of color, bright like petals on my skin. In my mouth, accidental chunks of lipstick tasted like Barbie doll.

I pressed my gluey hands to my face.

When I was done I lay down on B's bed. It all smelled like beauty products, that anonymous female scent that we rub onto ourselves to blend into a wet, aggregate femininity, to smell like a person but not like any person in particular. I recognized this specific scent on her sheets, a body lotion sponsored by the actress who peels her face off in those commercials. It was a body lotion I used and was used to smelling of, and this bed smelled just like my own bed, drowsy and thick with nights of repeated sleep. It occurred to me that I shouldn't have destroyed all the products in the room because I'd have nothing left the next day to make me look like myself. But it was too late to do anything about any of that.

It seemed early to go to sleep, but in a country like this, sprawling all over a yellowing span of land, there must be hundreds of thousands of people secretly sleeping at inappropriate times, times when they should be working or eating or otherwise fueling the total human enterprise. I thought of all those individual unconscious bodies sinking into themselves, slumbering away in the broad daylight of their drawn curtains. I thought of all the hidden spaces: the sewers, the closets, the lightless stomachs and wombs. Warehouses where stock sits silent, the dark interior of a Mickey Mouse costume, the caves of hibernating bears. I imagined the great diffuse blandness of these spaces, soft and dark like a concussion, and I closed my eyes and rolled myself over into the dim center of sleep.

WHEN I WOKE UP IT was to the thought of a dark eye, singular and large enough to sink my whole body into, the tail end of some dream I couldn't recall. The eye was so close that I could touch it just by tilting my upper torso a few inches forward, but instead I was trying to lean my body away from the blackness, inside of which I saw a scatter of dim shapes, squiggles, and lines that looked whitish through the dark liquid murk. I didn't understand why I was pulling back, twisting around before it, then all at once I knew. I was looking for my own reflection in its glassy curve—but there was nothing of me in its surface, nothing underneath. I strained to see, and in straining my eyes slipped open onto a place I didn't recognize: the light too bright, the smell of plastics. I rubbed my face with the palms of my hands, and when I pulled them away I saw them smeared with red, pink, purple, blue. Then I remembered, and I knew it was only a matter of time before B found me. And when she did, what would I say? What would she do?

When she pushed the door open, I shut my eyes.

There was silence for a few seconds before she padded into the room in socks, over to the bed so that I could feel her shadow resting on my skin, then to the window for a moment, then to the dresser where I had left sloppy entrails of color lying there for her to see, and interpret, and do something about. I listened for her voice but heard nothing. Then a few soft footfalls and I felt her again, over me and sinking down, bringing her eyes to the level of my own, releasing soft, stale breaths that stirred little strands of my hair. In the ebb and stutter of her breath, I could hear that she wasn't angry with me, wasn't struggling to hold back any surge of emotion. She was studying me the way we used to study the insects together, the miniature dramas of ants and bees. She'd be searching my features for any residue of tightness, for the tiny strain of muscles holding a face in shape, for traces of fakery.

The body is divided into voluntary and involuntary muscles, ones that you use and ones that essentially use you, make you throb internally and drive your life forward in a series of small movements that you couldn't stop if you wanted to. The ball of my eye trembled beneath its lid as I tried to concentrate on the muscles that would hold it still. The situation inched forward despite myself.

I could feel my eyelid begin to twitch.

My eyes spasmed open onto B's face, pale and so close to my own that her features were clear, exacted. Her sharp lines cut through my blurry vision.

"Were you having a bad dream?" B asked.

"I was just sleeping," I said. It was terrifying how gently she had spoken to me.

"You looked like you were having a bad dream," she replied. "I didn't know people slept like that, frowning and twitching. I thought you'd sleep more beautifully."

I didn't know how early it was, but she was already made up, her big eyes rimmed with black stuff that clumped to her lashes. I realized now that it had been stupid to think that destroying her makeup could do anything to separate us: she would only make me go to the store to buy all of it again. There was no way to wreck her without wrecking myself. Maybe there was no way to definitively wreck anything anymore. No firm cores left to target, only an endless springy meshwork replenished by phantom hands. I squeezed my eyes shut. This was what I had been striking out against all this time, an endless repetition of faces, when all along I should have been seeking and striking the hands behind them.

"Are you angry?" I asked B, who was still crouched down, a tight ball of a person.

"Why would I be angry?" B asked me.

It felt like a trap.

"Because I destroyed your things," I said.

She held still, and when she spoke she spoke with tenderness.

"It doesn't matter," she said coolly. "I can always use yours instead."

She leaned forward, continuing: "What matters is that you broke this stuff because of me. I made someone do something they wouldn't have done on their own. You did all this for me."

She paused as though she were listening for the first time to what she had just said. Then she nodded, reaching out to grab my wrist.

"You really care," she said.

I looked at her big, black-rimmed eyes. They had a moist, invertebrate vulnerability to them, their wet centers exposed. They opened and shut, surrounded by a twitching of hairs like thin legs, dark encrusted. Here was a person who should have been familiar to me, whose hand wrapped around my wrist should have prompted a deepening sense of recognition, thoughts of our past together, feelings. Instead, I was having trouble seeing her as anything more than a compilation of parts, each of which seemed strange and new and known at the same time. They were perfect prosthetics, modeled on her own original hands and face but with no investment in the person they were meant to imitate. I could destroy her with as little feeling as it took to tear up a photograph. I pulled my body upright in her bed.

"I'm late for work," I said, and I stood, pushed past her narrow body and into the hall, out the door, into the world outside.

THAT DAY AT THE OFFICE, I worked from the desk of my choice rather than the usual freelancer's cubicle. The desk I chose was farther from the air conditioner, closer to the window. From it you could swivel your seat and look out at a tree that was in the process of dying, its lower boughs bare in every season. The cubicle was mine today because almost everybody who worked here was out sick: one with the flu, another with tonsillitis, three others with some kind of stomach bug. It gave me the feeling that there was something wrong out there, something that was many different things. My direct manager had something called pelliculitis. Instead of giving me the day off, he was managing me via a series of Post-it notes I found stuck up throughout the office. The Post-its told me that the first thing I should do today was proofread next month's issue of *New Age Plastics*. There was an article in it that was in pretty bad shape. The second thing was to proof this week's *Fantastic Pets*, double-checking its pagination. Then, if I had time, organize the supply cabinet. When I went to the break room to get a cup of coffee, I found a Post-it on the coffee machine that read:

HEY, WOULD YOU MIND GRABBING ME A CUP OF COFFEE? HA HA! JUST KIDDING! OUT SICK WITH PEL-LICULITIS. —STEPHEN

New Age Plastics was a magazine devoted to the spiritual uses and properties of different kinds of plastic. Next month's issue was titled "The Healing Properties of Polystyrene" and featured interviews with an artist who made naturopathic jewelry from old Styrofoam takeout containers and an entrepreneur in Nevada who sold home-brew polystyrene tea that he claimed cured arthritis, imbuing the drinker's joints with all the fantastic resilience of this light, durable plastic. The pages were riddled with errors, per usual—the New Agers wrote in unraveling run-on sentences without punctuation, or they punctuated only with exclamation points. But my boss was right, this article was particularly bad. I couldn't even tell what it was about through the maze of vagary and repetition. One sentence in particular seemed important: *The duo meanings of plastic are as one, bendable/changeable on the one hand and destructive on the other.* This sentence appeared over and over, and when I crossed out a duplicate I'd inevitably grow uncertain of my decision, writing *STET* in the margin beside it, only to cross that out again a few moments later, and again, and again, etc.

The problem, I had to admit to myself, was not necessarily the article. As I tried to perfect the pose of someone just like me hunched over a desk proofreading, I was aware that it was hard to keep reading over the sound of the thoughts in my head. It was as if my thoughts were on channel seek: B's tender face. C's confused one. A full Sunday dinner obscured beneath white sheets. Covered in dead ants. Smeared with blue glitter and gelatinous pink. A round, luscious Kandy Kake, hazily remembered. I was salivating strangely, as if my tongue leaked. I thought I might be coming down sick, too. And even as I thought this, I knew it was not the normal kind of sick, where the body rebels against the foreign element within it. The foreign element was not yet inside me: there was still time to do something, though I didn't know what. It was enough to make me cry.

I texted C: *Crazy night with B. She's losing it for real. Call me?*

When I left the office at four thirty, C still hadn't replied.

I walked back home a new way that day, a way that lacked sidewalk but promised to keep me safe from B in case she was staking out my normal route, which snaked past all the gas stations and my two favorite Wally's Supermarkets. The new way followed the highway. I walked in the ditch when the cars came, breathing in their after-smell of nail polish or nail polish remover, scratching my shins on rough blades of gutter grass. It took longer, too, this way—but the difficulty was worth it. I could be alone with my thoughts, even if all my thoughts right now consisted of panicky, uncontrollable images of things I wanted or feared. Out here by myself, I could try to devise a plan.

When I finally reached home, slick with sweat and covered all over in dull gray dust, I had no plan. I started to head around to the staircase that led back to our apartment, but I stopped myself. It was dusk, and the darkening sky made the indoor spaces glow brighter by contrast. I stood in the driveway before my house and looked up into it from outside. I saw the visible fragments of my bedroom furniture, the unmade bed, the empty mirror. I saw the kitchen counter from a strange new angle, the Formica peeling off the side in a way I had never noticed when I was up there living. From the outside, the inside of our house looked like a stranger's. It looked like any house I might peer into with B, sitting on our roof and making fun of the stupid things they owned, the stupid things they were doing.

I didn't realize that I had been backing away until I stumbled over a jut of asphalt at the end of our neighbor's driveway. I turned around. I was back at the house across the street, the still-abandoned house. My safe house.

I walked across the lawn to the front door and eased it open gently. I walked over to the sheeted-up couch and lay down on its lumpy white surface. In my mind I said a silent good-night to each of my absent family members, only I didn't know their names so I called them Father, Mother, Daughter Who Does Ballet. I rolled onto my side and pulled my knees up toward my chest for slumber. But before I fell asleep, I texted C:

Am I seeing you tomorrow?

Are you mad at me?

Are you okay?

I haven't heard from you in a long time.

THE NEXT MORNING, I WOKE and all the objects were lit up with early daylight, soaked in a brightness that turned their surfaces stark and self-evident—except maybe for the shadows they cast to their sides, the hollow and unhollow centers, the undersides cold where they failed to find the light. The bottoms of things hid themselves against the ground. Otherwise, the world splayed open to my eyes and felt mostly safe. I checked my phone and there was nothing. I decided to walk over to C's house to look in on him. To give him another chance to be a better boyfriend or get him to give me another chance to be some kind of girlfriend. I wasn't going to work today. The thought hadn't even occurred to me.

Each time that I had gone out with C, he had picked me up in his beat-up white coupe and driven me over to his condo, a trip that took about twenty minutes with traffic lights and stop signs. It was a complicated path he took, full of turns, and I wasn't sure I could follow it exactly on foot. But I felt confident that I would recognize the way there from landmarks that I had stored in my memory over the months we'd been dating. Here was the piece of curb where he used to park and idle his engine while I said my good-byes to B and told her when I'd be back. There at the end of the block was the bent stop sign where someone had totaled their car last Fourth of July.

As I began walking, I kept track of the things I knew, the geographic features that let me know I was going the right way. I saw the azaleas in the yard of the pueblo-style ranch house and the golden retriever in the red collar. On foot each block seemed to take forever, and when I reached the larger roads it felt like I would never again reach an intersection or a landmark, it felt like I was walking the same steps over and over, until suddenly a traffic light would appear in the distance and I would be comforted once more by this proof that I was on the right track and making good progress. As I walked, I rehearsed what I would say to C when I saw him, what attitude I would take toward the fight we had the night before he disappeared. I thought about B waiting alone for me back at home, and about the family whose house I was living in now, a family I truly considered my own even though I wasn't sure they knew this yet. I imagined them standing in their freshly sheeted home, just about to leave, looking around them, and asking one another, *Where is she? Is she coming with us? Does she know it's the big day?* I knew in my heart that this "she" was me. I thought about their phantom love for me, light and airy as the love of ghosts. I thought about the pamphlets I had found on their counter, pamphlets for the Conjoined Eaters Church I had found out about at Wally's, pamphlets with titles such as "BOUNCING BACK FROM SELF-EXILE" and "THE PROBLEM WITH YOUR LIFE IS YOU."

When I finally reached C's condominium complex, my feet were burning and tingling at once and my throat felt like a single lump of pain. I must have been thirsty, and hungry. I would ask C to feed me when I found him. I pushed open the front metal gate and walked in, stepping over pointy metal spikes that sank into the ground when you drove on them the one way and pierced your tires when you crossed the other. I turned right at the geometrically trimmed juniper bush and left at the second left, where a lonely sprinkler jerked back and forth, watering a patch of concrete. When I saw the right group of condos, I headed up the stairs toward the top-right unit just left of the corner unit. I gripped the metal railing with a pink, sweat-filmed hand.

At C's entrance at the top of the stairs, I knocked and knocked. I made a high-pitched, terrible sound by dragging my fingernails down the door. I pleaded. I texted a series of question marks, nothing but question marks, until the screen of my cell phone looked as though it were glitching. I slumped down and sat on the concrete, thinking it'd only be a while before someone saw me and expressed concern, before someone did something about me. But that time didn't come.

I waited there until it began to get dark, and then I left to walk back home, emptied out and light-headed, not sure whether the salt on my body was from sweat or from tears.

WHEN I FINALLY RETURNED TO the house across the street, I felt relief and certainty. This was the place. There was no other place like it in the world. I had everything I needed here: peace, quiet, pamphlets. Everything except food. And my makeup, which was back across the street in what used to be my bedroom. I stepped softly over to the window and looked up into the warm yellow lights of my old apartment. It looked so much safer from over here, with a twenty-yard buffer. I thought I might even be capable of going back inside if only I could wait until the lights went off and B went to sleep, reducing my chances of seeing her to zero. I settled down on the couch in front of the sheeted-over TV to wait. I pulled the TV sheet back, uncovering its large, dark lens, and found myself distorted in its surface, sitting there watching myself watch myself. Time passed and the rooms of my old apartment went entirely dark, one by one.

Then I crept out across the street, past the old oak by my bedroom window, around the driveway to the staircase leading up to our two-bedroom apartment. I turned the key so very slowly in the lock, I opened the door with both hands on the knob. At the top of the stairs I knew I needed to check both bedrooms to see which one B was sleeping in—I had to do it without turning on the lights. I crawled over to her bedroom door, body low to the ground, and listened at the crack for the sound of sleeping. After a few minutes I was sure that I heard it: the sound of no sound, the sound of a stilled throat, the whisper of breath through the nostrils, almost imperceptible. Now I could sneak into the kitchen and grab some oranges, sneak into my bedroom and grab my makeup before leaving forever, victorious.

Then I heard a voice from behind me saying my name, again and again, insistent like the call of a bird. I turned.

She stood staring, gaping as though struggling to believe what she was seeing. It seemed to be her: the tiny mouth, sharp fingers, a voice like water falling on tin. These were parts of the old B, the one I knew. But the self-assurance, the way she leaned forward, extending a hand out toward me as though she thought she was helping, out and into my own space: this wasn't my frail friend. When the pamphlets instructed me to discern duplicity, was this what they meant? I looked at her, at the traces of varicolored eye shadow that clung to her eyelid. Errors were piling up in her. She needed sorting.

"What?" I said in a flat tone.

"Where were you? Where have you been?" B asked plaintively.

"I was staying with C. Because you were angry with me," I said.

"I wasn't angry," said B.

The silence hung around us, heavy and dark.

"Most people would be angry," I said.

"We're not most people," she said. "We're closer than that."

"Closer to what?" I asked.

"Closer to each other," B said. "Closer to being the same person. Like, if you destroy my things, you're destroying your own. Our lives are twined together."

"Twined, twined, twined," I said. *What a strange word,* I thought. It reminded me of the pamphlets.

"Are you making fun of me?" B asked, her face confused but also irritated.

The things we said slid past each other without making contact, failed to land or fit together. It was like C's porn videos, where soft, listless actors carried out their roles while thinking of something entirely unrelated somewhere beneath their faces. You watched them fucking and all you learned was that they were fucking. One body stuffed the head of another deep into a pillow and began its pounding: It was what it was. These bodies were universally compatible, each to each, so the minds would be, too. There was nothing any of these naked bodies could do to truly surprise each other.

I fantasized sometimes about an inverse pornography in which all that mattered was what was going on within what appeared to be a successful fucking. Everything would look the same, flat and happy, but as a viewer I would know that one of them felt an uncomfortable friction that they were concerned would turn into a rash, the other was worried about their unbalanced relationship, not sure what to think about or focus on, wishing they were fucking someone more energetic and distracting even if it was all staged. These innards would be exposed in a voice-over recorded by the actors directly after filming and spliced into the video during postproduction. You would know all the things that the body, in its busy activity, kept hidden.

But since C had disappeared, the fantasies that obsessed me were all the worst things I could imagine at any given time. In one fantasy I look over at the TV in the middle of having sex with C and I think I see our reflections—but then I see that it's a video of the two of us. But as I watch longer, I see that it's actually a video of C and someone else wearing a wig that looks just like my own hair, which starts to come off the head, revealing real hair beneath that also happens to be similar to mine, only blunter, darker. The hair on the wig is so familiar. This hair is soft and tangly, silky like a little girl's. It even has the same cowlicks as my own, a small one at the front above the forehead and a deeper one on the back of the head. That's when it hits me that it's no wig, it's my own actual hair. And then I wonder what's happened to the me that used to be inside it.

B was still crouched down, staring at me and waiting for me to agree with her. I felt a pressure in my muscles that might have been an urge toward flight or just the effort of holding a body perfectly in place. I felt waves of heat sweep my body from the head down, heard something sizzling behind my ears.

"I mean," she said, "how would you put it?

"Is something wrong?" she asked. "Is something wrong with us?"

She couldn't even understand why we might have a problem, and in this way she proved that she was the more innocent person.

"We can talk about it?" B asked.

For a second, I thought we could. It was a long second.

Then I lurched to a sitting position and pushed past her to my bedroom. The room had all my things in it, but when I looked out at it, I didn't feel like I was in the right place. My shoulder pulsed where I had muscled her aside. In my mind, I heard a shadow of the sound she had made when I pushed her over. A bird call, thin as a twig. It was the sound of injury uncolored by anger or fear: she still couldn't imagine that I was struggling against her.

I stood in front of the mantel. I knew that everything in this room belonged to me, but I couldn't shake the feeling that someone had moved it around or swapped it for identical objects, slightly off. To my right, the TV spooled out colors and light and sound that I couldn't bring into focus. I saw Kandy Kat's hollow cheeks and drowned eyes. I saw what seemed to be a darkened face, one eye black and one eye white, spinning dizzily on-screen. But that made no sense. It must have been a Kandy Kake, from the longest of the Kandy Kakes commercials, the one where Kandy Kat clones himself to sneak into the Kandy Kakes factory, sacrificing one of himself so that the other can sneak past the security Klowns and into the glorious troves of sugary-sweet treats that lie beyond. I tried to remember what happened next: did it end in a Kandy Kat embrace, their weak and wobble-thin arms wrapped around each other like a coil of wire? Or was it something worse, the two tearing and scratching at each other's identical bodies, trying to destroy each other for the sake of a single Kandy Kake smuggled from the factory grounds and ready at last to be devoured? I felt strongly that I had once known the correct answer—it was in me somewhere, even if it couldn't find its way out. I looked to the TV screen for help, but the cartoon was already over. All there was now was a pile of fur and the parting slogan, displayed on-screen in bright, bobbing words:

IT'S NOT YOU, IT'S THE FOOD.

EAT BRIGHT.

The light in the room shifted almost imperceptibly, and I knew that B had entered, clogging the doorway with her thin frame. Her face was wide open and excited, as if she thought I were about to give her a present. I kept my head where it was, pointed forward and staring. I held still. Any movement I made would be proof that time was passing. Any movement would suggest that something would be happening soon. I had an image of myself walking toward an unsheathed knife, its tip pointed straight at me: I didn't want to, and yet this image of myself understood that it was the only place to go.

Outside my bedroom window the streetlights came on, spilling yellow light into the darkening blue. Breath quaked my body. I couldn't do anything without driving the situation between me and B forward by notches, one step and then another. I heard the floorboards creak as she took another step toward me, contaminating my presence with her own. Everything she did seemed calculated to push me into the future.

Said the voice to my far right, almost out of the range of peripheral vision: "Are you okay? Is something wrong? Do you want to eat Popsicles?"

I reached out and touched the bundle of hair on the mantel, the lopped braid that B had brought to me and left in my hands. I squeezed it in my hand and drew it toward me. It had a yielding shape to it, like a stuffed animal with no limbs, head, or face. I pinched a bit of its smug torso and pulled. Hair like black taffy in the palm of my hand, with a blunt scissored edge to its ends. I wished that someone would catch me with it, to see me and shame me and stop me from doing this to myself. But there was nobody else: it was just me and B, her eyes large and confused and searching me for what I was about to do with her gift. Between my fingers the hair felt slippery, motile. As I tried to wad it, it unspooled. I knew I had to move faster.

Forming the hair into a cohesive mass was a losing task: single hairs drifted from the bundle, falling in slow motion to the carpet. Twisting the bundle made the sound of flesh opening up onto barren sand. I wrapped the stuff around my finger until the wad was the size of a walnut, but when I pulled it off it swelled up in my hand and I understood that this was going to be difficult no matter what. I looked to B's face, saw her eyes dark and frightened like little gaping mouths. Then I stuffed it in. Tongue clinging to the dry fiber, gums wettening but still sticky, struggling to stay slick. There were bits hanging out, but I couldn't open my mouth or I'd risk losing the whole thing. I tilted my throat back and tried to choke it down. I put my thumb and fingers on opposite sides of the neck and stroked down, the way I used to get my dog to swallow a pill hidden in a lump of peanut butter. At the back of my throat it stuck like a wet rag at the threshold and I had to cough it up a bit, gasping around it, needing much more saliva to get it down.

I rested the wad at the wet front of my mouth, behind the teeth, and I thought over and over about taking the first bite out of a Kandy Kake, cracking that fudge shell with my teeth and feeling the orange-scented syrup ooze out from under the thick skin. Digging my tongue through the oily stuff to the inner Kandy Kore, hard and dry as a bone, turning slowly to mush as my saliva soaks in. Sinking my teeth through layers of acidic sweetness to the woody pulp beneath, the crack of it in my mouth like a bone snapping in half. I looked up at the ceiling, opened my mouth, and pushed it in with two fingers, until I felt the furry ball lodged so far down my throat that it would be more work for it to find its way back up than to go, gently, in the peristaltic direction. My feeling of it disappeared completely when it reached my stomach, except for a heaviness, a sort of burden or weight I carried now that may only have been psychological. The fullness felt like it would never leave my body.

I grabbed another handful and shoved it in, using the left hand to round up stray bits. The hair was rodenty in shape and flavor. It was becoming darker and darker outside all the time, bit by bit. I couldn't make out the sheen of the hair anymore, just an anonymous blob, two shapes twisted into each other darkly. I turned around. There was a pale oval in front of me, swathed in dark shag, stuck through by two dots symmetrically placed and a thin patch of darkness at the bottom center. It was B's face showing fear, a shape I'd never seen it take.

THAT NIGHT I SLEPT, FOR the second time, in the house across the street. And the night after I did the same thing, ditto the night after that, and all the other nights until the night I became a Conjoined Eater. I felt better there, more like myself. During the days I walked two hours to C's condominium, where I waited for him. His absence made my heart grow fonder: with each day that I waited, he seemed like a greater and greater guy. I thought to myself that I didn't need to talk to him, not about B or anyone else, I didn't need to talk to him at all. I just needed to see him once, even from a distance, and I'd be able to imagine him again. If I could imagine him, I could imagine talking to him, telling him about the fight and the pamphlets and all the makeup I crushed, without actually having to explain the things I knew he'd have questions about.

In many ways, having this imaginary C back would be better than the real thing. The genuine, unimagined C would want to know why I was keeping the Eater pamphlets, storing them in bed with me, when I had always hated strange and unprovable claims. He would want to ask how I could possibly think damaging B's property would return our relationship to normal. He was always able to take the few simple things in my life and make them sound like trouble. It was his ability to trouble me that made me prize his comfort. I could imagine him hearing me out, tightening his jaw, nodding his head as he rubbed a hand up my back, saying, *I know you did the only thing that seemed reasonable.* I wanted it so badly that I almost thought it could save me from all the other things I wanted.

I wanted C. I was alive with wanting. I wanted to find him and hug him until his bones bent in on themselves like cheap patio furniture. When he pulled up in front of his house in his battered white vehicle, I would finally open the car door and step out into the bright, sun-ridden air. I'd walk up after him as he went to his front door, and when he slid the key into the lock I'd wrap my arms around him from behind. I'd press him up against the door with my whole small body, the sharp handles of my hips jutting into him, rubbing against his jeans. I'd shove my front against the contours of his back, force his chest tight up on the door. I wouldn't let him turn around to face me. I hoped he'd recognize me just from the shape of my body, the bony snag of my pelvis, the lumpiness of my nose and chin prodding at his spine.

Then I'd speak to him, directly into him, into his back. I'd tell him that after a long time not knowing what to want or how to want him properly, I had figured it out. We were fine: it was the rest of the situation, the other characters, B in particular, that was darking us all up. B was encroaching on my very structure, confusing my body with the presence of her own, sending her ex to muddle up my sense of the one I loved. The only way back into our lives was to ghost ourselves like they had in the house across the street, ghost ourselves immediately and get our bodies to a Conjoined Toxicology Center, where they'd tell us which bad feelings were our own and which had been planted by those who wanted us duped. All we had to do was give ourselves up and we could begin our second life together, a life in which nobody else would be around to keep us apart.

But waiting was hard work. I was sleepy all the time, I ate nothing but oranges. If I wasn't eating something while I watched for C, I'd find myself hard asleep, numb to the moment when he'd return and open his house back up to me to tell me where he had been, why I had done the things I'd done, and what I'd do next. I had to be peeling an orange, separating out its segments, pulping them within my mouth, or I'd end up still, deadlike, gulped into dreams. An endless sequence of oranges passed into my hands to be disassembled.

My eyes ached in the heat and my left lid had started fluttering uncontrollably. It was a little like watching a silent film, the way it made the world twitch jauntily in and out of darkness. I walked up to C's front door, feeling my knees wheeze as I moved. When I got there, I didn't know what to do: I had already rung the bell, had already knocked so many times that the side of my fist felt cold and tingly all day long. I dug around in my pockets. I found a tube of lip gloss, tinted raspberry with little sparkles in it. Extracting the wand with a wet popping sound, I stared at the blank slab of door. Then I wrote. I wrote:

THE PROBLEM WITH YOUR LIFE IS YOU.

It felt right, but looking at it, I wasn't sure what I meant by it. Then below it I wrote:

CALL ME.

I put the gloss back in my pocket and legged my way back toward home, my new home, the house across the street from my old home. When I looked back behind me, C's condo was unchanged. You couldn't even see the writing on the door at this distance. If you looked hard, you might notice that something over there looked slightly wet.

I thought of the orange pulp in my stomach, cuddled against a nest of B's hair, and shuddered. I tried to retch quietly, but my stomach only rubbed up against itself inside me, scratchily like two pieces of wool felt. I knew that I looked like somebody in need of desperate, anonymous help from strangers. But there was no one around to look at me, no one around to see.

☺

MY NEW LIFE HAD THE benefit of simplicity. If I wasn't over at the condominium complex staking out C's apartment, I was in the house across the street sleeping. Or I was at Wally's buying supplies for the next day. By supplies I just mean oranges, the oranges I tore through one after another until my lips and cheeks and fingertips were numb with stinging.

Night after night, I was zeroing in on the daily moment at which Wally's ceased resembling itself, the few short minutes where the shelves shifted into their new, perplexing positions. For the last week I had been overshooting and undershooting, discovering new slices of time that were just like any other: the same lights fluorescing a soured white, same tinny music seeping from the speakers, pop songs with all the words gouged out. The food chandelier hung heavy in the front of the store and swung slowly, deliberately, as though someone had come by and pushed it once, a very long time ago. As many times as I had come to Wally's, I had never seen someone swap out the food in the food chandelier, and yet it was different every time I saw it. New things had appeared in it when I left the store, things that hadn't been there when I came in. But this was a minor mystery compared with that of C's location, which had yielded no answers: nothing but waiting, and more waiting, and time.

The new plan was to find a way into C's apartment and wait for him to come in, to interrogate his objects, to do the things we used to do together as though there were still somebody to do them with. Generally: to be no longer on the outside wishing a way in, but at the end point already, wishing for others to trap themselves in with me. I came to Wally's in order to find the thing I'd need, whatever it was, to wreck the lock and pry open his door.

I saw a Wally's employee wearing the Wally's Hospitality Hat, the oversize foam mask made in the shape of a young boy's grinning, freckled face. A Hospitality Hat was like an ordinary hat in that it fit over the top of the head but also featured an extensive frontal flap with contoured nose, eye, and cheeks that was designed to be pulled down and over the openings of the face. Hospitality Hats were implemented so that customers would always be able to count on seeing a familiar face when they went in to shop at a Wally's, no matter how far from their home branch they might be. The system wasn't perfect: some Wallys were fat, others thin, some had jarring voices, some had breasts. But by removing a few of the variables from customer-employee interaction, they freed both parties to treat each other with the pretense of recognition, with amnesiac familiarity. GOT A PROBLEM ASK A WALLY read the sign overhead.

I had many problems. I looked down the aisle, toward the Wally that was standing at the other end, taking down notes on a clipboard. The fake face he was wearing hung down over his clipboard, freckled and permanently grinning. I wanted to ask him for help, but the Wally's corporate policy stated that employees were not allowed to offer help to customers, only a generalized form of aid. A sign near the store entrance read:

WEAKNESS THRIVES ON HELP

Insofar as all Wally's products might be deemed an aid to the human condition, a Wally might find it prudent to suggest to the customer additional items whose purchase might offer benefits, so long as said employee resists abridging the customer's individualized buying journey. Delivering said customer to their primary product goal shall be deemed an act of harm on the part of said employee, and a detriment to desire evolution.

Feed a man a fish and he'll imagine himself content, allow him to purchase a wide range of non-fish items and he will feed for days.

An ideal buying journey took at least an hour to complete. This Wally wouldn't be able to shorten my path, but he might be able to hint at what sorts of products might be near the product that I wanted to buy. Though it was possible that he wouldn't know himself, he could at least give me more to look for.

"Hi," I said to the side of the oversize foam face.

It swiveled toward me. The crest of each upended cheek was the size of one of my shoulder blades. Shadows sank into its fleshlike form. Each dimple could have swallowed up one of my thumbs.

"Welcome to Wally's," it replied.

"I was hoping you could provide me with product aid," I said.

"Tell me about your product circumstances," he said back.

"I'm looking for a large thing about the size of a crowbar, and also of about the same weight, shape, and material," I said, making a levering motion with my hands. Sometimes it was best to be vague. By being vague, you could occasionally give a Wally room to help you.

"I can recommend Salad Smotherin's," he said, "a new line of salad dressings from Rexall, the nation's leading manufacturer of paper products. Or a frozen dinner from Stewwart's."

I made a dissatisfied customer face.

"Aisle fifteen and aisle four," the Wally continued. "Both are delicious," he said, turning back to his clipboard.

"I need something heavy," I said, "and strong enough to break a lock."

"This week," he replied in a smooth and well-rehearsed tone, "we are also promoting the new Peapple by Nutrisco Foods. Passionate about fresh produce? Or are you a food explorer, looking to sink your teeth into a piece of the unknown? Peapple is a revolutionary new fruit combining the crisp texture of the apple with the velvety mouthfeel of the peach. Flavorwise, it's the pineapple's second cousin. Funwise, it's second to none. Brought to you by the manufacturers of Nutrisco Sea Nuggets."

"I need a crowbar," I said, "or something exactly like a crowbar."

He looked at me.

"Miss," he said, "I think you'd better continue along your buying journey."

It felt like a personal slight. Wasn't there a human being inside that Wallyhead, someone who knew the pain of losing the one they loved or, more precisely, being unable to find them again? A human person who knew the desire to hack through something hard and unyielding to get to the one you loved, hack through the one you loved, even, to get at whatever they kept inside? He must have a lover of his own, some man or woman or animal whose absence hurt like a presence, some person that he poured himself into like a mold to remind himself of what he was.

I wanted to tell this Wally what I was feeling. I wanted to tell him about an idea for a commercial that I'd been having, over and over, during the afternoons when I waited for hours, sweating, staring, seated in front of C's apartment. In this commercial I'm wandering around inside a wet and glistening space that I come to recognize is a body, though I don't know where I am in it. I'm still missing C and I know he's not around here to be found. I know that, but for some reason I can't stop looking for him. And I'm trying to claw my way out physically, pulling at nodules and hanging bits with my hands, but nothing will move for me until I find some tubes that I can wrap my miniatured hand around, they must be for blood. They're a meaty color, liver bruised blue, their texture springy like mattress foam. I'm tugging on one as though it were a handle on a locked door and suddenly it separates, crumbling like dampened cake in my grip. The ground heaves beneath me. Then I hear a growl of pain all around in what I suddenly recognize is C's voice. There's no way to tell him I'm in here and no way of getting out that won't hurt him, tear him open and apart.

I wanted to tell this Wally what I always see at the end of the commercial, a slogan materializing over my head, hovering there weightlessly, the letters illegible from below, the phrase too large to see. I wanted to tell him about this feeling, this feeling that everything is already ruined and I'm selling something I can't even comprehend. But when I looked up, searching for him, he had already disappeared.

In the next aisle over there was window cleaner, peanut oil, fruit snacks shaped like carnivores. The blue-raspberry color of the window cleaner sat against the peanut oil, bright as new brass. They didn't belong together, they had been stranded there, separated from their kind. Yet these items shared purpose. It was overwhelming: all the colors and shades of colors in between, asking you to fall in love with them, hold them in your hands, and take them home.

At the end of the aisle, a Wally was down on his knees, filing cans into the shelf. He had a young body, skinny, tall, wider at the shoulders than at the hips. It could have been C in there, and suddenly I felt like it really was: C hiding in plain sight, C watching over me in the grocery store aisles, C in disguise learning things about me in secret the way I always had wished to learn things about him. I wanted to walk up to that Wally, separated for the moment from all of its kind, and say to it all the things that I had been wanting to say to C: *Show me what you are when you're not around me. Let me see how you look when I'm not looking at you. Tell me everything I'm not supposed to know, and don't leave out any of the things you don't know yourself.* I wanted to extract one secret from him, it didn't matter which. I would put my hands all over that fake face and squeeze it to feel the bones underneath, bear down on the micromesh that veiled the real, living eyeball beneath and press until it blackened. On the next day, I would search this town for someone wearing on his naked face the bruised eye that I had designed for him. From a swarm of identical heads, this inner head would become distinct to me, singular, a head with a personal connection.

I moved toward the man, arms out to my sides, but he retracted, his body positioned for escape. He didn't know if I was about to hug him or hurt him, and to be honest I didn't know either. I heard his breath, heavy already, rasping through the mesh mouth of the Wallyhead. He stood up and hefted his box of product up in his arms, tilted sharply to one side as the product slid over; it must have been something heavy, like cans. Then he shuffled backward away from me toward the back of the aisle, turning at last and ducking one or more aisles over before I even had a chance to ask my question. Why had he left so quickly? Maybe he remembered me.

WHAT DO YOU CALL THE things in the supermarket that are refrigerated, that you look down into like an open casket, and are full of light? I was standing near one of them, feeling the cold rise up from within its bright, clean white. Inside there were chicken breasts and wings and assorted soda tucked into crevices of the body pile, half buried beneath shrink-wrapped Styrofoam trays. I picked up a soda and a package of raw chicken in each hand and moved them to the other end of the cooled box. I did it over and over again, like a punishment. I was making a path to the bottom of the cooling unit, where there might be something like a crowbar. I was following my product instincts. They told me to dig right here.

When I saw there was nothing underneath the chicken and soda except more soda and then a smooth white epoxy, hard as tooth, I started moving my pile from this end of the unit to the opposite end. I had patience within me. A hand on a pack of chicken breasts reminded me of C, the squish of him, the way he differentiated himself from this cooling unit or that shelf. There was a Wally standing near me, watching, but I kept on redistributing the chicken, fixing my gaze on the cold meat, suspecting that what I was doing wasn't allowed but hoping to do it for as long as possible. Finally, he spoke.

Through his Wallyhole he said: "Excuse me. Hello. At Wally's we pride ourselves on creating a flexible shopping environment, insofar as products have no fixed place. Which we believe inspires creativity. At Wally's, Consumers are Creators. We say that."

He paused. He must have been waiting for me to stop moving products around, which I would not do until I was more certain of what was at the bottom of this bin.

"Nevertheless," he continued, "there are boundaries that we do *not* allow the customer to flex, in this case the placement of products in both an area-specific and storewide sense."

I compromised by moving the products more slowly from their old place to their new.

He began again.

"We can all agree," he said, "that a man's home is his castle. At Wally's, we wish for your supermarket to be your castle as well. And, like a king in his castle, we wish you to do nothing, or as little as possible. We would rather you feel at home."

"I don't feel at home," I said, finally putting down the chicken flesh and sodas and staring the Wally straight in his face.

"In my home," I said, "nobody tries to divert me. If I wanted a crowbar, someone would tell me where to find it. Or maybe I would already know," I added.

I was bluffing. I didn't have a home where people treated me in this way, a home full of the things I needed. I hardly had something resembling a home at all.

The Wally just stared at me. It made it worse that he was staring at me with his real eyes, rather than the eyes of the Wallyhead, which were fake, shiny plastic with no actual holes for light to pass through. In the center of the forehead was a circular aperture smaller than a dime, through which a Wally's employee could glimpse a portion of the customer he or she was aiding. But to get a full view of a person through a Hospitality Hat, you had to tilt the foam face up toward the ceiling while looking down hard, angling your head within so that your line of sight passed straight through the mesh netting of the mouth. I couldn't see anything through the meshwork, but from the sharp twist of his head I knew he was examining me.

I was turning back to the refrigerator bin when he spoke again.

"Tell me about your product circumstances," he said.

With my mind I was digging through what I knew about myself, trying to find a chunk of language that would tell me what I wanted and needed and was asking for.

"I just want something that makes me feel like myself again," I said.

"Not myself as I feel right now," I added. Right now I felt like a person learning that a surgeon had left a pair of scissors inside her during an operation.

"I had someone once," I began, watching through his foam face for signs of recognition, sympathy. "We were fantastic together. He really understood what I was all about, what I was like inside. This was because, inside him, he was the same as me. Maybe not on the surface-most inner layers, but deep down, the deepest, tiniest part." I scanned his mesh mouth for a reaction, but there was none. "Then something horrible happened to him, and I'm still trying to figure out what it was."

The Wallyhead listened, pointed intently toward me.

"He lost himself," I explained with a touch of defensiveness.

I added: "I'm trying to find him."

"And what do you want from us?" he said, his voice a little gentler, a little wider somehow.

"I just want to get into my boyfriend's house and see if he's there, or not there. I don't need anything to happen once I've found out, you understand, I just need to know whether we're together or not, and if not, if it's because of me or because something dark and mysterious has befallen him," I said.

"If it's dark and mysterious, that's okay too," I added.

I said: "Something came into me, or my life. I need it out of me, as soon as possible."

I looked up at the Wallymouth. A single eye gleamed, not unkindly, through the dark netting. The head wobbled around slowly in what I chose to interpret as a gesture of sympathy.

"I can show you to a crowbar," he said.

"I thought you weren't allowed to do that," I said. But I wanted it: I wanted it enough that I didn't care if this Wally got punished for it.

"We aren't," he said slowly. "But I can show you to something better."

"Kandy Kakes?" I asked.

He just stood there for a second. The large foam head looked as though it were looking at me, which I knew meant that he was looking someplace else. Then he started walking.

He led me out of the aisle and into the aisle adjacent. There were jellied fruits suspended in plastic containers, glowing orange, yellow, pink, as the light pushed through them. I thought he might look back to make sure I was still there, but he didn't. I understood that it might not be a simple thing to look around in a Hospitality Hat, to change the orientation of one's head so radically. The foam plastic would chafe against cheek and neck. It would press warm and humid to the scrub of his pinkening face, eventually it might rub the skin away, showing the deeper pinks, the bluish-lilac tint belonging to the subdermal layers of skin. If he moved too much, his face might erode entirely. I trailed behind, several docile steps behind, watching his body clench and loosen with the motion of walking.

"When does the food chandelier get changed?" I asked him.

His body twisted toward me slightly, but the bulk of it kept walking as before.

"Do you know when you're going to get more Kandy Kakes?" I asked.

"Are these really the questions you long to have answered?" he replied.

I looked around us at all the veal.

The veal section had changed. In the weeks since it first appeared on TV, Michael's face had propelled veal to new heights of desirability: Men identified with his confusion, with the somber melancholy of his paunchy stomach and cheeks. Women wanted to feed him. He reminded the elderly of past versions of themselves, still ravening for living matter. And children finally had something they could understand when they thought of veal, that meat whose name wasn't a kind of animal or a substance that came nuggeted, pattied, or shoved onto a stick. Veal had a face now, where before it had nothing. And while Michael's face had once been an artless and unexceptional slab according to the personal accounts of grocery store employees and other witnesses to his robberies, image-capturing technology had transformed it into an object of fascination, something to stare at, a face that yielded up more over time.

The veal section had tripled in size, and Michael was everywhere: on stickers and cardboard signs that hung from the ceiling, mugging zanily all over the promotional Veal Wheel. He was a grinning caricature pictured next to the logo for the Regional Council for the Protection of Veal and Veal Imagery. Below his face, the text read: THE MAN WHO STOLE VEAL . . . AND GAVE IT TO THE WORLD. Veal's new slogan was short and underexplained. Each package was stamped with a single repeated phrase:

THE LIGHT MEAT.

Ending up with the Michaels gave me that old feeling of having someone around, someone familiar and friendly who I wanted to talk to. I looked into each pair of his eyes and tried to feel for the one that was most familiar to me, most like the Michael from the poster I had swiped or, even better, the sad, slabby man from C's television who I had watched cry through the rounded convexity of the glass screen. It depressed me to think of him living by the will of the Veal Society, kept in some room and taken out only when they wanted to extract more images from him. For his sake I hoped that he was okay, that these images were recent. I stared at the most Michael-like face of the bunch until I noticed suddenly that the Wally was stopped next to me, watching the same advertisement with an intensity that matched my own.

"Do you follow Michael?" he asked me, wiggling his large foam head on its axis a little.

"I've watched him," I said. "I have a poster of him at home."

"Customers love Michael," said the Wally, nodding. "His face brings new ones each week, and more the week after. They come with their own shopping bags. Some bags have his photo on them. They come and they shove bundle after bundle of veal into their bag. They come to see his face and they buy because they hope to take away a piece of it. We don't mind. We could stop it. Often when they leave with the veal, they take other items with them. This grows our veal proportion. We need the veal, but we can allow some to leave the store in the hands of customers."

"But isn't that what a store is for?" I asked. "To be emptied out by customers?

"And then restocked, of course," I added. It was important to me that he could tell I was a good thinker.

"A store is about something greater than selling," he said. "If you looked only at the surface of the word, you could say its primary purpose is storage. That surface is its core."

"Why do you need the veal?" I asked.

He indicated with his arm the expanded veal section, as if that were an answer in itself. An unbroken aisle of meat, every gap filled, every crevice stuffed with packages of flesh shining wetly like rosy chunks of quartz. Coolers of veal shivered invisibly, releasing a sheen of cold mist into the air. A tremble of vulvar pink, the color of an innocent child's gums. Freezers full of frosted flesh cast a low blue light.

"Wally's is collecting veal," I said, trying to extract words from his gesture.

"*We* are collecting veal," said the Wally. He leaned on the word *we* as he stared down at me through his open mouth.

"That doesn't make sense to me," I said.

"It's one of the only things that make sense," he said soberly. "What qualities unite and divide all the products in this store? Either they are good for you, or they work ceaselessly to destroy you from within. The categories of fruit and vegetable and grain are meaningless in the face of this single superior distinction. It does not matter whether a tomato is a vegetable with seeds or a fouled-up fruit, it matters whether that tomato will hasten your ruin. This is what they should print on the nutritional labels, the ingredients list. This is the only category that is truly important to know, and knowing it is power."

He continued: "We know what happens to the man who swallows arsenic, to the child or dog that keels over with a plastic bag shoved down the esophagus as far as it can go. The cause and effect are blatant. Most substances machinate more subtly. They suffocate the tinier parts of us, parts you can't see. Strychnine has an effect life of minutes. Alcohol has an effect life of hours. What is the life of a half pound of potatoes inside you, how long will it work away at you, sabotaging you in ways too small to perceive? Minuscule objects are breaking in you at this moment. You can feel them, even if they can't be seen or heard. The things that have gone wrong inside of you are whispering to each other beyond your hearing, too softly to stir the surface of your eardrum. They are whispering in the other room like your parents used to when you were just a child. A single moment of clarity could cure you.

A single taste of some pure and holy food could return you to your originary nature, your ability to discern good from evil as simply as one looks up into the sky and sees that it is blue. But there is nothing pure and holy in this world." I heard my breath loud in my own ears, so fast that it sounded to me as if I were running from something.

"There's nothing wrong with me," I said in a hopeful way.

"No, of course there isn't," he said comfortingly, peering down through the black mesh mouth. "You're like everyone else. A ghost trapped in a body, loving what kills it. Wouldn't you rather love what is right for you instead? Wouldn't you like to find out what that is?"

"I don't understand what you're saying," I said. "You're talking about C?"

The little transparent pipes in my mind were breaking one by one, spilling forth a caustic blue fluid.

"I'm talking about you," he said. "I'm talking about who's running you. Is it you, yourself, or someone adjacent, so similar that even you can't tell yourselves apart? Tell me, do you ever look in the mirror and mistake that face for your own? I see you and I perceive that the very edges of your body are a blur. You don't know where you end. You are nibbled at by a vagueness. By saying this, I in no way am referring to anything like an aura. This is a sign of the disintegration of your organism under pressure. Tell me, is there someone in your life who's been sharing your life too closely? A friend or a loved one? Is there someone who's been taking up your time and not giving any of it back? Have you made certain they're not stealing light from you? That the darkness from their body has not permeated your own by way of your common air, proximate water, shared furniture, et cetera?"

I knew he was talking about B.

"I did have a friend," I said.

"And your friend trespassed upon you," the Wally replied.

I nodded. His looming foam face seemed bigger now, closer.

He continued: "I sense another attachment, too. Someone who made you feel like a ghost within your own living body, someone who you are haunting. You see their separation from you as an act of harm, but you should examine the harm within you. Trace it. Source your sadness. Doesn't it begin in this person, absent though they may be? Their oozings in you, their memory turning to rot. The ghost of this person haunts you, and you cannot flee in body."

He reached forward his fleshy pink hand and placed two pink fingers against my temple. His skin was incredibly soft, like it had just been unwrapped, like I was the first thing it had ever touched.

He continued: "But you can flee your mind."

I didn't understand anything. Behind the Hospitality Hat, red became orange, orange turned pink. The colors bled sweetly, like a thing dying softly in the forest alone. By the time I understood it was the product shelves sliding on their tracks, shifting into their new positions, it didn't even matter. It didn't make a difference what different things were; just having them move across my visual field, casting their shadows on my retina, was enough for me to feel like I had known them deeply.

"Haven't you been sensing this?" said the voice in front of me. "Don't you want to be one with yourself? To have a double ownership. To know just once with surety that when you breathe, when you eat, that you are the only one inside you breathing and eating? That you are you, and no one else."

In the gap newly created by the sliding shelves, where the plastic cups of jellied fruits trapped in firm syrup had once been, and behind the head of the Wally whose voice radiated from within me, pouring out from my skull as though I were the speaker rather than the listener, I saw the bodies of Wallys working away at something, heaving boxes of something dense that hit the ground with moist thuds.

"I don't know," I said.

"You will," it replied.

The bodies were loading the boxes into a truck. The bodies were shouldering them heavy, like cases full of flour or ground bone, cases of liquid-soaked rag. On the sides of the boxes I saw the KANDY KAKES logo and underneath it the words:

HAVEN'T YOU NOT HAD ENOUGH?

I saw the EXIT sign glowing over the dark hole they carried the boxes into. I knew that there probably wasn't anything good inside that hole. Wherever my neighbors had gone that afternoon, silent and sheeted, it hadn't been in pursuit of happiness. Otherwise they might have looked happier. But what I found hopeful about that hole was: It was a hole. I could put myself into it. I could avoid detection, and in its dark inners I could pretend to forget myself. Whatever I had once had with B or with C was gone; if I wanted it back, I'd have to dig my way back into them.

It would be difficult, and there was no guarantee that they'd be willing to hold still to let me do it. I felt the thinness of the fiber binding me to myself: like a loose thread hanging from a hem, I could tear it off. I'd leave them waiting around in the heat for me, the ones I half loved, wondering what they had done to scare me off. Something rattled in my hollow. When the Wallys in their masks handed me the sheet, I took it. I let them help me unfold it, stretch it out to its full length. I let them drape it over me, shift it back and forth until the eyeholes fell over my eyes and I could see them all, their identical Wallyheads bobbing around me at slightly different heights. I let them blank me out.

I took one step forward, then another, then another another another.

WE SAT LIMP AND SILENT inside the hold of a white cargo van that sped along the highway. The van was a common make, rectangular and white with two long, tinted windows so we could see out and nobody could see in. It was the most popular model of cargo van on the road these days: according to the ads, one was sold every five minutes. Dozens had been bought in the time that we'd been driving. A funny chemical smell hung in the air, polyurethane foam, the smell of Wallyflesh bodying out the masks that the cultists continued to wear even though we were no longer in a Wally's, even though it was prohibited to wear the Wally's uniform outside of the store, where it was considered an unauthorized use of a trademarked visage. It was still bright outside, but fading. Slices of the world, anonymized, shone from around the corners of drooping Wallyheads as we drove someplace that I couldn't even imagine. I pictured a black, light-filled room. I thought of the house across the street, minus the house, minus the street.

For the first couple of minutes, the little slivers of outer world meant something. They were the stop sign on the way out of the Wally's parking lot, the second stop sign after the bend in the road that plenty of cars ignored, the willow trees lurching over the fenced backyard of a woman recluse who only left the house wearing a pretty silk scarf draped over her head, the ends clutched together beneath her throat by a hand that could have been very old or fairly young. She went as far as the mailbox, never farther. B said she was probably a former movie star with an obliterated face. B was obsessed with obliterated faces, she thought they made for a great story. If B were here, she would whisper into my ear that each one of the Wallys had lost their faces in gruesome grocery store–related incidents. But that kind of thinking was why I was here in this van and she was wherever she was. B didn't understand that the dangerous part of having a face was showing it off, not losing it. To see your face spread onto the faces around you, absorbed by others. The masks on these Wallys kept me safe the way the sheets over my neighbors had kept us all safe from seeing and then replicating their sadness, safe from taking them within. The masks were prophylactic, emotionally speaking. These masked men were going to bring me to a cleaner place, where things were more sharply distinguished from one another and where I would finally have the space to figure out who I was without other people nudging me all the time into the shapes they thought I should have.

After a minute or two in the van, we could have been anywhere. Tree-shaped trees blurred behind the shapes of the other people slumped in the van like captured things whose only experience had been to be captured again and again. Thinking of them in this way made me feel warmly collegial. Beneath their masks and uniforms, they could be people much like me, with anxieties about those closest to them and a weird misplaced hunger for something intangible that could be satisfied only by snack food. They might have someone they were running from, or someone they were running to, even though they didn't have any idea where that person might have gone or why. Of course they wouldn't be, beneath their foam shells, exactly the way I was. All of them were male, possessed of soft, foldy bellies that crested and troughed beneath their red Wally's polo shirts. They looked ample, arms and torsos pressed together. I wanted to push myself in among them, sneak my bony elbows up into their surplus, and fall asleep there, warm and forgotten and surrounded by the lingering scent of cheese, cardboard, and laundry detergent.

It was hard to think of the right thing to say when I had never said anything to these men and they had never said anything to me. I didn't know whether to express sadness about my past or positivity about my future with them. I looked around me in the back of the van: eight men in foam heads, six cases of Kandy Kakes, five or six tarps spread beneath us, balled-up newspaper, and two units of twine, brittle and straw colored. I looked at everything outside the windows. They could have been driving me in big loops around my own town and I wouldn't have known. It all went flashing by, increasingly green but still just visual slush, reminding me blandly of other places I'd been without causing me to remember them in detail. I figured that I'd better start feeling like this van was my home.

"I don't know about you guys," I said out loud, trying to sound upbeat, "but I for one am completely excited to eat a Kandy Kake whenever we get to where we're going."

Nobody replied. The only sounds then, as before, were the tires turning against the road, rubbing themselves out on it, and the low drone of the engine. Outside the window, the trees passed by—not faster, not slower, but the same.

3

☺

GREAT. ARE WE ALL SETTLED? *Fantastic. Tremendous. I can tell this is a good bunch. A tremendous bunch.*

Words spilled tinny from the overhead speakers, a deep and ballooning male voice undercut by the squeal of outdated equipment. In the cavernous room, our bodies turned toward the sound in different directions: we didn't know what we were looking for or where we would find it. It was a conference hall, bounded by movable beige walls and wine-colored carpeting, the carpeting dotted by little shapes that had gone blurry, diamonds and triangles with no points. Through the vents in my sheet I saw a tacky chandelier shining weakly above us, faint in the enveloping daylight. I shifted the eyeholes to try for a more complete view, but it was all parts and pieces: a white sheet or some dark gap cut into it, the graying carpet, the steep emptiness above.

Right. Now. Oh. Eyes to the front, please, eyes to the front. I'm right over here, folks. In the center. By the podium. Right in front of you.

The voice came from all around, but I tried to turn away from it and look toward the light. Turning into my dizziness, I found the brightness of the outdoors, rectangled through large glass panels. A breeze swayed the long, faded burgundy curtains hanging in front of tall plate-glass windows, curtains that must once have looked expensive, important. Now they were nubby with lint and the glass behind them was dusty from the outside, which made the things you saw through it look fake. Birds looked like an echo of birds, fat white clouds looked as if they were there to sell you fabric softener or air travel or health insurance. And there at the middle of it all: a plain wooden podium with angled microphone, an averagely tall man covered in what looked like a standard-issue white sheet but was actually of a luxuriously high thread count. He shuffled in place—or maybe he was doing something more impressive, it was hard to tell beneath my covering. Besides a small patch of color below his eyeholes, an insignia that I had been told stood for his decision to renounce his mouth, he lacked obvious markers of authority. Even with his features and limbs hidden beneath loose white, he gave the impression of being overweight and soft, a body like a sofa. *Great, okay,* said the voice, which I understood originated in front of me but which seemed to come from all around, pushing from the outside in. *Let's begin. Greetings to all of our new recruits, and Welcome. Or should I say Unwelcome. I'll explain that later. I'll be your Regional Manager, reporting to the General Manager and by extension to the Grand Manager himself.*

A few scattered claps that faded on their own.

You are all here because you have seen through the falsity of your everyday lives. You've seen that there is something real beyond the appearance of better and worse, buying and selling, brother, sister, husband, wife. You've seen that there is an arrangement of Darkness and Light that, like a shadow cast upon the wall, gives an illusory coherence to our lives and bodies. Or to put it in a friendlier way: You folks understand that there is more to life than life itself. Namely, there is Nothing.

Here, the speaker paused and I gathered that something was supposed to happen. I looked around me at other swiveling heads. Behind me, someone whispered a question. "Do they mean there isn't anything, or that there is something and it is nothing, with a capital N?" they asked, and fell silent again. From the silence there rose the sound of a cough and a couple of people clapping experimentally toward the back of the room. He nodded at us. The applause swelled. Our speaker raised his hands to indicate that we should be quiet.

We are gathered here to begin a journey of self-discovery, that is to say discovering what is inside yourself. Is it good? Or is it a toxic sinkhole, poisoning those around you? We'll find you out. Together. Here at the United Church of the Conjoined Eater, we believe that there is nothing more hazardous to yourself than being yourself. That burden should be shared. We believe that the quickest route to self-improvement is self-subtraction. Shed those unsightly remembrances. We believe that you contain a perfect being of radiant Light within you, a ghost that you were meant to become. You aren't yourself, more and more: and we can help you achieve that. Any questions?

I looked all around me, pressing my hands to the sides of my head to hold my eyeholes on straight. I had questions. There were still some things that remained unclear to me. But scanning the room, I saw only nodding bodies, white lumps bobbing at the top ends of people who all seemed to understand what was happening. I looked back at the podium and nodded my own head in turn.

Great. That's great. Let's move on. There are only a few simple rules here, all designed to keep you folks safe. First rule: You show up at staff meetings on time and ready to participate. That means volunteer your own experiences, ask a good question, or just stand up and applaud someone who deserves it.

Second. There are no changes to your partner assignment. No way, no how. When you file out of the conference hall you'll be given a room number. This is where you'll be staying. There'll be another person staying there with you. Perhaps they will be there when you show up, or perhaps you will be there for them. This person shall be your right hand for the rest of your time with us. Can you change your right hand? You cannot. For all you know, they might as well be you. Remember: Conjoined.

"HE WHO SITS NEXT TO ME, MAY WE EAT AS ONE!" shouted a fragile young female voice at the far right end of the room. More applause, and louder, one person whooping tentatively. I joined in, even though I could not say that I knew what I was clapping for, only that it seemed hopeful. In the midst of this new and mysterious information, I felt a confusion that was unlike my everyday confusion. It was the confusion of a newborn thing learning how to live.

The last rule I have for you today will probably be the most difficult one. In the life you left behind, you were asked to remember everything: your wife's birthday, your husband's preferred brand of soap, your best friend's boyfriend's name. Now we are asking you to unremember, as quickly as possible. This means unremembering not only your wife's birthday, but your wife as well. This means unremembering what you used to do for a living, what you used to own or wear. Most of all, it means remembering only what we have here within the Church, objects and people of verified Brightness.

I felt my sheet jerk across my face, blocking my vision. Someone was tugging on it, trying to get my attention. I turned right, readjusting myself, to find my eyeholes exactly level with a pair of eyes, brown like my own. Height like my own, body like my own. I had a strange, excited feeling that I had found myself: I was real, I was really there. Then the voice of a full-grown man came muffled through the front fabric that was his face.

"What do they mean, 'unremember'?" he asked, his voice urgent.

I pointed at the podium to say that he should listen, it would totally be explained.

"Do they mean forget?" he asked.

I shrugged from under my sheet and pointed again. Other sheeted people were glancing toward us now, swiveling their heads or tilting their bodies around.

"Because I don't know how to try to do that," he said, sounding increasingly upset. "I mean, I could stop talking about it, but I couldn't stop *knowing*. I couldn't do that. Nobody could do that."

He grabbed my arm and I shook him off.

"You're nothing like me," I said to him loudly, so that everyone around us could hear. I wanted them to know: though we may have looked alike with our white sheets and brown eyes and same heights, I was made of a wholly different kind of material. He was in Darkness, groping around for what these rules might mean. Now that I was here, now that I had escaped myself, I would be Bright. I would do the rules to the letter, no question, and their meaning would become apparent as I saw what they made of me. In all my life, I had never known what life demanded of me. Now that I knew, I would do it even if I didn't really understand what it was for.

It means unremembering the capitals of states and the denominations of currency and the nuclear power plant. All our troubles began with the power plant. It means unremembering anything made with chicken, which is a highly toxic Dark meat: even thinking about this substance can cause irreparable harm to yourself and to those around you. And most of all it means unremembering yourself: waking like an amnesiac to a world beauteous in its unassociations with pain, worry, strife. When the world is clean it shines Bright in its blankness. When the body is clean it rises ghostly into the Light.

I looked around for the man who had accosted me, but he was lost, reabsorbed by the throng of sheets. His questions had made me miss something in the Manager's speech, something I didn't know how to get back. Maybe I could ask my partner what I had missed, what other dangers I needed to avoid. Maybe my partner would be nice and not remind me of anything dangerous. Then the applause broke out all around me, loud and unhuman like the waves or the rain, and it was a moment before I remembered to join in, flinging my hands together in front of me, clapping until they hurt, trying to create in real life the small picture of an ideal Churchgoer that I had in my mind.

As we thronged from the room, sheets dragging across the carpet, someone stopped me and gave me a slip of paper that read *E38.* "Your room assignment," she said, her voice upbeat but not inspiring confidence. As I filed out the doorway into the corridors beyond, I saw a slight, sheeted figure up by the podium being reprimanded by the Regional Manager. I couldn't help thinking it was the man I had met before, the man who was my size, the man who made me miss that key part of the speech

I needed to become the ideal person I had come here to be, a person who wasn't.

IN THE HALLWAY OUTSIDE THE conference room, it was easy to pretend I knew where I was going: I followed the others, who filed unanimously toward a tight, cramped back staircase painted a nostalgic shade of mint. We were all new intake, fresh bodies for the Church to process, but as far as I could tell I was the only one who didn't know the layout of the building. The others navigated it by instinct, down flight after flight of stairs, taking the sharp turns of the staircase with ease, while I let my body get pushed along by their collective motion. I couldn't understand how they knew what to do—it was the first day and I had already fallen behind. The crush of bodies was a slow river of white, crowding our way to the goal. It reminded me of something I might once have seen on a nature documentary, the spawning of sharks or salmon.

We skipped one unmarked entrance after another, then suddenly the sheeted bodies were passing through a blank doorway painted glowingly green. In this new, subterranean corridor our unified motion disintegrated. Eaters split off to look for their assigned spaces while I pressed my back against the wall, trying to breathe, trying to fake a type of composure that would indicate that I was brimming with Light, quick to shake off the Darkness. It was while I hid here, in plain sight, that I began to notice that there were other Eaters like me who were not adjusting well. There in the midst of a traffic of white, they stood frozen, staring ahead of them or covering their eyes. Backs hunched, heads down in their hands, they looked as though they were wishing themselves out of this place or mourning their lack of know-how. Some came out of their stupor on their own and headed casually to their quarters; others were collected by low-level Managers and led away.

Then I saw a flash of skin in the white throng and some blue and green. In the sea of white, these colors looked wrong, a stain that was somehow moral. It took a moment for the colors to resolve into the shape of a human being, but when they did I recognized him instantly as one of the Disappeared Dads I had seen on TV. He had vanished while watching his eight-year-old son playing soccer in the park. He wore a green plaid button-up shirt and blue jeans, and he was pacing around the crowded floor with his left hand in his pocket and his right hand up to his ear as though he were talking on a cell phone. "No can do, no can do," I heard him say out loud, again and again. He looked the same as he had on the news, only his face was vividly pink.

As I watched him talk on his imaginary cell phone, I saw a pair of Managers come up next to him, sheeted up in coverings that bore the shape of the Renunciation Mouth. They spoke to him, poked at his exposed flesh. Their voices were muffled, but I could tell they were trying to get him to put his sheet back on. "No can do," he said. "I gotta be comfortable. I gotta be comfortable. No can do. Have you seen my slippers?" They looked at each other and grabbed him by the arm. Gently, firmly, they pulled him out of my sight, into the crowd beyond.

I looked around and saw a girl next to me, who had been watching them, too.

"Did you see that?" I asked.

"No," she replied.

"It was one of the Disappearing Dads," I said. "Hank. Or something."

"I don't think we're supposed to remember that," she said, sounding nervous.

"Where do you think they're taking him?" I asked.

She shook her head.

"Do you know where E38 is?" I asked.

But she was already walking away.

BY THE TIME I FOUND E38, my partner was already inside waiting for me. I had expected a room, but what I found was more like a medical examination tent, set up within the larger central space for emergencies. Instead of walls we had curtains: deep red curtains made of cheap velvet, strung up on metal rods that shook when someone heavy walked by. There was a small collapsible table and a rolling rack for holding an IV or a coat. A steel-rimmed mirror in the corner turned out to be a to-scale painting of the curtains, so that you stood in front of it expecting to see yourself, and instead you saw Nobody. One double-size cot done up in stiff red sheets sat in the center of a room that was barely larger. A girl lay atop this cot, sheetless and splayed out in the center like a starfish, so that she took up roughly the entire space. She lifted her head and glared at me.

"You're late," she said.

"I got lost," I said.

"How could you get lost?" she asked. "We got directions at the meeting."

I thought about explaining the guy, the guy who made me miss part of the speech, but instead I just shrugged.

"I'll help you next time," she said. She peered into my sight holes and added: "It reflects badly on us when half of us is late."

I took in her small, heart-shaped face, the pointy chin, the dark hair cut in a long, blunt bob not all that different from my own. She had dark brown eyes like mine and skinny, fragile-looking arms. In a taxonomy of women we would have been side by side. I wondered if she was pretty: I was so far from remembering how that concept worked and what it looked like. I wondered if she was prettier than I used to be.

"Shouldn't you be wearing your sheet?" I asked.

She looked at me strangely again.

"They explained that, too, in the speech," she said. "Were you even there?"

"I was there," I said. "But a Dark person in the audience inter-rupted my access to the information."

"Okay," she said. "I'll explain it, but you need to avoid situations like that in the future. Every interaction with Darkness brings down your Light levels, and you can pass it on to me too because we are One Person."

I nodded, and she explained. This small shared space was the only place in the Church where we were allowed to appear un-covered, sheetless, our sticky limbs exposed to the air. This was for some or all of the following reasons: The fabric that shielded us from rays of Darkness also interfered with the production of vitamins that we needed in order to keep living, at least until the day when our living was complete. Or our bodies needed to see another body every once in a while, see their naked face and little white teeth, to remind ourselves that we were not yet ghosts, only flesh pointed toward that goal. Or the sheets were primarily a way of communicating, we needed them only in the gathering places as a statement made to one another that knowing one another even as little as we did was a temporary situation, bound to end soon. Ultimately, seeing our partner sheetless helped to erode our memory of our own particular face, which was unviewable within the Church owing to the lack of mirrors.

I pulled the sheet up over my head and let it fall to the floor, crumpled. It was a relief—to pull the sheet from my body, to peel it from me where it had fused to my skin and yellowed, to expose my tingling arms to the air—but somehow it annoyed me to show my face to this strange new girl. She reminded me of B, consuming my face with her eyes, thickening the air with her presence. To see her lounge around in her skin as if it were the only natural thing to do highlighted how unnatural anything was for me now. I decided to call her Anna, which wasn't so far from my own name. It was palindromic, which seemed to suit someone who was destined to become my mirror. It was short and easy to remember. It was the name I had given to my favorite doll, the one that I asked my mother to throw away after I noticed something overly human about its eyes.

My hair clung to my skin like a bark. "You look exhausted," Anna said, sitting forward on the cot and looking at me hard from both eyes. "Much more tired than me. I'll work on getting my face a little bit wearier, but I always tend to sleep well. I think it would be better if you'd work on getting some more rest. The closer we are in body and appearance, the easier it'll be to merge our life."

I didn't say anything.

"If we are as One Person, spread out over two bodies," she said in a pert, authoritative tone, "we'll halve our load and ghost much earlier."

"I know," I said, but I didn't.

Then from behind me I heard the sound of the curtain being pushed aside, and a dinner tray slid into our space, its contents obscured under a gleaming metal cover. I picked it up and looked out into the corridor to see if another was coming, but there was nobody there.

I turned back to Anna and told her: "There's only one."

"Of course there's only one," she said. "We share everything now."

I looked down at the shining tray. I had no idea what it might be. A purer food, probably, or maybe a less pure one if they wanted to test our powers of distinction. I had to remind myself to keep my hopes down, that it might not be food at all—though the thought made my stomach ache with hunger. I took a breath and then I lifted the cover off the tray.

What I found there was a small heap of Kandy Kakes, twelve of them piled on a white plate. They were just as I had pictured them over the last few difficult months: a double squiggle of frosting-flavored icing gracing the dark, hard surface of its chocolate-armored puck. Just as I had pictured—only, if possible, even more beautiful.

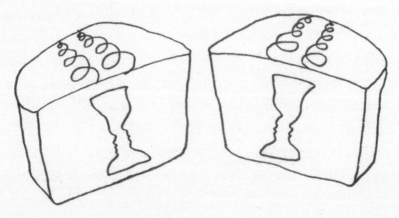

I almost couldn't believe this was really happening. I would grow clearer, thinner, Brighter, a more perfect vessel for my ghost. I felt a great burden lift from me, the burden of worry over what I was, what was becoming of me. With the help of these Kandy Kakes, I would finally become better in the Bright future ahead.

"Why are you crying?" asked Anna, annoyed.

I tried to explain: "I've waited so long for these."

Anna shrugged. "Well," she said. "Congrats."

I picked one up and brought it to my mouth. Of all the things I had wanted in my life, these were the only ones left. I felt my body grow hot, then cold, then hot again: I wanted to cram them all whole into my mouth, force them down. I breathed in their scent of hard, waxy chocolate and stale orange. My throat was wet and wide and tender.

Then I bit. It was harder than I liked, the casing exactly as impermeable as the ads boasted. I shifted it toward the back molars, where my jaw was a little stronger, and managed to pierce the chocolate armor, crush it a little, so that the syrupy orange-caramel filling began its seepage into my mouth. The orange goo tingled with sweetness against my tongue.

I looked up and saw Anna watching me.

"It's delicious," I said.

She nodded and blinked.

As I took up my second Kake and third Kake and bit down through their Choco Armor, I tried to remember only this moment, this present moment that was continually ending, this moment illuminated by the safety and Brightness of the Church, but I couldn't help it. Even though I knew it only harmed me, only hindered my progress, I was thinking of my old life, of the way B used to watch me eat. I'd be reading old sections of the Sunday paper while eating a bowl of cereal, and every once in a while I could look up to see her eyes on me. The look in them was something strange. She stared at me like I was doing something new that she wanted to do very badly. She stared at me like I had performed an ugly miracle. She stared at me like she'd be practicing it later, in her room, alone—standing in front of the mirror and chewing exaggeratedly, cowlike, biting at the air.

THAT NIGHT, I WOKE TO a feeling of hunger that verged on pain. I rolled over on my side and clutched my belly in toward my center, as though compressing the organ could fool it into thinking it was full. I sat up and looked at Anna, slumbering peacefully beside me in our double cot. I needed to eat more, and I knew if I woke her, she'd talk me out of it. Anna found it easy to follow all of the Church rules. But as long as I was eating the approved food, I reasoned, it shouldn't do too much damage to my Brightness levels if I ate another serving or half serving. I eased myself out from under the covers and put on my shoes and my sheet. I slipped out through the red velveteen curtains and snuck through the hall to a neglected-looking service elevator. Inside the elevator, the button panel was all blank. I pressed one at random and hoped it would take me to a floor with food on it.

Through miles of Church corridor, on floors where broad windows looked out on a massive parking lot, dark and featureless like this immense building's even larger shadow, on floors that had no windows and thrummed with the sound of machinery far underground, I searched for food. The structure was clean like a hotel or office building, the carpeting clean and dustless, but there were things piling up in it that didn't belong: a tilting pile of sequined decorative pillows blocking what looked like an unused elevator bay, cardboard boxes lined up in the hallway that turned out to be full of jars of beauty cream, the one with the commercial where the bird escapes from inside the woman. The creams were heavy and full, store-ready in their crisp red boxes, but when I took off the lid the cream's surface had a deep swirl in it: not a machine's smooth finish but something made by hand.

The upper floors had crisp steel numbering and panes of cold glass that revealed dull gray interiors. In the middle, the halls were motel-colored, sullen beige, with smooth neutral doors marked by small brass numbers. The lowest levels of the building—where I wandered, hiking my sheet up to move more smoothly, hoping to find a familiar letter on a door, or any letter at all—looked like a series of bunkers, avocado green and overlit, the signage on the walls outdated and peeling. Each new part of the Church I saw made me think it had once been something else: a hospital, a corporate hotel, an office complex. Even stripped of its former contents, the deep structure of the building held traces of its former use. I wondered if the other Eaters who passed me by could tell by looking at me what I had once been, what I had once bought, what couple of categories I had once belonged to.

On floor six, a tall man under an extra-long sheet with a ragged hem stopped me in the hall.

"What are you doing in Section Six?" he asked, holding me in place with two fingers on my sternum.

"I was just looking for some food and I got lost," I said.

"No additional food," he said flatly. "Where are you supposed to be?"

"E38, I think," I replied, thrusting my scrap of paper out from under my sheet and toward his eyeholes. He read it, turned it over, handed it back.

"Who gave you this?" he asked me.

"I don't know," I said. "Someone in a sheet.

"I'm new here," I added.

He looked at me, blinking through his holes, and when he spoke he sounded as though he had decided to do me a kindness.

"You aren't allowed here," he said in a reasonable way. "You're not cleared for it. These aboveground floors have a high minimum Brightness level. You won't meet this level, if you ever do, until you've spent a good amount of time working down below."

"Is there a chance I'll never reach this level?" I asked.

"Not everyone reaches this level," he replied. "More than half never leave the basement, until they are passed back out into the world."

"I hope to go all the way to the top," I said. To the final level, whatever that was.

As if he hadn't even heard me, the tall man pointed at a stairwell down the hall.

"You need to go ten floors down," he said. "Ask for E Wing. Don't tell them you tried to sort yourself up within the building."

I nodded, but I could see from the nonalignment of his sight holes with my face that he was no longer thinking of me at all. It made me remember C, how in his calmest and most relaxed state I could tell exactly what he was thinking about just by following where his head was pointed. By tracing his line of sight and fixing myself on that same TV show, crumpled sweatshirt, or cardboard pizza box, I could feel like I shared his mind, that our minds were one. I always wanted that intimacy, immediate but at a distance, as though our love were as swift and expansive as television.

I felt a sharp pain. Someone had hit me hard on the shoulder, I felt it down to the socket.

"Stop that," the man said sharply.

"I wasn't doing anything," I said.

"You were remembering," he said. "It was blatant. You put us all at risk."

"It just reminded me," I said, about to explain.

Suddenly he was backing up, pulling his arms in toward his chest so that his body under the sheet looked even more like a Halloween ghost's, swaying slightly as he retracted his body, shuffling, toward the opposite end of the corridor.

"No," he said. "*No*. You take that elsewhere. Take it back to the Darkness. We don't want it here." The smooth, round eyeholes, unchanged, contradicted the fear I heard in his voice.

He had almost reached the stairs. He turned his back on me to open the door and dove into the stairwell, slamming the door shut behind him. I heard the sound of his footfall on the stairs, running from me, fleeing vertically into safer and purer levels of the building.

I stood there for what might have been a half hour. My breaths were tiny, the air around me was still. I was afraid to move my body or my mind. I didn't know what would happen if I began remembering again, but I could tell from the man's reaction that it was something to be feared. C would have said this man was nuts, but I knew there was wisdom in his reaction. For as long as I could remember, there had been something going wrong in me: I did what I didn't want to do, I wanted to do things that I knew I didn't really want at all. Something in me did wrong when I needed to do right: the man who had fled was just the first person to see this in a tangible, physical way.

There was an uncontrollable amount of me within myself, and I didn't know how to stop it. I had missed some key part of the Manager's speech that explained how to unremember. Worst of all, I could feel it there inside me: my past. Even in its barest sense—recognizing a color, identifying a face—it worked Dark within me, before I even knew it was happening.

But then like a Bright gift, I recalled that a better me dwelled inside the me I was. I could feel it there, faintly: a version of myself with no past or present, just a feeling of Nothing about everything. Nobody else had seen me here in the sixth-floor hallway, so I would return to Anna and E38, eat the instructed portions of food, and try once more to live a life of genuine and luminous Brightness.

THE NEXT MORNING, ANNA AND I sheeted back up and went to our Church jobs, beginner jobs that were assigned to the newest converts because they didn't require much specialized training in the dynamics of Darkness. We spooned beauty products into beauty product containers by hand, a task performed better—and less messily—by machines. Specifically, we spooned TruBeauty gels and creams into TruBeauty containers in a large, open room that looked like it might once have been a gymnasium.

The Church owned shares in TruBeauty and a few other companies, like the company behind Kandy Kakes and the furniture company responsible for the large decorative pillows that were piled in the hallways and workrooms. We could do a lot of good, they said, controlling the movement of Dark and Light goods across this country, collecting the Bright things in one place and the shadowy ones in another and then keeping our own bodies as far away as possible from the bad things. We could do a lot of good for the people of our Church, they said, hoarding them away from a dangerous and variegated world, bricking them in with a wall made of Light. And then there was a need to keep bringing money in for as long as we all still had physical bodies requiring physical food that could only be grown, stolen, or purchased at a store with government-issued American currency.

I looked all around the Spooning Room, a gigantic, light-flooded indoors that felt more like an outdoors, and tried to imagine how much money it meant for the Church. Surrounding me, sitting on the floor, standing, cluttering the glossy pine floors with the dragging ends of their cloths, were sheeted-up believers. They huddled around industrial plastic containers of face cream, body cream, eye cream, esophageal cream, scooping spoonfuls and screwing shut the lids. The room looked wintry and cold; frosty evening light fell a deoxygenated violet over acres of white. In the sky-sized space above our heads were pigeons huddled silent in the rafters, and from time to time one took flight from one side of the room to the other, casting a small traveling shadow over our pale, upturned faces.

All around me, other Eaters spooned vigorously, with a good attitude. I struggled with my sheet, trying to push the parts that were the most like sleeves farther up on my arms so that I wouldn't get beauty cream all over my coverings. They slid down and I pushed them back up. I readied a bared hand for spooning and then I plunged my spoon deep into the vat. The hem of my sheet dragged in the gelatinous white and I pulled it out, wiped it off, readied my spoon again, and plunged it in, more cautiously this time. I filled one pot and then another with TruBeauty skin cream, the edible throat slickener that I remembered from commercials when I was still a Dark body, ghostless and clouded by misinformation. I remembered the bird, a white dove fighting its way into the woman's mouth, scrabbling at her face with its small talons, grasping for a clawhold. How the woman tried to smile around its body, her mouth entirely filled, her jaw straining at its limit. And how B used to inch closer to the TV while it played until she was on her knees before it, fascinated, the blinding white of the bird and beautiful face turning her own face pale like a corpse. I shivered and rubbed at my skin.

I didn't have to look up to know that a Manager loomed over me. I could tell from the hand that protruded from beneath his sheet, a hand gloved in white latex. He leaned over me and bent to examine my work. His long white sheet brushed against my face and clung to me there, where my skin was damp with sweat and sticky with the edible cream, which seemed to end up everywhere no matter how clean I tried to be. I saw his gloved hand come toward me, its finger a vague hook glistening in tight plastic. It stopped an inch from my cheekbone, hovered there. And then it came closer. He was scraping a patch of cream from my face, scraping it with force, and I knew that he was doing it not for the benefit of my face, but to see what was underneath. As he crouched down and peered at the spot he had excavated, I willed myself to think Bright and clear, to think only about my ghost and its pure yolklike perfection inside me, or about the wisdom of the lessons and how they confused me and twisted my thoughts into useless, harmless shapes, or about TruBeauty cream and how I should spoon it better and faster and neater and not think about how this same product had touched other parts of my life, Darker parts that I shouldn't be thinking about. But there was Darkness in my thoughts, and I knew he could see it. I closed my eyes and imagined an egg. His breath had a curdled smell, it stuck to my skin. Suddenly he straightened up.

"You're full of murk," he said, speaking down to me from his full height.

I looked up toward his face, sought out the eye and mouth holes that swayed an inch or so in front of his actual face. At the edge of a hole I saw an eye I thought I had seen before, blue and watery.

"And you're making a mess," he added, swiping his arm around at the irregular blotches of beauty cream that marred the floor and stained my white sheet a thicker, heavier white. "Try being more like those around you," he said as he walked away, "and less like yourself." I looked around the room. Everyone else did seem to be doing a better job, a cleaner job. Then from across the room I thought I saw Anna sitting at a different spooning station; I recognized the frayed right corner of her standard-issue sheet and the smooth, lazy way she scooped, as if it were easy, as if she were only lying around in our room, staring up at the ceiling and practicing her emptiness. A Manager paused by her station and patted her back. She looked up at him as he looked down and they were both nodding at each other, nodding as though they had just made a decision together. I thought of B's face pressed jealously against the window as she watched me walk away with C, my hand seeking around for his. Steering him away from her in the drugstore when I spotted her there, down on her hands and knees and reading the backs of boxes of hair dye. I thought of her face smiling out at me from under my haircut, and as I did I could feel my skin growing thicker, foggier, leathery tough. I couldn't seem to stop it; the memories came uncontrollably. I stopped spooning, squeezed my eyes shut.

When I opened them, it was to the sight of a tall, heavy-looking Eater in a newcomer's pristine white sheet. He was wandering back and forth on the warehouse floor, stopping other Church-goers, grabbing their shoulders, and shaking them gently, asking again and again: "Have you seen my car? A green hatchback. Have you seen my car?" I looked at the spooners around me. We had all stopped spooning, all turned our faces toward this alarming man who, in his forgetting, seemed somehow also to be suffering a seizure of remembrance. I could see on all of their faces that it was uncomfortable to watch him suffer so from his own unsheddable Darkness, but I felt worse than the rest of them. I knew I was closer to becoming him than becoming the well-adjusted Eaters to the right and left of me. I knew I was only a few remembrances away from letting something Dark slip out again.

As I watched, the Managers surrounded the remembering man on all sides. "Have you seen my car?" he asked them as they closed in on his bulky body.

The Eater to the right of me must have seen my concern through my sight holes. She leaned toward me in a confidential way.

"The Dads usually burn out early," she whispered. "Nobody knows why. Some people think it's because they can't shed their memories properly. They're too tied to the things they were responsible for, the things they owned. Even though that's what they came here to escape."

I looked at her and nodded. The Managers were dragging the man off toward the warehouse's outer door. The man had stopped asking about his car and was now just sobbing blurrily, a wet patch forming on his sheet near the face and shoulder.

"What happens to them?" I asked quietly.

"They are expelled," she said matter-of-factly. "Banished to their former lives. Returned to the toxicity of the world outside. You cannot have those kinds of things going on around purer, Brighter people. Allowing them to stay, even in a separate area, even in a neighboring building, would hold us all back."

I looked out at the outer door, glass paneled and sleek. In the squares that opened up onto the outside world, I saw thousands of small leaves twisting in the breeze, the worn gray asphalt and curb, empty plastic bottles and cans sitting in clods of browned-out grass. I saw at least twelve different things that I knew were killing me at varied rates, driving me insane, rendering me toxic and flawed. A shiver ran down my spine. Whatever it cost me, whatever it might take, I had to stay in the Church.

I WAS STANDING IN CONFERENCE Room F waiting for the day's speech to begin, waiting for our Regional Manager to step up and give us the day's new lessons on what to avoid, what to remember, what to forget. Anna had offered to stick close to me and explain the nuances of the speech so I wouldn't make so many mistakes in the future. "Every slipup of yours causes me to slip too," she said. "Remember that." I knew now that I had to follow her instructions to the letter if I wanted to stay in here, where I was safe from the Darkness and the toxins and, most important, from myself.

It was late afternoon and we still hadn't had lunch; people stirred a little less than normal as they stood. They moved drowsily, their sheeted forms tilting in the light like there was a person trying to keep awake somewhere beneath. From across the parking lots that darked like lakes through the middle of the business center, we saw other buildings like our own, mirrors to those on the outside, and we saw small people entering them and leaving them.

In the room, a scent like diet cola sweated from our bodies, sweated out through the skin and was absorbed by the white fabric. The sound of a generator weighed heavy in the air, filling the room though all the windows were closed. Light filtered in through the standard-issue sheet I had been done up in, through the very transparency of the cloth itself. We knew we were safe in here, or we thought we were, or we felt we were, or we wanted to feel we were. Through eyeholes I watched my fellow Eaters, the white of their coverings melding together to form a thing that looked like a mountain range in the snow, dozens and dozens of peaks rising sudden and urgent from out of the white, the points eerily rounded, as though they had been hammered down.

We were packed tight together and the air tasted moist and personal, like a kiss from the mouth of a stranger. Dozens and dozens of us, new and old, waited restless before the empty podium. We swarmed it like ants around a gob of jelly, trying to figure out how to wring from it the thing we wanted: a glimpse of the Regional Manager, the Manager's favorable attentions, the words from his mouth that raised us from our situation and into a better one. These blank periods of time before the lesson began were difficult to fill. They were uncomfortable and boring. We wanted to watch one another, judge one another, determine whether we were better than each other and worthier for advancement. We wanted to feel lucky, feel hopeful, feel closer to our ghosts. But in this sea of white, it was hard to see any trace or trait on your outside that made you different from anybody else.

The white mounds in front of me begin shifting, turning their torsos laterally beneath their shrouds to look around, swaying before me like mountains in the wind. Then I see our Regional Manager making his way through the crowd, cutting his path from the catering entrance toward a thick swath of admirers who part just a little to let him through. They all want to feel the force of his body on its way, they think that some of his Brightness will rub off in the friction. The Manager, trailed by a couple of assistants, grasps his head with both hands to keep the eyeholes in place as he moves. He's walking slowly, like he thinks he has a majestic air. But he's not that tall, not especially graceful. All he is is Bright, Brighter than the rest of us. We know this because we've been told, we know even though it doesn't really show up through his sheet, a sheet of higher quality than ours—hotel-quality luxury thread count, thick and creamy with satiny details at the hem that drags along behind him. He reaches the podium and his assistants scurry out from behind to sort out the train of his sheet so that he won't trip as he turns to us to speak. The Manager gives us all what I assume is a look of appraisal, though through the eyeholes it can be hard to tell. At moments like this he looks so ordinary it is hard to believe that he, alone, has the knowledge necessary to midwife our future selves.

Then he raises his hands grandly and addresses us all:

HE WHO SITS NEXT TO ME, MAY WE EAT AS ONE!

I look at Anna, standing next to me, already shouting the words back to him, already joining her voice to the total volume of the crowd, shouting and shouting in perfect unison like one great white sprawling person with a single monstrous voice. Anna looks so happy through her sight holes, her eyes bugging out enthusiastically, her mouth pressing feverishly against the inside of her sheet as she cries out again and again. She looks so happy and so Bright.

I reach down and I take her hand in my own. I clasp it. I work my fingers in between hers and twine us. And then I lift my head up to shout.

INSIDE A BODY THERE IS no Light. Blood piles through with no sense of where it goes, sliding past inner parts, parts that feel something but know nothing about what they feel. What they sense they send up through nerve channels to the brain, a cavefish-pale organ with no nerves of its own. Inside a body, thoughts that never touch air, never reach Light, thoughts that end in a suffocating Dark. The damp basement in a horror movie into which a teenage girl sinks slowly, the stairs groaning beneath her weight, her voice thready and red as she says the name of her boyfriend out loud, over and over again.

Inside a body there is no Light, so the Eaters teach that you must shine your own through Righteous Eating. The diagrams illustrate it beautifully: a female torso in cross section, set on its side like a fish on a cutting board. Small cubes of black and white fall down its throat in the direction indicated by an arrow, the paths of the body marked out in bold white lines, highway lines. These black cubes represent food, the bad kind that starves the ghost within you so that when it is its moment to emerge from your soft shell, to come from you into the world and carry out your project more perfectly than you had ever dreamed, it will die trapped and weakened in your body that has been a prison to it forever. White cubes are the good kind of food, the kind that can save you—if not in this body, then for the next.

Inside the schematic woman, food cubes are destroyed. They release their own benevolent and malevolent ghosts. Dark food travels down to the protective organs in which the ghost gestates vulnerable and sleepy; it clusters to their outsides and strangles what sleeps within. The good food, by contrast, breaks into shafts of differently colored light, bright like fireworks, and this light illuminates the body and nourishes the ghost within. *Imagine this, they say, how radiant you become when you eat Bright. How beautiful, how durable and long-lasting. The colors that can't be seen, working brilliance inside you, preparing you for your ghosting. Colors more beautiful than any of the colors you know.*

I used to lie in bed at night with my hands on my belly, feeling the blood crowd through, wondering what was taking place within me. Now that I had been illuminated, I lay in my cot, sideways like a baby in the womb, and when I rested my hand over my central organs I knew precisely what lay beneath. I knew that the flawed and sad feelings, daily dissatisfactions and pangs of despair, were just my ghost's way of kicking within me, kicking to test its independence, kicking to tell me it wants to be let out.

I fell asleep dreaming that it would split me open someday soon, like a green shoot piercing the husk of a soiled bulb.

FOR THIS LESSON, TURN YOUR *attention to the borders of your own body. If you are Stage Four in a state of peri- or proxi-ghosting, this session may not have much to offer you. For those operating at Stage Five or higher, or if you are already experiencing the feeling that your skin-barrier is penetrable or not really there, engaging with this lesson's material could reverse you five to twelve decastages, and result in harmful physical symptoms such as retching, increased heart rate, elation, suggestibility, joint and liver inflammation, and epidermal crusting. If you or anyone you know fits this risk profile, please inform an attendant immediately.*

Now, to those of you remaining with us today, welcome. I'd like you to close your eyes and concentrate on your edges, how they feel, how steady or firm. Where does your profile end, and is the ending blurry or rubbery? Trembly? Vibrating sharply? You'll notice that your husk stiffens up, turns turgid, when your body channels memories of your Darker past. You feel queasy, don't you? This is because thinking of your past instantly activates all things the you of your past came into contact with, from the innocuous to the severely toxic—especially the severely toxic. Your past life was like water in a stagnant lake: slow, cloudy, full of silt and particulate. Light could not push its way in through the murk. This is not to say that your past was one of total Darkness, just that the mud mixed with it so thoroughly that you cannot draw one single cup of water from that poisonous lake that is fit to drink. In each sip there will be a mouthful of dirt to choke you. That's why we're here today: to help you to filter from your bodies that Dark matter that interferes with your progress toward an ideal ghost state, that stalls the eventual discard of your body husk. We can sanitize your past in the present, if you are willing. Results contingent. Who has questions? If you have questions, raise your hand. An assistant will be over to deal with you.

I lay on my back in the center of the gymnasium and tried to breathe. I tried not to do anything that could look like I was raising my hand. I intended to know what I was doing and to do it perfectly. I pictured a perfect student and tried to resemble her physically. I tried not to look at the ceiling or toward the voice of the instructor. I tried not to look like anything, tried to feel like I had lost myself among the other supine bodies lying limp on the floor. I tried to concentrate only on the idea of Light and the ghost within me, not on my memories, which were as mottled as ever and seemed to be with me all of the time. The Managers moved between us, checking up on our progress, their sheets brushing across our faces and mouths by accident. I could feel Anna in the room, somewhere in the room, executing the exercise rather than worrying about its execution. Today the air had a frictive quality that ground against my skin, and I was glad again for the protection of the sheet.

I'd like to start by asking you all to focus your ghost pointers on the object at the center of the room. Keep your eyes closed.

Focus with your inner eye, with your ghost's eye. As I'm sure you all know by now, the object at the center of the room is an orange, an ordinary, everyday piece of fruit. Oranges, in and of themselves, are neither Dark nor Bright. If you had to put them in one category, they'd be Bright—but barely. Eating an orange is about as beneficial for your future ghosted self as brushing the lint from a sweater. It basically doesn't matter. Oranges, however, are a popular American fruit. They show up in our grocery stores, in our Little League games, in our sack lunches, in the moments at which we are the weakest and lowest. They are a major player in the collective Darkness of our former world, and as such they are one of the most dangerous objects you could encounter or think about: the very notion of an orange is guaranteed to bring up dangerous memories thick with harmful people, places, and objects.

Gaze upon your inner thoughts, the ideas and memories evoked by this fruit, and you will see how they tend to bring into this clean, sanctified space remembrances of a corrupted time, in which Dark objects mingled indiscriminately with the Bright and your ghost was in a state close to atrophy. Recall, BUT DO NOT THINK OF the Dark feelings of that time, which are now gone: feelings of loving them too much or not enough, never loving them the right amount, of wanting them to give you space and then feeling unloved, of saying you understood what they were saying when what they were saying only made you feel more confused and more alone. Remember: DO NOT REMEMBER your past. PERCEIVE your past as you would perceive a dark stone or flower resting at some distance from you. THEN CAST IT FROM YOU WITH FORCE.

Now, I'll show you a couple techniques for filtering and refurbishing mental material. While your past should always be regarded as toxic, these techniques, practiced continuously and with escalating intensity, should allow you to interact safely with the objects found in our little haven. Let's start with a basic, fairly neutral memory. I'd like everyone to call to mind a memory from their past, let's say from the past five years, let's say it's an ordinary day rather than a special occasion, and let's say it takes place in a kitchen. DO NOT REMEMBER this memory, simply inspect it and take stock of its contents. When does it take place? Who is present? What types of objects and colors are near to you, far from you? When you have one of these in view—say, the location, that kitchen—I want you to work on turning that location into this location. This might be subtractive, if you know a lot about this location you used to occupy, or additive if you don't. For example, you were once with your sister in a bright, cozy kitchen whose walls were covered in a decorative paper depicting marigolds in bloom. You looked into your cup of tea and saw the dead husk of a spider resting at its bottom.

First, eliminate the sister or sisterlike object from this memory. Whatever you thought of her at that time, she is nothing more than a sister-shaped impediment to your progress now. You could begin by introducing a particle of blankness near her face that expands to swallow her whole, from her needy little mouth to her chewed-down toenails. Or you could "black her out," overlaying her location with a square or scribble of black that disencourages the gaze. Perhaps the easiest method is to look away. Try it. This may take a couple of tries.

All around me I heard little sounds of effort, trapped groans and squeezed breathing as we tried to expunge loved ones from our own private scenes. These filtering sessions were painful; I found scratches on my body afterward, I had sore muscles in my forearms and calves, I must have pulled them trying so hard to hold still. I was working on a memory from earlier last year, from before I knew there was any life other than mine to escape to, before I knew about the Darkness and the Light, before things had gotten so bad. It was a memory in which I stood in my kitchen while somebody who I tried to imagine was not B suggested we eat something that was not Popsicles. I had eliminated her face and hair, now a fuzzy space tilted atop the thin neck and words came from it, though I no longer knew what they meant.

Once you've worked at the eradication of persons, try a background substitution. Borrow from our pure and Light-filled surround. Instead of your childhood wallpaper, think of our glossy white walls. The more your memory of that place comes to resemble this hall of Brightness, the Brighter you'll be in memory, and in your current, evanescing iteration.

I turned the gray walls crawling with small, historied stains into a stark white expanse like the one in this room. I took out our cheap plates with the yellow rim and put nothing in their place. Even with these markers scrubbed clean, I couldn't help knowing who it was, when it was, what was happening. What was B doing? Was she looking and acting like me? Had she seen C, and how far away was he from where she was now?

Recall the parable of the knife: There were two brothers, identical in temperament but divided in spirit, each bearing much enmity toward the other. With their father's death, they made to split his property equally in half. They were fortunate, for their father possessed two of each thing, every object set next to its twin in his ample abode. They commenced to halve his estate, and the portions were made exact—but for a single carving knife that had no partner. The two argued bitterly over this knife, whether to share it in increments of time or split blade from hilt and go their separate ways. Finally, proffering the knife's edge to the throat of his sibling, the eldest suggested that he would take possession of the knife in its physical manifestation, while the younger might count himself the owner of the knife's intangibles: its sharpness, form, and afterlife. They quickly parted ways, the eldest mounting his horse and pointing himself toward the village, while the younger lay supine, bleeding his life out at the side of the road. But the bargain was in the younger man's favor after all: while the eldest prodded dully at supper with his lump of inherited matter, the younger lived far better in heaven with his knife at his side, singing knife-songs to the heavenly gathering and putting holes in the angels, one by one.

KEEP GATHERING, LEARNING, CLEANSING

YOUR GHOST RUNNETH OVER

With that, our Manager exited the room and there were no more lessons for the day.

AFTER A MEAL OF SIX Kandy Kakes, I headed over to the Greeting Hall for my shift processing the new recruits. Anna was already there, washing her hands beneath hot water in preparation for the formal bath where we'd wash their soiled bodies. Wherever I intended to be, it seemed like Anna had always gotten there five minutes before. She looked up at me as I walked in, then back down at her washing, violently down, as though she were washing the me from her. It was clear Anna had started to resent me, believing that she could rise further and faster on her own, which was probably true. Since we had arrived, we had risen up in the Church, but not so far up.

On the other side of the metal garage door I could hear the new recruits stirring in their holding pen, writhing in a collective fidget, asking timidly for food or water. I was full of anxiety and fear in these moments before processing began. The Darkness they would carry in beneath their fingernails and on their feet, dissolved into the slick of their mouths and eyes, their unchecked speech containing within it unedited and uncleansed referents to the Dark world I still remembered, though I tried not to. The inevitable stream of questions that they would ask and that I could not answer—they made me feel like I knew less than they, less than anything at all.

At the hour mark the door lifted and the recruits came in, blinking up at the bright fluorescent bulbs overhead that rendered their bare bodies in shades of sickly yellow and cream. We peeled the sheets from them and exposed them, blinking, to our Brightness. Inside the Greeting Hall they swarmed aimlessly, they crouched and covered their heads with their hands, they stopped in the middle of the room and stared above. Their naked faces were open and searching hungrily for direction, and I was grateful for my sheeting, which kept us apart. As a greeter it was my job to grab them one at a time and guide each through the different steps of the bath, the salt bath, the sand bath, the white bath. I grabbed a girl by the wrist and turned her around to face me.

She might have been thirteen, fourteen, with flat blond hair that dribbled down across her chest. Had she decided to come here, or had she been decided for? I grabbed her other wrist and looked for her eyes. "Are you ready," I said, "to purge the Dark from your body, to eat only Light, to cut from your flesh the double of your own self and cast it out to starve in the wild?"

In the whites of her nervous eyes, blood vessels stood out like red thread. "I guess," she said.

Good enough. I took her by the wrists to the salt bath, instructed her to lie down and thrash around like a bird in a dry stone bowl. I heaped cup after cup of salt upon her moving body and helped her rub it into the areas where Dark tends most to accumulate: the armpits, elbow pits, the areas behind the ears and at the nape of the neck, the Dark folds where hair entraps particulate malaise.

As I bathed her in hard, scouring white, her face twisted into a shape designed to keep the salt out. It was only after I had moved her to the sand bath that I realized her mouth was not just assuming a protective stance but was working itself toward speech. She moved to wipe her mouth with a limb, but her movable parts were as silty as everything else, the sand caked to her fingertips and wrists, her small floral lips. She nudged at the air with her head, eyes fixed desperately on my own, indicating that she wanted me to brush the sand from her lips with my own hands. I looked down at my hands. My fingers poked out from beneath the edges of my sheet. They looked older than I had remembered, with deep lines near the joints and a cracked pattern spreading all over the backs. I had lost track of time. I didn't know how long I had been in here, how much older I had gotten. My age, like my birth and upbringing, was a forbidden topic. Inquire instead, said the Managers, into the agelessness of your ghost.

I indicated to the girl that I was busy doing other things to her, important and necessary tasks, required tasks. I waved my hands around in an imitation of washing and then held a quieting finger up to my lips, up to the spot on the sheet where my lips would be if it were a face. I readjusted my sheet and tried again to push the sleevelike regions of my covering up past my elbows. I leaned forward toward the tub and scrubbed with fine pale sand at her back and arms, her shoulders like bone handles to grip as I cleansed her of her past. But she kept looking at me with that needy look, sucking her lips in again and again. Her tongue emerged and pushed at the grainy stuff around it. She tried to eject from her mouth a globe of spittle that split her lips and came out dark with damped sand. She gagged into the air near my hands as I worked to hold her neck still for the cleaning. She struggled and twisted, retching aimlessly. I was having trouble holding her in place: my sheet was sliding off, I risked showing my face to the entire room.

"Please," she said in a soft voice that crumbled, "I have to be at soccer practice."

Recruits came in like this all the time, people of all ages with only the haziest idea of what they were doing here.

"There is no such thing as soccer practice," I said. She looked confused. I added: "It'll be better for you if you forget there ever was."

"But my mom said. Ask my mom," she insisted, her voice louder, pointier.

I shook my head and let go of her for just a second to tug my sheet back on center. Then I grabbed her by the shoulders and maneuvered her from the sand into the white bath. The white bath used to be a dairy bath, mostly milk, some yogurt, but researchers at the Church had discovered a toxic quality to milk. If milk was said to nourish the flesh of a human baby, it was bound to be suffocating to the infant ghost. Milk had been outlawed. Now the white bath was flour diluted in water, a passably milky liquid that had to be stirred constantly to keep it from separating into thin, cloudy liquid and a sticky, bottom-dwelling paste.

I hoisted her from under her arms and staggered her over to the white bath, slid her in one leg at a time while she looked up, saying to me over and over again, "Find my mom, ask her, please. Tell her I need my cleats. Don't forget my cleats. I don't want to wear my tennies and have Amanda Marcos do an impression of me falling on my butt during the kickoff. Where's my mom? Is this a doctor's? What are you doing to me?" Her talk was drawing stares from the other recruits and, worse, from the other processors. I felt their eyes on me like a fever. I had to quiet her before someone else decided that I was a bad worker, a bad worker because I had a bad recruit.

Her naked body projected through the white like pink islands rising out of a thick, blank sea. The flesh quivered, sent slow ripples through the thick. I leaned down, brought my face close to hers, lined up the holes in my sheet with the hole through her ear, and tried to speak as kindly and sweetly as possible. I told her that maybe someone she had once considered her mother had brought her here or maybe not. The idea of her mother was obsolete, it belonged to a doomed world headed cheerily toward total Darkness poisoning. She was lucky to be here with us, lucky to have found a way out of her doomed self. I rubbed her back in small, comforting circles. When I looked into her face for signs of peace and understanding, I saw the small black pupils shrinking in the center of her eye.

"My mother is where?" she asked.

I tried to think of a new way to phrase how alone she was.

"Do I know you from someplace?" she asked even more uncertainly. Her body lurched forth from out of the bath as she tried to see through the sheet holes to find my face. One glistening wet white hand shot under my sheet, grabbed at my bare wrist, and sought around on it, as if she were trying to find my pulse.

"I know I know you," she said. "Please—from Forest Hills. The condos by the big Wally's, the one with the bank in it and the ice cream sandwich bar. The condo complex where they just planted all the trees, those little trees that need to be held up with slings and rope. You have to remember me. I saw you there. Getting into your car. Going up to that door. You looked sad. You have to tell my mom to come get me."

She was full of Dark. The only thing that could come of listening to her was misinformation. What I thought I had lived had been a bad dream originating in a sick body, like the sorts of nightmares you have when you sleep with a high fever. I had always lived here in the Church. Was the name Forest Hills familiar? Was it more familiar than any other name? Was it someplace that I had been, someplace I had slept, someplace I had lived in? Could that have been where C lived, where he used to live, maybe where he still lived today? Sometimes I had the feeling that he was here in the Church, only the building was so large that we had never been in the same place at the same time. A Manager watching me from across the room shook his head slowly, and I knew that I had messed up, stalled the processing, dredged the past up within myself, and Darkened up where everybody could see me.

I looked down at my work as though nothing had happened. I picked up the pitcher for cleansing her internal passage. Darkness sloughed fairly easily from the body's outer covering, it was sloughing the inside that would take months and months of laborious and intensive Uneating. In a few minutes I would be finished processing her, but she'd still be far from Bright, far from an adequate shell. For that she'd need to reverse her commitment to herself. She'd need to become like Anna, who I could sense as she worked at the other end of the room, executing her cleanings with a quick and rough touch, turning out the new recruits one after another, each one of them bringing her closer to her promised end. I sank my pitcher into the deep, bland white and filled it with white water, warm thick flour water, and I held it up over her head for the pour. I held her chin with my left hand as the white ran down, and I said to her gently: "You were born to Nothing, you were mothered by Nothing, you were fathered by Nothing, you are child to Nothing." Beneath the thick liquid I could see her blinking, the eyelids fluttering shut and shut again as they tried to keep out the white that would not stop coming.

"Your safety was Nothing, your hopes were Nothing, you made no mark, and any gap you left behind closed up a few hours ago," I said, feeling inexplicably sad, inexplicably because I had said these words hundreds of times and knew it to be the truth. "You knew nobody, and nobody knew you," I said, and as I said it I was seeing C's face horizontal next to mine, in the morning before we had gotten up, his eyes fixing on a freckle, a spot, a stray hair at the corner of my mouth.

"But now we have you. We see through you to the person you always were," I continued. I squeezed my eyes shut. "The better person. And we will find that person for you, and get them out."

THAT NIGHT I LAY IN the cot next to Anna as we waited for our check-ups. On the other side of the red curtain I could hear the Inspectors wheeling their carts into the curtained spaces to inspect our bodies for ghostliness, pulling aside covers, rearranging the sheetless limbs on their squeaky platforms. Anna was lying down, manufacturing memories unlinked to her past. Her exposed face was waxy and still, her eyes closed, hands folded over her belly. Her mouth tightened and loosened very slightly, sometimes pulling into a short smile, which gave her the look of a child playing at being a funeral corpse.

I was lying on my side, pretending also to manufacture present memories, but what I was really doing was thinking about the girl I had handled earlier that afternoon. I hadn't felt well ever since I had heard her mouthfuls of fake recognition, her description of that half-fleshed place that was beginning to feel more and more as though it could be C's apartment complex. C's neighborhood had always been a bland place—doors, sidewalk, maybe trees or maybe not. The sun went up there, after a while it went down, and the whole time there were cars coming and going and staying still. But as I tried to remember if I had ever been in a place specifically like the one she described, seen that specific girl's face watching me from the periphery, it all began to feel more possible. Even if I hadn't been there, I had been someplace so similar that nobody would be able to tell the difference.

The Inspector came, pushing aside the heavy crimson curtain and assessing our bared, inert bodies with satisfaction or dissatisfaction, I couldn't see which. He rearranged his glossy, sateen sheet around his body and pushed two hairy arms out from the white. A large and expensive wristwatch shone gold on his left wrist, no longer working, its hands still. He lifted Anna's limpened wrist as she smiled up at him Brightly. He turned the wrist over and opened up a lab notebook to a page flagged with a small red tag. He wrote numbers in the margin and sketched in red pencil the topography of her veiny underwrist. He turned her arm back over and took a small flashlight from his tool case, shone the light on her forearm, throat, cheekbones. "Great," he said, "looks like you're really thinning out. I can almost see something moving, a little bit of a kick forcing the flesh around." Then he pulled down the covers and illuminated her lower belly, where the pale and freckled white skin cased her gut and viscera. In the shadow of him, she tilted her head from side to side as though she heard a secret music, pleasant and mellow, played at volumes too soft to hear.

He packed the flashlight away and pulled out a small, slim rod, tapered like a chopstick, and dragged it lightly over her arm, shoulder, torso, leg, long strokes like a razor. He looked at the rod and put it into a plastic bag, tucked the plastic bag back into his toolbox, wrote numbers in neat columns on notebook paper. "I'm seeing good texture," he said, neck still bent, pointing that large sheeted head toward the notebook in his lap. "Smooth, even, very flat. Good transparency, as I said before, improving. We also call that diaphaneity. Just a fact. If there is one thing you could work on, I'd say it's hardness. Think brittle, or bony. Like a shell or fragile porcelain cup. In nature, successful eggs are almost always a compromise between protection and vulnerability. Meditate on that. And as always, keep thinking Bright. Are your memories shaping up?" he asked, turning the page in his notebook.

"Extremely well," said Anna. She looked over at me. I looked away.

"I suppose it's your turn," the Inspector said, his back still facing me. His shoulders shook slightly as he wrote in his book.

"She's not doing well," said Anna.

"I'm doing great," I said.

"She's not doing great," Anna said. "She's very troubled."

The Inspector turned and pointed his eyeholes toward me.

"You have a stormy look," he observed.

"Test her properties," said Anna, sitting up sharply.

"Don't listen to her," I said, trying not to shout but probably shouting anyway. Anna shifted around, twisting her body as if she were about to get up. She had this look on her face that was like no look I had ever seen before. It was a thing that reminded me only of this place, uniquely, and no place else. It was like pity, like the weaponized pity you have for a thing you are about to crush, but she was scared of me, too. I wondered if this feeling had ever been seen on my face by someone else that I hoped to crush. The Inspector was leaning in toward me now, trying to get a view of me through the better, larger hole in the sheet.

"Why don't you want to be inspected?" he asked.

"It's not that. Please don't listen to her. She's trying to destroy me," I said, reaching out maybe to touch his clothed forearm, then drawing back. Touch was forbidden; it passed memories of touch and feeling. Touch was too persuasive.

"I'm not," said Anna. "I'm just trying to protect us all. She's leaking Dark thought all over the place. You must feel it," she said. She was making a kneading motion in front of her with two bony hands, as though the Darkness were in the air and she were wringing it out.

"I feel something," he said. "It's true."

He looked more closely at me, as though I might have something written in my eye, a note from the manufacturer or instructions for use.

"She has these dreams in the middle of the night. They're not from here. In them it's like she's hugging someone, over and over again. Sometimes like she's eating something long and choky. These aren't things we have here, or can do here. She's bringing them in. She can't leave herself behind. She, like, adores it. She's spilling all over me. You have to do something about her." Anna was running out of things to say, but she never slowed, she started again at the beginning, there was no air, no breath, between her words.

"She's wrong," I said, trying to jam my voice in between the gaps in her own.

He peered at me encouragingly.

"She's doing it," I said. I tried to think of specifics.

"Sometimes I'm sitting here working on my unmemories, and I'll see her looking at me with this look of recognition. Not a normal recognition look, like 'I see you every day.' It's like I'm a long-lost sister to her," I said. I added: "I see it in her face."

"That's inconclusive," said the Inspector. "That could be your work."

"But it's not," I said. "I'm pure and Bright. I sought out my differences and overwrote them. I replaced the background, the foreground, the characters, the situations. I was born here, in the Church. I have always been here, in the Church."

"She had a weird interaction with a new recruit today," said Anna.

The Inspector swiveled toward her.

"Describe," he said.

"I saw her take a new recruit through the three baths, a teenage girl. Blond. Halfway through the second bath the girl got spooked. She started trying to use her eyes. She looked at *that* processor"—Anna pointed at me with a finger as straight and brittle as a twig—"and she started shouting she knew her, she knew her. And said a lot of junk about some apartments and some car."

"That wasn't about me," I said. "She couldn't even see my face."

"She didn't have to," countered Anna. "The past was thick on you."

The Inspector cleared his throat.

"How," he asked, "did you know it was her if her face was properly sheeted up?"

Anna sat back and looked smug.

"She's my space mate," Anna said. "I know how she moves, her size, her shape. I know it because I know everything I've seen in here. It's all I know."

My throat had a choke in the base of it. I didn't know what to say, but I could tell that I was going to lose.

"We'll need to give you a survey and see if you're marked for sortdown," he said, not unsympathetically. He rooted through his toolbox for the papers.

"Okay," I said. I closed my eyes and tried to think about this place and nothing else, this room and nothing else. Inside this dark, cramped, red-curtained room, I lay and built a red-curtained room in my mind, I put myself in it with the Inspector, and I left Anna out.

"All right," he said. "I've got it. Now just answer these questions to the best of your ability."

"Okay," I said.

"Here's the first one," he said.

DO YOU EVER FEEL LOST, DESPERATE, OUT OF CONTROL IN TERMS OF YOUR THOUGHTS, OR AS THOUGH YOUR FEELINGS HAVE FEELINGS OF THEIR OWN?

"No," I said. "I feel even and Bright. My feelings are pretty much responses to what happens in the daily management of Darkness. Feelings of fulfillment when I work. Et cetera."

He paused as he wrote down: *No. Feelings of fulfillment.*

CHECK INNER AND OUTER BODY FOR TRANSPAR-ENCY. DO YOU NOTICE AREAS OF INCREASED OR DECREASED APPEARANCE ON ANY OF THE TOP TEN BODY ORGANS? DO THESE FLUCTUATE AS YOU OBSERVE THE WORLD?

"Oh," he said. "This one's for me. Hold still, I'll be checking your diaphaneity."

He pulled out the flashlight again and held it up against my throat, arm, torso. He leaned in and squinted, adjusted the eye-holes from side to side.

"You're murky," he said. "I'd say sixty percent cover. Not good. Now think about your mother or father."

I tried to think about them. Then I tried not to. I couldn't tell what I should try to do. I could feel Anna at my side, smirking, as he got out the rod and ran it along my length.

"Also, soft. Hard in places, but that may just be the bone."

He sat up and took the numbers down on paper. It looked as though he were shaking his head, there, beneath the cover of his large flapping white sheet.

"Okay," he said, "last question."

CLOSE YOUR EYES. IT IS A NICE DAY. IMAGINE YOU LOOK AROUND AND THEN UP. WHAT IS IT LIKE UP THERE? DESCRIBE IN DETAIL.

"Um," I said. "I don't know how to answer this."

"To the best of your ability," said he.

"All right," I said. "Well, I guess it's high up. The top is far away. It feels safe. Not like anything is going to cave in. It's a good day. People are full of Bright all around me. And I guess it's nice up there, the normal kind of nice. It's a happy color like blue or something, and free of toxins."

The Inspector was writing furiously on the sheet of survey paper.

"You said blue?" he asked, not looking up.

"Blue," I said.

"We don't have blue here," he said. "Blue was removed due to its toxic effects. We have white ceilings. Sometimes gray. Or with industrial support beams, steel beams. We have red curtains. These are all acceptable answers."

"My answer wasn't acceptable," I said. I had intended to say it as a question, but I already knew what he would say.

"No," said the Inspector. "It was not. It's a holdover from the outside, where they have blue. It's an indicator that you are almost certainly bringing in other things, more dangerous things, from outside as well."

"What if this was the only one?" I asked hopefully.

"I'm sorry," he said. "You'll still have to be sorted out. We'll reassign you to some outside work, nothing too dangerous, hopefully. Some kind of halfway job where we'll try to offer you at least partial protection from toxicity. Maybe at a factory. Who knows." He looked at my face. "You'll still be fed well," he said. "Kandy Kakes."

I didn't know what to say. He was packing up and moving on to his next inspection. Next to me, Anna sat in silence. He paused at the door.

"You'll probably have a final meal here. Move you out tomorrow morning. Someone will let you know where you're going, I think," he said. And then he was gone.

For a second I lay still. Then I writhed around, side to side, moaning. After some moments I quieted and turned to Anna.

"You destroyed me," I said.

She didn't say anything.

"Now I'm sorted down," I said. "Everything I worked for. All the memories I undid. How clean and Bright I got. Now I'll go back out in the world and be degraded in an instant. My ghost will shrivel. I won't live on. You killed my ghost," I shrieked.

Anna just shrugged her head around in a big fuck-you kind of way. As she rolled her head around on its slender stem, I saw her collarbones and shoulder blade sliding past each other like pistons in an engine. Each bone had a stark drop shadow underneath.

The fleshier body parts had eroded, and now she resembled a beach cliff, sharp edged and towering above stretches of vanishing sand. Every day her body looked more like B's—more like B's but less each time I saw it, as though every person I met were an echo of one I used to know.

"I have to protect myself," she said. There was something not quite apologetic in the way that she said it.

"From the Darkness?" I asked.

"From you," she said. And she lay back on her cot, folded her arms, and gripped a bicep in each hand. She closed her eyes and her mouth tightened into a slim little line. I could tell that she was back at work perfecting her memories, isolating the little pockets of outside Darkness and filling them with plain, clean Light from within this place. I thought for a second of trying to undo her, trying to make a greater Darkness happen to her. But then I just gave up. I looked over at the fake mirror at the fake reflection of the blood-red curtains and it was as if I were already gone. Something was burning behind my eyes. I thought it was anger, but then I realized it was tears.

THAT NIGHT I WENT TO my last meal in the compound in the Grand Cafeteria, which used to be a Wally's, which was now just a big, thingless space lit up by supermarket fluorescents that turned everything beneath them an insomniac white. We ate there once a day, and after eating we went back and slept on our double-size cot curtained off by velvet red, slept on one of hundreds of cots that filled the room infirmary style, making it look as though we were all in a massive emergency of some kind that never ceased or lessened. The line for food was already long, twisting through the spaces between those Eaters who were already eating, standing there with their sacks open and their mouths clogged. I thought I recognized some of the bodies, but that might have been a mistake. Stranger or nonstranger, all Eaters acted more or less alike, did things more or less the same way. I wondered if any of the others were having the same problems as me beneath their crisp white sheets, if they too were experiencing dizzying pulses of longing as they thought accidentally on their past lives with its warm bodies and delicious, treacherous food. If they felt their thin, glassy skin go opaque when they remembered the people of their past.

I queued up with my empty sack and waited my turn. Food was done by weight: nine units for a large man, three for a child. Someone with a body like mine took six, though there were days when I got five, and actually there were more days like that recently, more and more and more. I held my sack forward while they counted them out. It was like Halloween, if Halloween happened twice every day and the only things there were to eat were Kandy Kakes.

Today was a five Kake day. I found some empty standing space and opened my sack. All around me other Eaters were doing the same, reaching in and rifling through their issuance, feeling it up with their fingers, searching around for edges within the gummed-up mass of Kandy Kakes, whose fudge coating was airproof and weather-resistant and impervious to pretty much everything.

We peeled them apart with our fudge-covered fingernails and felt the scrape of a Kandy puck beneath our clawing as the wet surgery sounds, sounds like the ones made by the insides of our own bodies, accompanied our digging. We lifted globs to our mouths and sank our teeth through the muck, bit down on that chalky layer of fruity cocoa and eked away at it with our teeth. We drooled into it, let it soak us up and turn our mouths ashy and dry. We let it drain us, waiting until it turned soft enough to bite. Then we bit it.

The Kakes rubbled on our tongues, tasting of chocolate and bone, waxy with fudge and greasy frosting, and at the same time not tasting like much. Tasting like less than we had expected, even though every time we ate one we expected less. The gathering space was full of people standing alone and facing in random directions, all wrestling with their own mouths. And when we had won at last, cracking the Kandy Kore to reach the sugary fluid within, we gagged on the bitter slick. My mouth was raw and scoured and tasted of biled orange.

I looked down at my sack, at the four that I still had to finish. Down inside me, in a place near my heart, my stomach quivered.

My new assignment had come in. The next day I would be shipped out into the danger. I would be leaving the compound for someplace else where there was no shield to protect me from Darkness, no purifying and Lightening baths, no safety from the toxic thoughts and feelings of normal un-Lightened people. But I would still be under the Church's protection, there was no reason to despair. They told you that sorting down wasn't the end. You were still doing important work, even if it was at the cost of your health. You were part of the hidden face of the Church, hidden beneath your normal face, and they told you that everything you did was in service of the Brightening of the world, especially when you labored away from the Church, like at a Wally's or a car wash or something.

So tomorrow I was assigned as a decoy on *That's My Partner!* I would be stripped of my sheet, my unghosted body displayed to hundreds of thousands of people in varying states of Darkness. I would dance with the other decoys, dance circles with them around our target and shield her from the gaze of the one she loved, shield her from recognition, from finding her way back into her own used-up life. And even though I hated that show, it was funny how grateful I was now to be sent out there to the shadows, rather than to the pitch Dark of the world I had once lived in.

THESE ARE MY LEAST FAVORITE episodes of *That's My Partner!* in the order in which I saw them. First, the episode where the man who loses his partner in the final full-nudity blackout round insists that he *did* choose the right woman and tries to take the decoy home. The decoy female looks actually terrified as he hoists her up and tries to flee the soundstage with her body heaped over his shoulders; she claws at him, trying to create an egress. Fortunately, a member of the security team Tasers him before he can get off-camera. Then there's the one where the couple loses but reveals at the end that they have a child together, even though procreative couples are legally barred from participating because of custody issues. The producers won't let them out of the contract, which stipulates that any shared property be divided equally in half in the case of a loss, which means that the dollar value of their son must be calculated exactly and matched by an equal amount of property taken from the holdings of whichever parent gains custody. You can see the studio lawyers and the producers arguing while the couple just stands around in the background, slowly coming to understand what they've just lost.

And of course: the one where the couple actually wins, but then you see that both of them look uncontrollably sad. You watch them notice the sadness on each other's faces. You watch them realize that the other person didn't want to win together and stay together—they realize that even before they realize they feel the same way themselves. They walk offstage together, ushered by the host, looking tired and holding each other's hands limply, as though they are handling raw, cold chicken breasts.

As for favorite episodes, I don't have any. I hate the rest equally.

In the bus with the other decoys, the sound of the vehicle blots out the noise of forty-nine girls breathing short and sharp. We're quiet and still, not because we were ordered to be, but because there's nothing to say. Over the last months, we've all done the same things, had the same experiences, and felt nearly the same way about them. Conversation among us would change nothing: someone could say, *Ten to twelve Kakes a day,* and another would reply, *Yes,* as if that settled it. You couldn't have distinguished us one from the other unless you had known us in our earlier lives, and even so you'd have to match that person up with one of our number, a head among other heads protruding from a single gigantic body. I'm the only one looking around and into the others' faces. I'm trying to see if any of them are excited about the journey, but it's impossible to tell. The girls around me have different hair colors and face shapes, different faces poking out from their heads. They all have the same body type: spookily thin. Their bodies weigh against your retina like light—you hardly feel it, you hardly see them at all.

The Conjoined Eaters now own eighty percent of *That's My Partner!* They own twenty-three percent of Fluvia cosmetics, several processing plants where food matter is enriched or impoverished, twenty percent of a major soft drink manufacturer whose best-selling product is a soda that puts you to sleep. They own sixty-seven percent of all Wally's stores, which means that six out of every ten you walk into are fully Conjoined facilities, all the foods grouped according to their Darkness content. And that number doesn't even take into account the different Wallyfronts that have only been infiltrated rather than illuminated fully, infiltrated by Eaters who mostly perform the functions of normal employees but also work subtly to redistribute falsity within the grocery store environment. It hardly even makes sense anymore to say that the Wally's empire is infiltrated by Eaters—our people have entered the essence of the company. An outsider would say that the Conjoined Eater has many faces—but I knew that it was a single face, only you couldn't see the whole thing at once.

Which reminds me of a story I once heard, about a beautiful woman with a daughter a friend of mine had once loved, and they never saw each other again.

AFTER WATCHING TMP! FOR THE first time at C's house, I came home to B and told her about the episode I had just seen. The female contestant made it out of the blackout room holding the hand of a man who everyone, audience and host included, thought was her husband at first. He was the same height, same sharp jaw, same lean cyclist's build, only without the slight beer gut. This stranger was probably what her partner had looked like four or five years ago. There was applause everywhere, and the host even started walking toward the happy woman and mystified decoy, his right arm outstretched in anticipation of a handshake. Then her husband wandered out looking confused, and the whole thing fell apart. I tried to explain to B exactly what got me down about it. It was that they had wanted to stay together. Or it was that she thought they had, she had been so close.

Said B: "I would do it. I've got nothing to lose."

"If you were on the show," I said, "it would be because you had something losable."

"I've never had something losable," B said. "Except maybe you now."

I got up to fiddle with something a few feet away.

"If C wanted to go on that show, I'd dump him," I told her. "No hesitation."

"Yeah. Sure," said B, unconvinced.

"I'd dump his ass," I said.

"I don't see what the problem is," B said. "Anybody would recognize you. I'm the one you should be worried about."

She had just come from a disappointing date with a guy that she had bitten only a couple of weeks before, who not only forgot her name, but forgot that she, brittle and pale, had been the one who sank her teeth into his left hand. They had a fight about it, even though it was only their first date. B told him that they had met at a birthday party in a nice apartment with the two fireplaces. They made out while listening to nineties R&B on an obsolete cassette player in one of the empty bedrooms, and then she bit him. He insisted that he would have remembered that and that she was acting crazy. Then she did it again, bit him on the arm so hard that she broke the skin, leaving little red notches that traced out the shape of a crescent moon.

OUTSIDE THE WINDOWS, EVERYTHING IS getting darker. First the yellow dies from the light, then the green and pink. The world is a blue version of itself, momentarily, before the blue snuffs out, too and it is all night. I'm surprised that it takes so long this time to get to the soundstage in Loyota Beach. I remembered the distance between Randall and Loyota being something simple, an hour and a half or an hour forty-five in traffic. We've been in this bus for almost six hours. But maybe there are lots of towns called Randall. Who knows if I was even in the one I had heard of, rather than one that had never existed to me at all. In the quiet of our full bus, I can hear the breathing of the girls around me, a continuous breathing with no chink of rest or silence in it because we are too many. Dozens of ponytails swing left and right in near unison in front of me, swinging with the movement of the bus. With my butt sliding around on the leather-print plastic of the seats, I feel just like a child again, safe in the understanding that anything bad that were to happen to me would be someone else's responsibility. Maybe that was the secret to happiness, I thought, being free of the responsibility of yourself. I look at the window, where my ghost face looks back at me, just a whitish-black outline on a black surface—free of my chin, which was too pointy; free of my nose, which was too lumpy.

One of the decoy girls starts differentiating herself from the others all of a sudden. She's breathing hard, looking all around at the inside of the bus. Then I realize she's actually looking outside the bus, at the things passing by.

"That's my house," she says.

No one moves.

"This is my neighborhood!" she says, louder. "I used to live here!"

Now she's looking into each of our faces, as though we could tell her whether she's right or wrong, or say, *Good job!* or something like that. It looks as though she is really animated and energized by what she sees, or what she remembers about what she sees. She must have good memories of living in this place, or someplace like it. I wonder what I'd do if I looked out the window and saw my old house, or C's old house, but then I realize that I might not even remember what those things look like anymore, and I stop thinking so that I don't have to be sad.

Inside the compound, everything had looked the same. Out here, all we register is an endless mass of alien sprawl. Maybe that's why nobody does anything about the girl shouting about her town: we can't even see her town, can't make it out amid all the outside that's going past. We aren't used to looking off into distances, only across the room. Some of us think she's just showing off. After a while, her energy damps down and her mouth shuts again. She sits back into her seat and looks like she isn't sure anything has happened after all.

When we get there, they stow us in a big room full of little cots arranged in two long lines, like in a Victorian infirmary, the space between them so narrow that you hit your knees if you try to turn around. I can tell they tried to make it look like home, but they got so many things wrong: the fluorescents are circles instead of bars, the cots have scratchy blankets on them that are just whatever colors instead of the bloody crimson we're used to. And then there's a big window onto the outside that they've covered up, but I can still feel that it's there behind the cardboard, changing color and content as the day goes on. I know that I'm going to be sleeping here for a certain number of days, but I want to go as long as I can before I touch any of the weird new bedding. C used to play a game with me called "What's the Worst That Could Happen?" where he'd ask me that question and I'd try to tell him. C invented it to show me that the scenarios I worried about were outlandish and unlikely to happen, but it turned out that he found my answers funny, so then we played it for other reasons. What's the worst that could happen if I touched these foreign things? I could forget the one place I still remembered very clearly, my bed in the room of beds at the Church of the Conjoined Eater.

We're far from the compound and they didn't bring enough Kandy Kakes for all of us, so I only get four. It's almost a relief, I think, pushing the Kandy silt around inside my mouth. Each one is just as difficult to eat, but at least the meal is over faster.

SINCE THE EATERS HAD TAKEN over the daily operations of *TMP!* there had been some changes to the music, the decor, the corporate sponsors. Instead of the plush, swirly fuchsia carpeting on the main stage, everything was black and white, harshly gridded. The floor was dizzy with contrasting tiles that sprawled hundreds of feet; it was hard to look at, and when you walked on it you felt as if you were on a boat. Instead of the blood-red curtains that divided the main stage from the musical stage, the curtains were dark, deep blue, the color of the ocean at a depth where there's still light, but barely, and the pressure would crush you like a plastic cup. Celebrity appearances made for higher ratings, so now there was a guest host, a new one each show, a recognizable celebrity who performed in the dance number and donated their likeness, who let the makeup artists inscribe them on each of our faces, one by one. Sitting in the television hall, we had watched the famous faces of singers, models, and movie stars waltz past the camera in multiple. We saw so little face in our daily life that seeing one made multitude sickened us with expression and the particularity of its parts.

There had also been changes to the format of the show. The musical number in the show's second challenge was far too popular to change very much, but the first and third challenges were in flux. The first challenge used to take place on a typical game show set, both contestants seated on opposite sides of a wall. After the preliminary questions ("What color are her eyes?"), each contestant was shown photos of body parts and asked whether they belonged to the person they loved or to somebody else. The highest-scoring contestant went on to the next round. Recently, the first round had become more haphazard. Sometimes the host asked the questions or showed the photos, but neither contestant was given time to answer: the round took minutes, and then there was an extended celebratory sequence where the couple was filmed enjoying some veal that they had been given as a prize or playfully spraying each other with cans of Slumbertime Soda. Often the round made even less sense: one partner was given access to a stocked buffet while the other tried to guess which foods they were eating from it. I saw one where the two players just sat on opposite sides of the wall, staring, until suddenly the host declared that one of them would go on to the next round. I had never liked this show, but even I could admit that our version of it was worse, in terms of entertainment value.

I LIKED SOME OF THE changes to the final round—for example, the fact that the all-nude blackout round no longer took place in the dark. Now the player wore a blindfold and their partner wore a gag, so that even if the player couldn't see the person they were looking for, the person they were looking for could see them and try to get near them. The success rate was just as low, but the charade was more hopeful.

Eaters made great decoys: we had consistent body types, were paid in Kandy Kakes, and had absolutely no schedule conflicts. We would be the first all-Eater decoy cast for an episode of *TMP!* We weren't the healthiest or most coordinated performers, though, and I could tell that the choreographers who worked with our bodies were getting frustrated. They were outside people. They looked at us and it was as if you could see the questions twisting around inside their faces. They took us first to a large, bright room with warm yellow wood floors that looked like living wood, but better. There were mirrors on all the walls, extending from the floor to well above our heads, and a wooden bar ran across them. The bar looked like it was there to demarcate, keeping us or our reflections from trying to cross into the other's realm. They lined us up and told us to keep our arms out while we kicked, for balance. They said it was a simple kick pattern to start, right and then left with the right foot, right and then right with the left foot. Then right, then left, then a right with the left, and after that two more rights. That wasn't what we called them back at the compound, where we knew that the right hand/leg was the Light one and the left was the Dark one and each could be located on either side of the body owing to random genetic variation and body baffles. But all right. Outside rules. We named our different sides with temporary labels that we would peel off later, once things were normal again.

The real problem was we couldn't see ourselves in the mirror. We weren't dumb, we knew what we looked like: I, for example, would have dark hair down to my back or possibly put up in a ponytail, a pointy chin, pale features, and lips pressed together or open, their shape a little like the shell of a clam or scallop. In our mirror line, I could pick myself out fairly confidently since I was second from the end, flanked on both sides by blond girls. It was just when we started kicking that it got confusing: looking for my legs instead of my face, I saw a mass of them scissoring away, some in sync and others badly off. I thought about my legs: What was I doing with them? Which set of mirror movements did they match up with? Was I doing well, or was I the girl third from the right whose ankles quivered as if they were about to snap? We weren't used to mirrors anymore. There hadn't been any at the Church.

We did better in the next room, windowless and dim and where the walls were just walls, not twinnings of our single selves. We learned to stand in a line without looking back and forth at one another and to do the simple kick pattern and then a more complicated kick pattern, right leg left, left leg right, right leg right left right. These musical numbers were supposed to require a lot of spinning and place swaps so that it would be more difficult for the player to spot his partner amid our shifting forms, but we weren't very good at spinning or swapping. We got dizzy. They modified the routine so that it included more arm gestures, especially gestures that would obscure our faces while emphasizing the mood of the song, but we still had to spin some and the dizziness was like a long, billowy fabric that fluttered out beautifully at first, filling the air with motion and color, until suddenly it caught up to itself, snagged, and drew tight around us like a noose.

I looked out across at twenty-four other decoy girls practicing their routine, putting their arms out like airplanes for the first turn, holding on to themselves for balance or comfort as they entered the series of tricky steps that would weave them in and out of the line, around and behind one another, shuffling like cups in a magician's trick. They clutched at their own shoulders, trying to hoist their bodies upright, but still they swayed. We can't help it. We are all, apparently, so weak. The choreographers told us that we were going to have to improve: they couldn't have one contestant dancing like a normal adult woman and forty-nine decoys flopping around like invalid children in a beginner's dance class. I tried to bring my chin up in a way that I thought could possibly look elegant, like an expensive lamp covered in gold and painted flowers and slender, breakable parts that extended off from the side.

The spinning girls spun before me, their bodies rigid, their arms out like little white spokes. I was spinning, too, spinning and weaving, and I heard the sound of their spinning and of my breath loud in the center of the skull. I heard them fall and pick themselves back up, the sounds softer than you'd expect, their bodies light like dolls. I heard little cries escaping their mouths when they thudded onto the floor and I saw them straighten their backs and begin spinning again and again. I craned my neck up toward the ceiling overhead and saw the fluorescents bearing down on us all, brighter than us and cleaner, too, like the floor of a hospital smelling of bleach and lemon grove. And then I fell, too, my eyes brimming over with light.

THE REAL JESUS ONCE SAID: *"If a kingdom is divided against itself, that kingdom cannot stand. And if a house is divided against itself, that house will not be able to stand." His first argument is that* WE BEGIN DIVIDED. *His second argument is that* WHAT IS DIVIDED CANNOT BE RECOMBINED. *What he did not say, whether it was for lack of adequate time or preparation, was that a person, self-divided, partitioned and full of doubt, will fall unless they are able to force that rebel element from its foreign home.*

What has the human body, in its infinite wisdom, done with the appendix, a dark organ, a wormlike sac fixed parasitically to the intestine? It has choked it gradually over thousands of years. Most scientists agree that the appendix used to be a sort of internal sibling nestled in the bodies of our predecessors—a sightless, speechless homunculus capable of counteracting the better thoughts of its host. In Jesus' time every citizen would have sheltered one in their guts.

FEED YOUR LIGHT. DWINDLE YOUR DARKNESS.

KEEP EATING THE KAKES!

I lay in my cot listening to tonight's Church lesson over the loud-speaker, thinking about the lesson, trying to understand why this lesson and why today, what is it trying to tell us about our current situation? If we decoys were unable to stand, if we happened to fall continually, did it mean we were divided houses? If we were, as the choreographers told us, the worst dancers they had ever seen, did it mean that other people, people on the outside, were more whole than us? That they had done a better job of dwindling their Darkness and that they had done it all on their own, without needing the Church, because they were simply better at being people?

The guest host was the actress from those commercials I used to hate, where they reveal her hiding like a skull beneath the skin of that nice lady who just wants a smoother, more radiant face. She showed up with two bodyguards and learned the musical routine in twenty minutes flat. She had wide cheekbones like a human cat. She was blond and about as pretty as she had looked on-screen, pretty in a pushy way: all of her features seemed to tell you she was attractive before you had a chance to gauge it yourself. I could tell she was curious about us, wondering why we weren't more curious about her. My body didn't hold curiosity for very long now: questions took hold briefly, tensed my muscles as they passed through, and relaxed them as they leaked away. But I looked at her stretching on the warm-up mat, drinking from a plastic water bottle. She looked like someone about to go for a jog, not someone about to smear her face all over other people on a TV game show. I walked to the other side of the room, where she lay on her back, holding her stiff, straight leg and pulling it across her body.

I looked down at her for a few seconds.

"Are you nervous?" I asked.

The beautiful actress from all those movies sat up and smiled at me.

"It's a piece of cake," she said. "All I have to do is dance around a little and look like myself."

I wanted to ask her why it was so easy for her to do this, how it could be so simple to try to be like yourself. I asked: "Aren't you worried about what could happen to you in a crowd of decoys? You could get lost."

"No," she said, laughing. "It's just a game of 'who wore it best.' Almost every time, I'm the one who wins. The only thing that's weird here is you're the only person paying any attention to me. Where are all you guys from? Did you grow up under rocks? In a third-world country? Were you homeschooled?"

I looked at her, and then I walked back to my side of the room, where all the decoy girls were busy sitting around. When I walked up, a flicker of recognition took hold of their faces. Then it passed.

LITTLE BRUSHES EKE AWAY AT my skin, leaving trails of color. They feel like insects on me, landing on me, dragging their light, stiff limbs across my face and lips and eyelashes. Insects of all different shapes, softnesses, teeming across my surface as though I were plant or soil. I felt everything but couldn't move. I opened my eyes and my face was different, I closed them and it all went black again. Each time I raised my eyelids, my face was two steps removed from what it had been before. I was a series of photographs of different, unrelated people, a yearbook that didn't even belong to me.

Someone put a palm on my forehead, the way a mother might check for fever, their hand cool and slippery. Then they pressed down hard, pushing my head back while another hand forced it forward. A scraping rim around the perimeter and a sound like crushing grass. I opened my eyes and another person's hair sat on top of my own, slipping slightly atop my slicked-down head. Now there was blond hair all around my face, touching my cheek, touching my neck, clinging down across my forehead. The hair was stiff, almost pointy. It bounded me on all sides, like a tiny room.

The blond actress came up behind me and gave me a sort of hug. She stayed there, her face above my face, her hair mixing into the hair of my wig and merging with it, making us look for a moment like a single monster creature that could be happy and sad at the same time. "Looking good," she said, beaming at me from the face that belonged to her. I felt for a second like she remembered me, but then she moved on and did it to another girl, and another girl after that.

From behind the dark blue curtain, we decoys slumped against whatever was around and listened to round one. If he didn't pass round one, we wouldn't be needed. Then we could take off our woman costumes and go back to our cots. We could close our eyes and dream of our faces as we remembered them, clearer in our imagination than in any mirror. If he did pass round one, then we would have to dance and spin in front of hundreds of strangers, and if we fell, we might lose even our assignment at the game show, where we labored in shadow but not in the real Dark. Through the curtain we heard the questions and the responses.

"Dark meat or light?" asked the host.

"Uh, dark," said a man's voice, without much hesitation.

"Good. A closet or a stove?" said the host.

"Stove," he said with confidence.

"Correct again," said the host. "Now: Africa or the military draft?"

I didn't understand. Maybe I would have if I were still with C. These were questions for outside people, people in love, not people who had misplaced their lovers. I wasn't the sort of person anymore who could watch this game show and make some sense of it. I couldn't even make enough sense of it to hate it. I could only dance around within its bounds and try not to fall down. I looked around for the contestant, the girl who was putting her relationship on the line; I wondered if she was worried. But at this point we were a sea of blond actress, and the little portions of face that offered particulars were hard to search out and read.

The deep blue curtain rose like a wall in front of me, but the way it stirred showed that it was unmoored at the base. It matched the identical blue sequined dresses we had been packaged in, heavy dresses that dragged down our skinny bodies. It throbbed every time the audience burst into applause. I looked at the curtain and I tried to see it as the deep red curtain around the little space where Anna and I used to sleep, the space where she was probably sleeping right now, at this moment. It was terrible the way resemblances ran wild through the things of the world, the way one place or time mimicked another, making you feel that you were going in circles, going nowhere at all. I looked forward to fully becoming my own ghost, which I had been told would resemble nothing and would look uniquely like itself.

The happy music played. He'd won round one. We were going to have to dance.

THE CURTAIN SLID OPEN ON our twirling mass, kicking in unison, waving in unison. We were a blur of blond and dark blue, we had a hundred arms. The sequins that swathed us bled together, a shitty ocean glittering with sharp points of light. I looked for the girl who had shouted about seeing her house and I couldn't find her. I looked for the blond lady contestant and I found her every-where, everywhere equally, there wasn't even one girl who looked more like her than another. The production department had done a really great job.

Now we kicked in a line, grabbing shoulders for balance. Now we did the move where some of us stood still and others wove in between us, smiling and waving. Now we all moved forward and back alternatingly, like children on a swing set, but not children, and no swing set. We let go of shoulders and began the spin pat-tern, raising our faces to the bright studio lights overhead that beat down upon our open eyes and turned the world bright and white and then a bruising violet color. We gulped down lungfuls of the air-conditioned studio air, the same air for all of us. We were all spinning, we were all blurs of girl and color. The thought made me calm: at this moment we were all decoys together.

Then we formed a single line one person wide. This was the beginning of the finale. From the player's point of view, we would look like one solitary girl moving toward him, but then the first girl would peel off and take her final position, and then the second girl would peel off, etc., until he had gotten a front view of each one of the decoys and also his partner. This was almost his last chance to point at someone and shout, *That's my partner!* because then we would go into the spinning leaps for the final flourishes, and after the final flourishes it would all be over.

I got in thirty-first position in the line and took a breath. We lurched forward, step by step, as on an assembly line. It took so long before it was my turn. The other decoy girls were probably tired, too, and aching from our shoes—but we were Eaters and used to our shedding bodies crying out for one thing or another. Then there were only four people in front of me, then three, and I could begin to see past their shoulders as I leaned left and right. The player was tallish and cuteish, with brown hair.

Then I felt my stomach turn over. There was no blood left in my body.

Because it was C standing in front of me: C with precision, C and nobody else.

All the decoys right behind me had piled into my backside, and the others were confused, craning their necks. I said his name once, and then again and again and again in different ways, wondering if he couldn't hear me because he wasn't really reacting, just staring, his mouth a little ajar. Then I remembered that I wasn't looking like myself, I was looking like the blond actress, so I grabbed at my hair and tried to pull it off, but I had forgotten it was pinned in, so it came only halfway off while I was shouting. I had to stop shouting to start taking some of the pins out, but security was coming up from the wings and I didn't have time. So I took both my hands and I tried to rub the weird makeup off. It was not like the makeup I used to wear, it didn't look like me. It gummed up against my hands, making my hands feel like flippers, mittens, stumps. And I got some of it off, I think, but I smeared most of it, and I looked at him and his face was not showing signs of recognition, but showing instead that grossed-out-but-thrilled look he used to get when watching *Shark Week* on television or really weird porn.

The decoy girls were looking aimless, sometimes staring at me, sometimes at C, sometimes at nothing in particular. They didn't know who I was or who I had been, and they weren't really curious. My hair looked a mess and my face was unintelligible, but then I remembered that I had one part of me that wasn't pinned down and marked up: it was only covered, temporarily, and it could be uncovered. I reached down and pulled the sequined dress up over my head and then I took off the sculpted bra that was supposed to make my top half like her top half, and the sculpted underwear that was supposed to make my bottom like her bottom, and then I waved my arms, and pointed to myself, and said: "See? It's me!" I couldn't think of anything any better.

C squinted at me as if he were trying to make me out through my body and my face and all the different stuff that had been caked onto me.

I felt like I might cry, only I couldn't quite believe this was happening. Technicians spoke into small microphones that wrapped like slender stems around their faces. The studio audience just sat there.

"I looked for you," I said. "I waited outside your apartment and I watched your door. I waited for you to come back. I was there all the hours of the day, every day. Except when I had to go to Wally's," I added.

"I was there," I said. "And you were never there."

Nobody said anything. Nobody did anything. C looked like he was trying to consider the possibility that I was someone he knew. His shoulders, usually slumped forward, had pulled themselves upward and back, as if they were trying to protect the rest of his body by moving it a few precious inches away from me.

Then one of the blondes took a couple of steps in my direction. She was looking deep into my face in a way that nobody had in months or maybe years. She was rifling through my face with her own, and it hurt. It almost hurt. It was like holding still for the dentist. Whatever she was searching for, her facial expression looked like she was having trouble finding it. She put her hand on my shoulder and I realized I was cold. I was shivering even under the hot lights. We were the same height in these standard-issue sequined shoes, and she had a pointy chin and big dark eyes the color of something I remembered having remembered some time ago. Her dry, bony hand on my arm reminded me inexplicably of autumn.

Then I felt it pushing on me, the knowing that this was probably B, must be B. B was the other contestant on the show, which meant that she was C's partner, which meant they had loved each other, or something like it, for more than the qualifying number of months. How long had I been gone?

As I looked at B, her face pulled itself together, like in a time-lapse sequence in a nature documentary, a sun rushing from left to right across the TV screen or a deer carcass turning its insides out as it slumped into bone and soil. It was her, her features heavy with familiarity. This had been my friend. From her face, it was clear that she couldn't quite place me.

"I looked for him all over," I said. "Did you know?"

"You might have had the wrong condo," she said gently.

"I've gotten lost there too," she said. "All the buildings look the same and it can be pretty confusing."

I stared at her. What she had suggested was possible.

"Is it you?" B asked, still sounding hesitant.

"We missed you?" she said tentatively.

It was possible. I hated her.

C HAD ONCE TOUCHED EVERY part of my face with his hands, with his lips and tongue. He had tried to find out how much of it he could fit into his mouth, licking my nose and then clapping his whole mouth over it, grunting as he widened his hold on my face. We practiced breathing through each other, sealing our lips together and relaxing the nasal passages, taking turns inhaling, drawing air through the holes in the other person's body, breathing circularly. We put our lips close and spoke down the other's throat so that we could feel the words trembling in our tissue, as if we had said them ourselves. We licked each other's ears, necks, teeth. He had tasted every part of me, even some of the parts inside, but it didn't mean anything now.

I walked along the side of the highway, where people had strewn plastic wrappers, soft drink containers, broken pieces of car. Headlights came and went like hours. I wasn't really dressed, but I could barely feel the weather on this body that still hung heavy on me no matter how I tried to shake it off. At the studio someone had thrown a black robe around me, one of those hair and makeup robes that hang dozens deep in the long dark closets of the soundstage. People had been arguing over what to do with me, standing there naked on the stage. I needed to leave right away: if the Eaters found me in this situation, where it was clear who I was and what I had done, they would make me a Tester or a Knowledge Leper and I'd never again be on the path to becoming my own ghost, which was the last thing I had left. I had to become something. I was nothing as I was.

If I stayed, I wouldn't have a choice. But if I could get to another Eaters compound, one where they didn't know me and wouldn't recognize me from the episode of *That's My Partner!* that fortunately had not aired yet, I could slip in and take a position similar to my last one, as a processor. I could slip in and hide myself in an inner room, wait there until things changed, until I had turned my body into its own disguise.

THE FIRST OF THE EATER Infotoons that I'd seen in the red room began with a simple white background. A cartoon fish comes strolling by on its back fins, upright like a human, with a sexy, wriggly gait. It's kind of dancing, wobbling from side to side, smiling a suggestive fish smile, when pieces of it begin to peel off: whole chunks, perfectly smooth and fillet shaped, exposing the whitened fish skeleton beneath. The more it wriggles, the more it comes apart. When the sticky chunks fall to the ground with meaty little thumps, cartoon people run up from behind and gather them up from the ground. You hear dozens of gulps as they slide the pieces down their throats, you see the lumps of food creep down, down, to the larger lump of the stomach. Everyone is doing it, filling their bellies with fish flesh, eating as much as they can hold. Everyone except the pretty cartoon girl at the back of the group. She's just watching. Her hands are clasped in front of her demurely. The fish topples over and lies still, which makes sense: it's all out of muscle stuff. Then, all the eaters begin to die. One by one they lie down on the ground and curl up like cooked shrimp, turning ashy and still. But the pretty cartoon girl is radiant, smiling with teeth that are very straight and very white.

She looks around at all of them, the people she knew, getting rigid there on the floor, and she's serene. Then she opens her pretty mouth and thrusts her whole hand inside, wriggling it around until she gets hold of something and begins pulling it out. It's the back fin of a fish, a ghost fish, whitish and see-through, emitting a pale green light. She pulls it out whole, fin and torso and fish skull, holds it aloft like a torch, and is more beautiful than ever. Her feet don't quite touch the ground. She's a living example of the benefits of Uneating, the highest of Conjoined techniques and one that we are all working toward, though we don't know what it is exactly. The message flashes on the screen:

ALL YOUR LIFE YOU'VE BEEN PASSIVE.

NOW BE ACTIVE: ACTIVELY AVOID.

I had avoided all the Dark foods, I had eaten whatever approved ones had been put to me by those who knew better. And then when Darkness had been discovered in those approved foods, I had stopped eating them, too. When approved food dwindled to the singular, I ate the only thing that was permitted. I had done everything that was demanded of me, and my progress must be going well, therefore. I should increasingly be resembling my ghost, my truest and most recognizable self. And yet it didn't quite feel like that was happening. I had seen the few things I cared about forget me seamlessly. I had seen the life I never really fit into heal up around my absence like a wound scabbed over.

I touched my face. I squished it around. I couldn't feel what had gone wrong.

UP AHEAD, I SAW A Wally's glowing with its signature red neon lighting, the burning bright bands outlining a Wallyhead whose mouth flashed open and shut furiously. What was missing from Wally's, what had always been missing from it, was the possibility of loitering there without purpose and without any money. That was what I used to have in the apartment with C, even with B: it meant that even if someone wanted to use you, consume you, they at least wanted to consume the parts more specific to you, parts you needed to spend some time digging out. My body felt cold and sweltering at the same time. My feet were lumpy and blue. Walking was difficult. The lights in the distance grew brighter and dimmer for no clear reason; my eyes felt sore just looking at them.

I climbed the hill toward the bright red light, the straps from my sparkly decoy shoes cutting the shape of a sandal into pale angular white feet the color of cavefish. I saw the inside of the Wally's, still miniature at this distance, bristling with activity: the Wallys double-stocking full shelves of food product, polishing the food chandelier, moving heavy boxes of stock from the visible area to the invisible, and vice versa. It was only when I got closer that I realized I had found a Wallyform instead of an actual Wally's. I didn't know exactly what a Wallyform was for, but the

Church had explained to me that they performed a very special role and required unique, highly talented employees. I had met Eaters who worked in them at the Church. They were trained in mime; they did everything gracefully. They even managed to make dismembering the Kandy Kakes look appealing.

A Wallyform looked like a Wally's store in almost every way. It was only when you looked for the flaw that errors began to surface. Employees bustled around at the checkout counters and the shelves closest to the front of the store, but the areas in the back, the bakery section and the swinging freezer doors behind which heaps of food sat in suspension, were desolate, backgrounded. The fruit in the produce section was perfect and unblemished, which was normal, since all Wally's produce was waxed, polished, and painted before being put on display. But this fruit was not only unblemished, it was identical: each pear like another, modeled after a Primary Pear and repeated over and over and over in the bins. As long as you pointed them at slightly different angles in the bin, it looked natural enough. As I walked up to it, I saw the sign on the door: CLOSED FOR RESTOCKING. The Wallys glided around within, unnaturally graceful, handling their items as though they were living things, baby animals or organs for transplant. They were Wallybaffles, trained Eaters who authenticated a Wallyform by performing in full view the customary gestures of a Wally's employee.

I was six inches from running into the sliding glass door when I realized that it wasn't going to open. Looking closer, I saw how hopeless it was: the seam between the two glass panels wasn't even a seam, it was just a line painted on solid metal, depth cues added with a touch of darker paint. Still, there had to be a way in. I knew this because I knew people at the compound who were Wallybaffles. They were special people: they managed to do even the small things, the Kandy Kakes consumption and the programmed vomiting, with a sort of lightness and finesse. They made the things they did look blameless and right. While I was at the Church they had showed up for weekly inspections, and that meant that they must have a way of getting inside the Wallyform and then back out again. I hit the glass not-door with my skinny fists again and again, then I went around to the windows in the front and hit them, too. I remembered from movies and TV that a human being striking a window could cause it to shatter, but the glass was too strong, or I was too weak. My body didn't do much anymore when I put it to things. I didn't even make much noise pounding my fist against the glass: the ones that turned to look dismissed me almost before they had swiveled their heads. I might have been a painting of a hysterical female, paused in motion and screaming decoratively. But my throat was going raw, and my hands hurt dully.

Then one of the fake Wallys inside seemed to notice me for the first time. He tilted his Wallyhead up and looked at me through his real eyes. Then he pointed toward a spot behind him, behind him and to the left.

I WENT AROUND TO THE side of the building. It was gray cement all the way up, cement bricks stuck together, and some dry grass on the ground, except where it had been worn away. A portion of the wall opened out and a Wally came into the outdoors. He was of average height, or at least not of a height anybody would comment on. I had to assume he was the one who had motioned to me.

"Hi," I said.

"It's you," he said.

This was true, but how could he know that?

"Yes," I said.

"You must remember me," said the Wally with a pleading tone that I recognized, though I couldn't recognize him.

I looked at him in what I hoped was an encouraging way. I wanted to recognize him. I wanted to give him that, counterfeit it, if necessary. My invertebrate face felt soft and confused by the order.

"We were at the Randall compound," he said. "I saw you every day in the corridor leading to the Testery. We looked at each other. Sometimes you with your mouth open like you had something to say to me. Once in the Big Room you gave me one of your Kakes. It was a nice gesture, I thought, even though nobody really wants more Kakes."

Had I done that? I wasn't much of an expert on myself anymore.

"Faces are a big part of how I remember people," I suggested.

"Oh, right," said the Wally, fumbling with his Hospitality Hat.

"You get used to the masks," he said, "I mean really used to them. Without them, I mean, there's a rawness," he added. He grabbed at the base of his throat and dug under the flesh-colored rim. He pulled it up and over, turning it inside out in the process, talking the whole time.

He added: "It gets so the normal air chaps your face."

With his mask off, he looked like someone I could have recognized but didn't at all. He was young and rounded, his freshly shucked skin glistening pink in the light of the streetlamp. He had a pouty little mouth, compact like a nose, and two swaths of hairless fuzzy cheek rising up on either side of his face. He looked nice. I could have known him if I had ever met him. He looked friendly. I didn't want to mislead him, but wasn't it kinder to pretend? It would be better if we all could come home to the wrong house, sit down with strangers to a dinner that wasn't ours, treat them like family because we didn't know any better. Then hug all their strange bodies good-night and go to the wrong bedroom for a thieved sleep. There would be nowhere you could go, nowhere you could run to, where you wouldn't be among family and friends. You would run from home, to home, inevitably. I should give that gift to this boy, whoever he was. And then I would climb him to safety, like a ladder.

"What was your name again?" I asked decisively.

"Chris," he said.

"Chris," I said, "of course. I remember you. Possibly you're the only thing I remember from those days. I looked for your ghost many times during the lessons, but probably you were always out of range. I hope you understand that I gave you that Kandy Kake only because there was nothing else around to give. If there had been other things, I would have given you something you liked much, much more."

"I thought that was the case!" he said, pleased.

"It was," I said.

"Look, Chris," I said, "I'm going to have to ask you for a favor. Someone who looks exactly like me has just done a thing on national television that the Church isn't going to be happy about. Obviously I'm a loyal, hardworking Eater, just another minus believer trying to choke down my Darker twin and transition the ghost to sole proprietorship. But for right now I need to hide. Can I hide in your product baffles?"

He considered this for a moment, searching my face for duplicity. He seemed to see something in me, whatever it was. Then he let me inside.

I WAS TRYING TO FIGURE out if there was anything in here that would tell me who I was now, why nobody saw me in me, why others saw someone I had never been. Chris still followed me, trailing ten feet behind and probably wanting to ask more questions, but the other Wallybaffles kept working as though I weren't even there. I passed so close to them that I could smell their sweat mixing with the treated foam plastic of their masks, and still they remained perfectly fixed on their work. I felt like a ghost haunted by another ghost. We wove through the aisles. I watched the Wallybaffles do their graceful shelf-restocking dance. They sank squatting to the floor, reached out, and pulled the product close in toward their chest. They paused, compacted themselves. Then they propelled upward again, to a standing position, from which they proffered the product, gently, to the shelf. From this distance, though, it was clear they weren't restocking anything. How could they? The products would overflow, choke the shelves. They'd need unstockers to take down the products they had placed, and if anyone from the outside were to see those, it'd all be over. So instead they rose and sank like ocean waves, hoisting product and then bringing it slyly back to the floor, where they would pick it up and hoist it once more.

I tried to find something a Wally's would sell that might be shiny enough to show me my reflection. Ever since C had failed to recognize me I'd been wondering if there was something newly wrong with the way I looked, if I had maybe begun to transluce or take on an ethereal look because of the ghosting process. The plastic-wrapped meats on their trays of Styrofoam were glossy, but not dark enough to reflect anything apart from my shadow looming over and onto their surface. The canned goods had flat metal ends, but the metal was dull and dark and I didn't even show up. Nothing in there looked out at me, all the objects stared deeply into themselves. I picked them up and put them back where they were. They were lighter than I expected, though lately I had been finding normal objects weirdly heavy.

Then I noticed the TV screens mounted on the walls. On-screen, an episode of *That's My Partner!* was playing itself out, the dancing girls smiling and turning and spinning, first in a front view, then overhead. They spun like sparkly gears around one another, glittering like sharp metal. I looked up at them grinning down at me and it seemed impossible that I was ever there at all. How could I ever have looked so happy, so graceful, so small? They were weightless, made of light. They were the color of the sky at hours in which everyone's asleep. Then their smiles started to come down: they were looking over at something else.

The camera angle changed, and there was a pale swipe on the screen, some shape moving in the blur, painfully white but stained by shadow. The blur convulsed and suddenly its edges were there, cutting the shape of a creature out from its background. A haunch collapsed inward, dark in the hollow and skinny like a dog. Above it a section that reminded me of moonlight passed through the gaps of a venetian blind, carving strokes of bright out from a dark room. The mass came into view, then blurred back out, the focus continually changing as if the cameraperson couldn't decide whether it should be on-screen or off-. I looked hard at it. It was the color of natural wax, pale and creamy. It had shadows in places, strewn through its smoothness. Then I saw. Those were ribs. That was the jut of a hip bone. It was a whole human body: female, naked, holding its arms out as though waiting for an embrace.

"That's my body," I said to myself, and then I realized that I was starving.

IN A DREAM YOU SAW A DOOR AND YOU REJOICED:

IT WAS THE SEEING, NOT THE DOOR,
THAT YOU CONSUMED

BLESSED IS THE MAN WHO WEARS A
FACE NOT HIS OWN TO SAVE HIS BODY
FROM TOUCHING THIS WORLD

AND CURSED IS THIS FACE, AND THE ONE BENEATH:

LIKE THE SOLE OF THE FOOT IT WILL BLACKEN

YOU ARE THE ONE WHO DID THIS TO YOU

TAKE YOUR OWN LIFE FOR EXAMPLE

IT MAY BE HELPFUL TO PICTURE THEM WATCHING
THEIR FAVORITE TELEVISION PROGRAMS
WHILE NOT THINKING ABOUT YOU

A PERSON IS JUST A BABY GHOST

CONSIDER THOSE WHO THINK OF YOU IN THIS WAY,
AND THE GHOST OF YOU THAT IS MADE

GET THERE FASTER:
BE YOUR OWN GHOST

"Chris," I said, "I need to eat something right away."

He looked at me sadly. He said nothing. I had to push him harder.

"Chris," I said, "look at me. I look like people who are about to die."

"You mean you're going to get ghosted?" he asked.

"No," I said. "Or maybe," I said, reconsidering. "I thought so. But this isn't loosing my perfected ghost unto the world. It's just ordinary dying."

He looked like he was about to disappoint me. His face had a downward thrust.

"Our food's all decoy," Chris told me. "It's all idea. It's made to nourish the ghost. Nobody anticipated having a use for real food here. We're a Wallybaffle."

I looked over at a pair of plastic-wrapped pork chops. Something had pooled in the lower-right corner of the Styrofoam tray, and I poked it. It was replica meat runoff, stiff and made of plastic. I hadn't noticed because all of it was wrapped in plastic already, and also I wasn't really an expert on food either, anymore.

"Plus, all a ghost needs is the Food Idea, you know. And we have lots of that around," he said, pointing at the aisles and aisles of fake plastic cookies, fake plastic chickens, fake plastic fruit.

"Do you have food breaks?" I asked. "With real food?"

"We have one at the compound once we get back," he said hesitantly.

He paused.

"And we have one while we're here," he said, brightening slightly. He hadn't figured out what I was driving at.

"And where does the food come from?" I asked.

He looked around, confused.

I looked toward the front of the store, where the checkout Wallys sprayed down and wiped their product conveyors with what I was now certain was fake water. I looked toward the back, where there were rows and rows of stock untouched, replete, not being messed about with by anyone. I headed back there. As I walked, the aisle closed in around me: my shoulders knocked against the shelves, the ceiling came down until I could reach up and touch it if I wanted to, but I didn't want to. I came to a wall painted like a half-scale supermarket. This was why nobody was doing anything at the back of the store: there was no back of the store. Just smooth surface and a little scene that I, with my clumsy, heavy, long-boned body, would never fit into. I ran my fingertips all over the hard surface of the wall, looking for a nick or button.

Then a piece of the painted world slid open, and we walked through.

SOME ANIMALS TAKE THEMSELVES AWAY to a private place to die, into the forest or under a raised wooden deck constructed of weather-treated pine. Are there animals that seek out the most public place to die, the greatest number of eyes to watch them lie down, roll over, stiffen? Is it true that all living creatures feel the instinct to survive, or are there ones that don't, only we know nothing about them because they die so swiftly, in utter silence, before they can be seen and recorded?

I was slumped, my back to the wall, looking out at the warehouse stacked floor to ceiling with large boxes of Kandy Kakes, which were themselves filled with smaller boxes of Kandy Kakes, which contained Kakes on Kakes on Kakes. In a cartoon these stacks would have teetered above us, but this was real and so they stood there, stretching upward like hard geometric trees. Now that I knew there was something wrong with me, and how wrong it was, each part of my body began its own respective panic. It felt as though all the bits of myself were fleeing to different corners of this gigantic room. In the empty space at the center, I waited for a better idea, but there was none. I couldn't do anything without a good strong impulse to survive, and what there was of that desire belonged to the bit of ghost I felt rattling around in my chest: my ghost, which had nothing to do with me, which resembled me not at all, which wanted me to be gone, obliterated, so that it might be free to be its absolute nothingness with absolute abandon.

Chris was milling about, looking worried. He kept trying to talk to me.

"Don't you want to go back to the store area?" he said. "I can find you some really nourishing decoy food," he said, "to feed your ghost. Fake chicken soup?" he asked. "Fake instant mashed potatoes?"

I was like the Kandy Kakes commercial where Kandy Kat just sits on the floor, starving and wasting away and staring straight out into empty space as the dust settles in his open mouth, coating his tongue. I was like that neighbor lady that everyone thought was a hoarder but who turned out to have almost nothing, just a TV and an antique bedroom set, in the apartment where she died alone of pancreatitis.

"I'm really worried," Chris said, looking really worried. "You don't look like you're thriving. Maybe you should eat one of these Kakes?"

"I dunno," I said. "I've had so many and I'm still going to die. I thought I would be fat by now, I thought they'd accumulate. I don't understand. I've been eating Kakes all day, every day. I should be fat."

Chris squinted at the back of a case.

"It's real," he said. "A bunch of chemicals, plus some flour and aspartame," he said.

"What about the sugar?" I asked. "The lard?"

He leaned close to read the fine lettering.

"The Choco Armor," I said. "The Candy Shrapnel. The fudge crust. The caramel-orange syrup core."

"No," he said. "Just chemicals, flour, aspartame, and some food-grade plastic."

I pushed myself to my feet. I read the label. Only sixty-five calories per serving, and a serving was two Kakes. I guessed it was a cost-saving strategy: real fat had to come from somewhere, and it took time and energy and money to squeeze the living oil from living things. Dead matter, on the other hand, was abundant and cheap. It was everywhere. Our world was made of it: life clung only weakly to its surface. How much energy was it taking me to squeeze those calories from these dead chunks of stuff? And if I ate enough of them as quickly as I could, more quickly than I could, might I maybe outrun this starvation, this steady ghosting of my body? Could I eat my way back into my own face?

I tore open the cardboard casing. Hundreds of them looking up at me like dull black eyes. My stomach leapt up as if it were trying to escape through my mouth.

It's no different from eating a piece of fruit or a chicken nugget, I told myself. But it was. Now that I knew, the Kakes all tasted of petroleum and soil, vitamin and dirt. I knew that I was eating the food of the dead—mineral, chemical, synthetic. I was no longer a member of the food chain. I was part of something else.

Chris popped up in front of me.

"This is great!" he said. "You've really made a full recovery. I think there's a color in your cheek. You'll be back to normal in no time! And I'll take you back to the compound, and we'll see each other again, every day."

I felt my stomach buckling already, telling me it was full. *You weakling,* I told it. *You will take this,* I said to my body, *and you will take whatever comes next, and when you're brimming over you will pack it down to make more room for more. You will pull the food from these objects and build it into me, remake me in edible plastic, turn me fake, too.* It was hard to swallow, and I couldn't breathe through my mouth anymore: the bitter orange seepage had formed a slick like flypaper at the back of my throat, a sticky cling that grabbed at the things I tried to push past. I closed my eyes and thought about the Kake. I felt for it with my body. I tried to seek out and zoom in on the living portion of it, the caloried portion. The part that had once been hacked off from a plant, then ground, powdered, processed, refined, enriched, and mixed in with all the other crap.

I concentrated on the biting and chewing. My body didn't want to: it felt like the food was filling me over, pushing against the backs of my eyeballs. What occurred to me then as I crouched on the warehouse floor, my mouth full, was that living wasn't a matter of right or wrong or ethics or self-expression. There was no better way to live, or worse. It was all terrible, and you had to do it constantly. I bore down, I tore in. I held my fingers over my mouth to steady the lips and keep the food from reversing. I held the image of the shark in my mind, tearing tearing tearing at the body of a seal.

Chris was talking at me still, spinning out optimistic Eater fantasies of what life would be like for us back in the cult. I stuffed another Kake into my mouth from the case. I was chewing less and less each time, trying to channel the shark. Between chewings I could hear him saying: *You'll come home with us in the white van, maybe we'll sit next to each other so I can make sure nobody messes with you. Then the next day we'll see each other in the corridor, and maybe you'll speak to me. Or not, if you don't feel like it, no pressure. But we'll still have this, this stuff we had*

*today. We can be people together, in secret, pretending that we're
not. We can be people, secretly, until we become ghosts.*

He reminded me of someone. As I thought on it, I realized that
someone was me—the past me, telling C all about how great our
lives would be if we moved in together or took a trip to Puerto
Rico. I didn't want to ruin Chris's vision of the future. You needed
a vision of the future in order to get anywhere; you couldn't live
life thinking you were always about to fall off a cliff. I didn't want
to tell him that I would never go back with him to the Church:
I would be going forward, forward by way of getting back to the
kind of life I used to have, only this time I'd live it better. I didn't
want to take his imagined situation away just so that he could
know something more accurate about his actual situation. Because what I was thinking now, what had come to me like an
entirely new thought, was that I could use him. I could make use
of him, as normal people made use of other normal people—for
love, for sex, for someone to care about your thoughts. He wasn't
the person I had dreamed of being with, but maybe that person
could be built from the raw material he contained. I had already
tried to escape, to avoid, to negate myself. Now I was ready to try
living.

I put a half-eaten Kake down on the concrete beside me.

"Hey, Chris," I said. "Come here."

Chris trotted over, helpful as ever. A good employee.

"Do you need help?" he asked, his pink face making a friendly
shape.

"No," I said. "I just need to talk to you."

I stood up. I put my hand on his shoulder and looked up into
his eyes.

"Listen, Chris," I said. "Do you love me?"

He looked hopeful and confused.

"Or," I said, "do you think you could?"

"Well," Chris said thoughtfully, "I think definitely. If you wanted me to."

"Okay," I said. "That's good. Do you want to come with me?"

"Sure," he said, "can do. Where are we going?"

"Someplace nice," I said. "Normal. We can live in a house with a roof and a kitchen, surrounded by neighborhood. We'll both get jobs. We'll never talk about them. We'll watch TV together, things like that. Okay?"

He looked puzzled again. "Okay," he replied.

"I'll call you C," I said. "For short."

"Okay," he said, rubbing his face slowly with the palm of his hand.

I knew he didn't understand what would be happening to him, but he'd come along anyhow.

"It'll be wonderful," I assured him. "You'll like it."

This seemed to put him at ease. He smiled at me, a pure and friendly smile, and walked off to continue his pacing.

I picked up my half-eaten Kake, and to my surprise, my mouth watered. I stuffed the half Kake into my slavering center. Over by the door, Chris walked around, wiggling his arms in optimistic motions and talking on about what our life would be like once we got back to the Eaters. He was so far away now, or maybe he just looked distant because we were imagining different things for our future. Standing small there among the boxes of Kandy Kakes that rose like brownish cartoon cliffs around him, he resembled the videos I'd seen of sea lions floating angelically among the kelp, black bodies filmed from below, their shapes cut out in bright sunlight, bodies mistakable for those of a human being. I felt the memory of a shadowy arm around me, a watcher again, sitting there on the couch with my boyfriend, watching the animals become prey. Somewhere there were giant whales feeding on creatures too small to see, pressing them against fronds of baleen with a tongue the size of a sedan. There were polar bears killing seals, tearing ovoid chunks from out of their smooth, round bellies. In the surrounding vastness of the warehouse, I heard something scratching against the concrete floor and knew there were rats here, scraping a thin film of nutrient from the dry packaged matter that surrounded them. Life was everywhere, inescapable, imperative.

ACKNOWLEDGMENTS

ALL MY THANKS TO Claudia Ballard, Barry Harbaugh, and Cal Morgan for their insight and faith, and to everyone at William Morris and HarperCollins who helped to make this book a reality. I am grateful to the Virginia Center for the Creative Arts, the Santa Fe Art Institute, ArtFarm Nebraska, and the hardworking staff of the Bread Loaf Writers' Conference for giving me community, support, and the gift of time.

Thanks also to Heidi Julavits, Ben Marcus, and Sam Lipsyte at Columbia for encouraging me to write what I could not yet write, and to early readers JW McCormack, Shayne Barr, Kimberly Wang, and Kathleen Alcott, who each embody a way of seeing that I wish I could make my own. To my parents for loving me and teaching me. And to Alex Gilvarry, a fantastic person to love.

ABOUT THE AUTHOR

ALEXANDRA KLEEMAN has written for publications including the *Paris Review, Zoetrope, Guernica, Tin House,* and *n+1*. She received her MFA in fiction from Columbia University and has received grants and scholarships from the Bread Loaf Writers' Conference, the Virginia Center for the Creative Arts, and the Santa Fe Art Institute. She is currently completing a PhD in Rhetoric at UC Berkeley. She lives in New York City.